NO LONGER APR 1 5 2023
SEA
OF
D0428378

LIGHTS . . .

Feeling a bit lik … he cast into the pool … es might eventually regret their cavalier attitude toward being filmed changing their clothes, Mia decided to keep a watchful eye on things, hanging back enough to stay off camera. Once inside the pool house, the group discovered a DO NOT ENTER sign on the door leading to the woman's changing room. "Giles insisted there's better footage if the guys and girls have to negotiate the same space," Lysette, camera resting on her shoulder, whispered to Mia.

"I'm impressed this place is so big it's got two separate dressing areas," Mia whispered back.

The dressing room manipulation appeared to be the line in the sand for Chiara. "No way am I gonna change in some gross boys area," the stunner declared. She ripped the sign off the door and tried pushing it open. "It's stuck."

"It ain't stuck," Nicky said. "Something's blocking it. Let me."

Nicky gave the door a shove, moving whatever the blockage was out of the way. Chiara stepped into the room. She let out a heart-stopping scream and then, to the shock of all, crumpled to the ground in a faint.

Francesca dropped to the floor to help her friend. Mia stepped over the unconscious girl to see what had cause her traumatic reaction and almost passed out herself.

The blockage behind the door to the woman's changing room was the body of Giles St. James . . .

Books by Maria DiRico

HERE COMES THE BODY

LONG ISLAND ICED TINA

IT'S BEGINNING TO LOOK A LOT LIKE MURDER

FOUR PARTIES AND A FUNERAL

Published by Kensington Publishing Corp.

A CATERING HALL MYSTERY

Four Parties *and a* Funeral

Maria DiRico

Kensington Publishing Corp.
www.kensingtonbooks.com

KENSINGTON BOOKS are published by

Kensington Publishing Corp.
119 West 40th Street
New York, NY 10018

Copyright © 2023 by Ellen Byron

All rights reserved. No part of this book may be reproduced in any form or by any means without the prior written consent of the Publisher, excepting brief quotes used in reviews.

To the extent that the image or images on the cover of this book depict a person or persons, such person or persons are merely models, and are not intended to portray any character or characters featured in the book.

This book is a work of fiction. Names, characters, businesses, organizations, places, events, and incidents either are the product of the author's imagination or are used fictitiously. Any resemblance to actual persons, living or dead, events, or locales is entirely coincidental.

If you purchased this book without a cover you should be aware that this book is stolen property. It was reported as "unsold and destroyed" to the Publisher and neither the Author nor the Publisher has received any payment for this "stripped book."

All Kensington titles, imprints, and distributed lines are available at special quantity discounts for bulk purchases for sales promotion, premiums, fund-raising, educational, or institutional use.

Special book excerpts or customized printings can also be created to fit specific needs. For details, write or phone the office of the Kensington Sales Manager: Attn.: Sales Department. Kensington Publishing Corp., 119 West 40th Street, New York, NY 10018. Phone: 1-800-221-2647.

The K and Teapot logo is a trademark of Kensington Publishing Corp.

First Printing: April 2023
ISBN: 978-1-4967-3970-4

ISBN: 978-1-4967-3971-1 (ebook)

10 9 8 7 6 5 4 3 2 1

Printed in the United States of America

To my wonderful readers. I can't thank you enough for your support and enthusiasm.
Mille grazie!

Chapter 1

If anyone had told Mia Carina that one day she'd wake up in bed next to a former male model, she would have spit whatever she was drinking out of her nose.

Yet here she was.

Mia enjoyed a languid stretch and was rewarded with an angry meow from Doorstop, the Abyssinian diva who commanded the foot of the bed and was not happy about being woken up by an accidental nudge from Mia's foot. Mia sat up and reached over to pet the annoyed cat. "Sorry, sweetie. I didn't know you were there."

Doorstop made a sound that in human would have translated to "Yeah, right" and repositioned himself.

The male model still asleep next to Mia muttered something unintelligible and then said quite clearly, "Bacon and grape jelly." Mia giggled. Shane stirred and opened one eye. "What?"

"You were talking in your sleep about work again. It's adorable."

Shane yawned and sat up. "What did I say?"

"Bacon and grape jelly."

"Right. For the Kiwanis Club breakfast in the morning."

"Practically our only event this month that isn't a prom, graduation party, or wedding."

Shane and Mia were coworkers at Belle View Banquet Manor, the party facility turned over to her "recovering mobster" father, Ravello, as payment for a gambling debt. Mia breathed a sigh of relief when Ravello asked her to help him run Belle View as a legitimate, entirely legal enterprise for the Boldano Family. She'd breathed sighs laced with lust and desire when Shane signed on at Belle View as operations manager. By Christmas, she and Shane had succumbed to their mutual attraction, but feeling guilty about the impropriety of a boss-employee relationship, they'd kept their romance on the down low for months.

Shane laced his fingers together and placed his hands between his head and the pillow. "Speaking of weddings, we need to find out if it's okay to give Jamie and Madison cash as a present. I don't see a bride in Connecticut carrying a satin sack for checks."

Mia chuckled at the reference to the most important accessory to a bride's outfit at the many Italian weddings she'd grown up with—the money sack. "At least not Madison's family. They're a little upscale for the sack. Nonna said that, in her day, sacks didn't even exist. People just stuffed the checks or cash down the bride's cleavage and, when that filled up, in the groom's pockets or pants."

"And now sacks are old school. Did I tell you

that for the Castro-Pradeep wedding, I have to print out business cards they can hand out to their guests with their Zelle, PayPal, and Venmo account information?"

"Ha. That's a wedding favor I didn't see coming."

Shane's extremely handsome face creased in a frown. "I still haven't figured out what to wear to the barbecue." He and Mia, along with Ravello, the Boldanos, and a Queens/Long Island contingent would soon be trooping up to Worthington, Connecticut, for a party hosted by Madison's parents in honor of the happy couple.

"Me neither," Mia said. "This is, like, a whole new world. Jamie showed me pictures of the Wythes' house, where they're hosting the party. It's old and white."

"Like Madison's relatives," Shane said with a sly grin.

Mia chortled, then wagged a finger at Shane. "Don't. Be nice, you. It's not her fault her family goes back a million years. Jamie said the house is, like, almost as old as the country, and her parents are super nice. They don't act entitled at all. But what to wear, what to wear. Hmmm . . ." As Mia pondered this, she tapped an index finger painted with sparkly gold nail polish against her lip. The other four nails were painted a soft sea green.

"They sail a lot in Connecticut," Shane offered. "Maybe stuff with anchors?"

Mia brightened. "Great idea. I'll see what I can find online."

Shane yawned, then leaned over to Mia, gifting her with a kiss that knocked all images of anchors and America's founding fathers from her thoughts.

"I gotta go home and shower before work. It's gonna be a day."

Mia sighed. "I know." Big Donny Boldano, Jamie's father and technically the boss of all bosses to the Belle View crew, had begged Mia to hire Jamie's older brother, Little Donny Boldano, to do something—anything—at the banquet facility. At the ripe old age of thirty-four, Big Donny's namesake was still trying to find himself. This was to be his first day on the job. Mia and Shane's plan was to let Little Donny figure out which angle of the catering business interested him the most and then place him there.

Shane kissed Mia again, then tossed off the covers and planted his feet on the ground. Mia followed his lead. Shane threw on his clothes and headed out of the bedroom to the stairs that led from Mia's second-floor apartment to the first floor. The couple slowly crept down the stairs to avoid disturbing Mia's grandmother, Elisabetta—who startled them by being in the two-family home's front vestibule, having just returned from a power stroll with the "Army," her friend group of neighborhood seniors. The octogenarian wore a bright pink velour tracksuit and matching sneakers. She greeted the couple with a *buon giorno*.

"Ma'am," Shane said with a respectful nod.

Elisabetta shook her head, perplexed. "I don't know why you keep sneaking outta here. You two been at it for months. You can stop now."

Shane shook his head. "I'm afraid I can't, ma'am. I have too much respect for you not to sneak out."

Elisabetta shrugged. "What is it the kids say now? Whatevs." Enabled by the ability to stream, a newfound affection for teen dramas and reality shows had led to an interesting vocabulary for an eighty-something.

Shane addressed Mia in the most businesslike tone possible. "I will see you at work, Mia."

Mia responded in kind. "I will see you there, Shane."

Elisabetta rolled her eyes as Shane headed out the door. "You're a big girl, *bella bambina,*" she said to her granddaughter. "You're allowed to have a boyfriend."

"You just said I was a big girl and a beautiful baby in the same sentence," Mia teased.

Elisabetta muttered something less flattering under her breath. "You're making me salty."

Mia burst out laughing at her grandmother's use of a slang expression popular with millennials for expressing frustration, prompting a dose of side-eye from Elisabetta. "Sorry, Nonna. But I don't even use 'salty' when I'm ticked off or upset. I'm too old for it."

"Meh, like it says on the mug you got me, age is just a number. And you know what I mean. You need a life. Especially after what you been through with that *figlio di puttana* you married." Elisabetta punctuated her ire with an angry spit, then bent down to tie a sneaker that had come undone. "I like that Shane. And I'll like him even better when he puts a ring on it."

Mia favored her grandmother with an affectionate grin. "Simmer down, Beyoncé. Shane and I aren't anywhere near that point. We're like what they call friends with—"

"Benefits. Yeah, yeah, I know. It's all over my shows. I'm not a fan of that friends with benefit *merda.*" Elisabetta rose to her feet with a groan. "*Marrone, queste vecchie ossa.* I'm gonna give myself a goal today. Get up once without groaning or cracking."

Elisabetta headed into her apartment, and Mia bounded up the stairs to hers. First stop was her bedroom, where she pulled the cover off the cage of her pet parakeet, Pizzazz. She opened the cage door, and while she added pellets to the bird's food dish, Pizzazz flitted around the room, mischievously dive-bombing Doorstop. The cat swatted at the bird but, used to her antics, didn't bother to do more than that, especially since it would have required moving from a comfortable prone position.

As Mia showered, she thought about what her grandmother had said. She did need a life—one she'd denied herself after her philandering husband, Adam Grosso, had gone missing with his mistress in a Miami boating accident and Mia found herself the primary suspect in their disappearance. After a few tortuous months, the mistress's body had washed up on a local beach to the screams of sunbathers. With no evidence of murder, the police wrote off Adam as missing at sea, and Mia hightailed it back home to New York. But the trauma of the experience and Adam's disappearance haunted her. It took meeting Shane for Mia to realize she'd been using the ordeal as an excuse to avoid giving her heart to another man—someone she felt deep in her soul would never betray her.

Mia stepped out of the shower. She heard Alicia Keyes warbling "New York State of Mind," indicating an incoming cell phone call. She focused on toweling herself dry and let the call go to voicemail. "Hey, Mee-ster." Mia's bright mood dimmed at the sound of Little Donny's voice and unwelcome nickname for her, coupled with his gloomy tone. "I'm gonna be late today. Sorry." The call clicked off.

"Way to start your first day," Mia muttered. She loved Big Donny, who was her godfather in addition to being an actual godfather. But at the moment, the fact that he'd dumped his son's early midlife crisis in her lap made her feel, well, salty. "Why do I feel this whole Little Donny thing is gonna be a disaster?" She said this to Pizzazz, following the parakeet to its commodious cage. Mia secured the cage door, gave Doorstep a pet, then put on black slacks she topped with a slinky turquoise tank top she insisted to herself she chose because it was comfortable on a warm day, and not at all because Shane once commented that it matched the bright blue of her eyes.

Downstairs, Mia found Elisabetta comfortably ensconced on a new recliner while watching a show on a new fifty-inch smart TV, both recent eighty-fourth-birthday presents from Mia and Ravello. A plate of almond biscotti sat on her lap. Mia perched on an arm of the recliner. "Whatcha watching, Nonna?"

"One of those shows about Hollywood. They're doing a story on something about a pilot. But I don't know where the planes are."

Mia, confused, listened to the show's host, a vapid D-list actor who'd found his calling as an entertainment reporter, wax on about a project about to start production. "He's not talking about plane pilots. He means TV pilots. That's when they shoot a first episode of a show they're gonna try and sell to the networks or streamers." Mia gave herself a mental pat on the back for knowing this. Fifteen years of subscribing to *People* magazine had paid off.

"Huh. What's the name of the show?"

"I missed that. Hold on."

Mia took the remote and rewound. She stopped after a minute and leaned in to read the screen graphic behind the host. What she saw surprised her. "It's called *The Dons of Ditmars Boulevard*. And it's gonna be filmed here in Astoria. They're gonna follow around a bunch of Family wannabes."

Elisabetta gave a sage nod and adjusted her wig, which she'd knocked askew with the comb she was using to scratch a spot on her scalp. "*Dons of Ditmars Boulevard*. I heard about that show."

"Really?" Mia shot her grandmother a skeptical look. "Why would you have heard about a reality show pilot they haven't even begun to make yet?"

"Because, Miss Smarty-pants—"

"Hey, an expression from your own generation. I didn't know you remembered any of those."

"Because," Elisabetta continued, ignoring Mia's good-humored dig, "Gabriella Pasqualini's grandson Paolo was gonna be on the show, and she told us all about it. But he dropped out to become a priest."

"Wow. I didn't know anyone did that anymore."

"It happens. You don't know because the *paisans* don't brag about it like they used to. But I don't think this *Dons of Ditmars Boulevard* show is anything to brag about, either."

"Agreed. Those shows live to make people look bad. Or stupid. Or both." Mia snagged a biscotti from Elisabetta's plate and planted a kiss on her cheek. "I gotta get to work. *Ti amo.*"

"*Ti amo, bambina.*" Elisabetta pointed at the TV screen. "*Guardare,* it's Ditmars Boulevard. Look at all those goombahs."

Mia glanced at the long line of teens and young adults as the show host's voice-over explained they were waiting to fill out applications that might land them auditions for the show. She shook her head. "What kind of nutjobs would want to be on some low-rent reality show?"

She was about to find out.

Chapter 2

Mia sauntered into work at Belle View Banquet Manor, still basking in the afterglow of her rendezvous with Shane. The glow faded when she saw the sign taped to the office door of employee-when-she-felt-like-it Cammie Dianopolis: Recording in Progress—Do not Disturb. Mia opened the door, engendering an outraged squawk from Cammie. Guadalupe Cruz, the Belle View executive chef, sat on a folding chair next to her. A professional-looking mic sat on the desk between the two women, along with a phalanx of expensive-looking electronic equipment.

"Morning," Mia greeted them with purposely faked cheer.

"Ma'am." Guadalupe, an army veteran who'd manned the commissary kitchen during a couple of Iraq tours, was still military through and through.

"Mia, you interrupted the recording," Cammie scolded. She crossed her arms in front of her chest and gave her boss the evil eye, pursing lips painted a retro shade of frosty pink. Cammie found her style in the mid-1980s and still wore it with pride.

Mia met the evil eye with a raised eyebrow. "And you are recording exactly what?"

"A true-crime podcast based on the murders that involved Belle View," Cammie said, jazzed about her latest venture. She gestured to the electronics taking up every inch of space on her desk. "I got Pete to pony up for top-of-the-line gear."

Pete was Cammie's ex-husband, Detective Pete Dianopolis. Pete wrote self-published thrillers under the pen name Steve Stianopolis. Assuming he'd immediately join the pantheon of hugely popular authors like Lee Child, he'd divorced Cammie to make room for the author groupies he expected to fall at his feet. Neither they nor the big paycheck he expected ever materialized, and he'd come crawling back to Cammie, to the benefit of her and Belle View. A cowed Pete would do anything to win Cammie back, including springing for pricey recording equipment or revealing the occasional clue in one of the murder investigations involving the catering facility.

Guadalupe stood up, her towering frame filling the room. "I got menus to plan."

"No worries." Cammie checked a piece of equipment. "I think we got a good take before Mia barged in."

"You mean greeted you on the start of the *workday*," Mia said, hitting the word "work" hard.

"This is work," Cammie replied. "Everybody loves true-crime podcasts these days. It's great free publicity for Belle View."

Mia grimaced. "Not sure how 'learn all about

the murder victims found in or around Belle View Banquet Manor' is great publicity."

"Normally I'd be with you on that, ma'am," Guadalupe said. "But thanks to a podcast I heard, I just booked a visit to a B&B that was the former hideout of a doomsday cult, so I'll recuse myself from this conversation." With this, Guadalupe departed, her chef's toque grazing the top of the door frame.

Cammie pondered a document on her computer screen. "Which do you think is a better title, *Catering Hall Killings* or *Killings at the Catering Hall*?"

"Hmmm . . ." Mia thought for a moment. "I'd go with, forget the podcast because more important things are happening today, like Little Donny starting work here."

"That's a terrible title," Cammie said with a pout. She placed high-end earbuds in her ears and pressed a button on a recorder to play back her interview.

With the Kiwanis Club breakfast in Shane's perfectly shaped, capable hands, Mia focused her attention on Little Donny, who showed up close to lunchtime for his first day at Belle View looking like he'd slept in his clothes, which it turned out he had. "I got a serious overhang." The Boldano firstborn rubbed his forehead. Little D, as he insisted Mia call him—"It's my new handle, clever, huh?"—was good-looking in a swarthy way. But at the moment, his rumpled outfit and black beard stubble gave him the look of a shipwreck victim.

Mia silently prayed for patience dealing with "Little D." "Everything okay?"

"If it was, would I be here?" he grumped. "My kid brother's getting married, and I don't even got a girlfriend. Which reminds me, I'm not working weddings. I can't deal with some other couple's happy time right now."

"Fine. No weddings. Not a problem. We've got lots of graduation parties coming up. Tonight, there's one for a bunch of kids from Queens College."

Little D shook his head. "Jamie went to Queens College. I only got through high school because Dad got one of his goons to hack the school's grading software and change my Fs to Bs. So, no working a graduation party for me. Too depressing."

"*Fine.*" Mia said this through gritted teeth, her prayer for patience unanswered. "We've also got a birthday party for a four-year-old coming up. Not a graduation, I promise. They're all still in preschool. Little kids. Adorable."

Little D shook his head and whimpered. "The way things are going, I'll never have children."

God help me. Mia sucked in a breath and slowly released it. She summoned a sympathetic smile. "Donny, if you threw yourself into your work, it would distract you from your problems. You might even make some new friends."

Donny sparked to this. "Like hot college girls?"

It was Mia's turn to shake her head. "No dating the customers."

Little D muttered an expletive and slumped in his chair. "What's the point of all this anyway? Why should I help other people make happy memories?"

Mia leaned forward. "That's the *whole point*—to know you helped someone create a memory that will live forever. And you're part of that memory. Donny, that's incredibly fulfilling."

The recalcitrant new employee responded with a skeptical "Meh."

No wonder his parents wanted this guy out of the house, Mia thought to herself. Despite being in his almost-mid-thirties, Little D still lived at home. This wasn't unusual in Mia's circle, where friends often lived at home until they married. Mia knew a woman who had three kids by three different boyfriends but had never married, so she still lived with her parents, as did her kids. Still, most had walked down the aisle at least once, if not twice, by Little D's age. "Tell you what," Mia said, "I'll find something for you to do that won't push your buttons. In the meantime, why don't you check out your office?"

Little D followed her with little enthusiasm to the small office they'd carved out for him off the first-floor Marina Ballroom, where Flushing Marina could be seen shimmering through the room's floor-to-ceiling windows, as could the LaGuardia Airport runway, where a 737 was coming in for a noisy landing. After depositing her charge, Mia scurried to her father's office, catching him as he returned from his daily lunch at Roberto's Trattoria. "I wanted to warn you, there may be another murder on Belle View property."

Ravello responded with an understanding grin. "Little Donny?"

Mia nodded. "He's Little D this week. He hasn't

even been here an hour, and he's already making me *pazzo*."

She detailed her frustrating conversation with the latest Belle View employee. As she spoke, Ravello used the back of his hand to wipe perspiration from his forehead. While her father was a large man, he was also preternaturally dry, plus he'd lost weight recently. It occurred to Mia that he was breathing heavier than usual, too. "You okay, Dad? You're a little not yourself."

"It's all this diet and exercise Lin's forcing on me," Ravello said, referencing his girlfriend of about a year, a federal prosecutor turned florist who owned a charming shop in Manhattan's East Village.

"That should make you healthier," Mia pointed out.

"I've been ordering seafood salad instead of fettucine Alfredo."

Mia's eyes widened. "Wow. Your system may be rebelling against the switch from heavy cream to lettuce."

"In more ways than one. I was in the restroom at Roberto's, and—"

Mia held up a hand. "TMI. Even for a relative. Any tips on how to manage Little D so I don't lose my mind?"

"Give him a little time to make himself feel comfortable here," Ravello advised. "Meanwhile, keep checking out bookings. Something will come up he can deal with."

After conferring with her father about a few other business details, Mia returned to her office and called up the Belle View calendar. She noticed Cammie had added a facilities tour to the schedule. Intrigued by the name of the potential future customer, she popped up from her desk and went to Cammie's office. "I saw a tour for a Giles St. James Productions on the sked. What's that about?"

"A production company is checking out Belle View's catering facilities for an upcoming event." Cammie checked her reflection via her computer screen, patting down a few errant strands of frosted blond hair. "I call giving the tour. I wanna pitch them my podcast."

"You can have the tour on two conditions: no pitching, at least not yet. Let 'em book here first. And Little Donny shadows you."

Cammie groaned. "I don't care if you're running a halfway house for mobster spawn, but spare me any extra work, like training them."

"Extra work implies you do any work at all. And those are my conditions."

"Fine," Cammie grumped. "It's a good thing this is the best job in the world, or I'd quit."

Mia left Cammie to deliver what she hoped would be, if not good news to Little D, then at least news that didn't send the lost soul spiraling further. She found him engrossed in an app on his phone. "I've got a task I think you'll like. A production company is coming for a tour. Cammie is leading it, and you can shadow her so you learn how to give them yourself."

" 'Kay." Little D held up his phone. "Whaddya think? Could this be the future Mrs. Little D?"

Mia glanced at the photo of an excessively made-up, half-naked woman lying prone on a bed.

"What app is this?" She looked closer. "D, this isn't a dating app; it's a porn site."

"Your point is?"

"No porn in the workplace." She gave herself props for not screaming this in his face.

"Fine." Little D sounded glum. "I just searched 'Hot Chicks.' I was too depressed to pay close attention."

"Well, un-depress yourself. I'm walking you over to Cammie. She'll give you a rundown on everything you need to know for the tour."

Mia personally delivered her reluctant trainee to an equally reluctant Cammie and escaped to her office. Thrilled about the possibility of a production company using the Belle View facilities, she texted Shane the news. He responded with a bitmoji of himself giving a thumbs-up. Not for the first time, it struck Mia that even his avatar was gorgeous. She debated whether to go with a response involving hearts, then went with something a little more businesslike. She edited her avatar so it better reflected her coloring of dark hair, pale skin, and bright blue eyes, something she'd been meaning to do for a while, and sent Shane an image of the avatar holding a movie slate. To her delight, Shane hearted it.

Curious about why a production company was scouting an Astoria location, Mia typed "Giles St. James Productions" into the search bar on her computer, then clicked on the company's website. The glamorous bio of company founder and president Giles St. James impressed her. Excited, Mia envisioned Belle View as the premiere Queens catering facility for a marquee Hollywood production company. She clicked on a tab marked "Projects," and her enthusiasm lessened. Despite the tony website, Giles St. James Productions only produced cheesy reality shows, including the pilot for *The Dons of Ditmars Boulevard.*

Mia chided herself for being judgy. And then tamped down a sudden feeling of foreboding.

Chapter 3

On the way home from work that evening, Mia tried to dispel her concerns about the production company. She never knew if her instinct for trouble was the result of growing up as a mobster's daughter or some form of PTSD based on the same reason. Either way, there was no cause for concern yet. The Belle View tour hadn't happened and might not happen at all. Plenty of prospective clients canceled appointments at the last minute. *Worry is paying interest on a debt you may not owe*, she told herself. Mia couldn't remember where she'd heard this saying and considered it a little complicated to unpack, but it did come in handy sometimes. She shelved all thoughts of Giles St. James Productions, replacing them with daydreams about her upcoming evening with Shane.

Elisabetta waylaid her the minute she stepped inside their shared front vestibule. "*Guarda.*" She held up a large bag stuffed with fiber skeins in a glaring cacophony of colors. "The crafts shop is selling grab bags for a buck. You should see my haul."

Mia followed her grandmother into the living room, where every surface except for the floor was covered with a hideous array of yarns. The crafts shop had clearly found a way to foist unsellable merchandise onto their senior clientele—shove it into plastic bags, label them a "surprise collection," and sell the bags for a dollar, offering a deal knitters and crocheters like Elisabetta would be unable to resist. The yarns were so homely that even her grandmother's little rescue terrier mutt, Hero, ignored them, choosing to hunker down in a corner of the room far away from the offending fibers. "I been crocheting all day. I made you a little something." Elisabetta proudly held up a tank top in a shade of brown that reminded Mia of the bark on a dying tree, with shoulder straps crocheted in a bright—and clashing—fire-engine red. "Pretty, huh? Try it on."

Mia responded with an impulsive wince she quickly hid. "Sure."

She pulled off her silky lavender top and thrust her arms into the tank top. Within ten seconds, she'd broken a sweat. The fibers were nothing known to nature and breathed about as much as a rubber wetsuit. Elisabetta glanced up and down approvingly. "Now you got something special to wear on your next date with Shane."

"Right," Mia said, wondering if it was too late to plead a migraine and cancel her plans with him. A text pinged with the message *I'm outside*, answering her question. "Oh, goody. He's here."

Elisabetta gave her a gentle push down the hallway toward the front door. "*Vai.* Go. Enjoy. I got more crocheting to do. Or knitting. Whatevs."

Elisabetta watched her granddaughter make a slow death march to Shane's car. Shane's welcoming smile turned into a jaw drop as he took in her top. "What are you wearing?" he asked as she climbed into the front seat. "You look like you're playing the part of a tree in a kindergarten play. A very sick tree."

"Long story, but"—Mia cast a sly grin his way—"I'm hoping I won't be wearing this for too much longer."

Shane matched her grin with a sexy smolder. "You won't. I give you my word as a gentleman."

Shane kept his promise, with Mia's hideous tank top quickly shed post-dinner at his place. He brought her home in the morning so she could arrive at work separately from him, maintaining the clumsy ruse of hiding their relationship from coworkers who knew exactly what was going on but humored them. Mia fed Doorstop and Pizzazz food and kisses, then steeled herself for another workday with Downer Donny.

But over the next few days, Little D confounded expectations by not being the worst employee ever to work at Belle View. His mob-adjacent muscle scored Belle View some great deals, although he had to be constantly redirected onto the straight and narrow path. "We don't *steal* it off a truck, we *buy* it off a truck," Mia gently reminded him.

"Bor-ing," Little D said, blowing a raspberry. "But . . . it ain't bad 'negotiating' with suppliers . . . in my own way."

"As long as you're using words, not actions, to make deals," Mia said, nervous about what exactly the Mob boss's son meant by "in my own way."

She caught a break when the Giles St. James Productions reps showed up for their tour and she could foist Little D on Cammie for the innocuous activity. First, Mia welcomed them to Belle View in her position of second-in-command to her father, who had taken the day off to do a healthy-cooking workshop with girlfriend Lin. "We love the idea of hosting a production company and know we have the means to meet your every need," she told Ariadne St. James, who'd introduced herself as the company's vice president and executive producer.

St. James was an attractive, elegant Brit in her mid-forties whose cool reserve pushed Mia's too-Noo-Yawk-for-her-own-good buttons. When the producer spoke, it was with the dulcet tones of a Masterpiece Theater host. "You have excellent parking facilities, something we're in need of. I assume any charge for that is baked into the overall fee."

"Absolutely." Mia cursed herself for how the word came out in her own accent, a nasal Queens honk.

To her relief, Cammie came tapping down the hall in her bright pink, circa mid-1980s heels with Little D in tow. Cammie exchanged greetings with Ms. St. James and introduced her charge. "Donny is a recent employee here. He'll be shadowing me to learn the ropes on leading a tour."

Donny gave a slight bow and offered his hand to the woman. "Donato Boldano Junior at your service."

Upon hearing his name, Ariadne's reserve

melted. She took his hand and favored him with a warm smile. "Well, Donato Boldano Junior, I look forward to taking full advantage of your services."

The gleam in her eye set off an alarm bell for Mia.

"We'll start in the Marina Ballroom," Cammie said, herding Little D and Ariadne, whose eyes were locked on each other, toward the space.

Mia waited until they were out of sight, then ran to Shane's office. "We have a problem. Or maybe we don't. I don't know."

"Okay," Shane said, understandably confused.

Mia detailed the sparks she saw fly between the Boldano offspring and the producer. "It was his name that made her light up. Not his looks, although he's plenty good-looking. But so not my type. And he's like a brother to me." Shane's glower motivated the sidebar. "The pilot the company's producing is called *The Dons of Ditmars Boulevard.* What if she wants to put Donny on the show?"

"She'd be a terrible producer if she didn't think that the minute she met him," Shane said, not making Mia feel better. "But even if Donny wanted to be on the show, you know Donny Senior would say no. Has Little D ever gone up against his father?"

"Never," Mia said, calming down. "He idolizes him. He'd never do anything against his dad's wishes. I feel better. Thanks." She took a step toward Shane and then backed up. "I feel an urge to kiss you that I'm not gonna act on."

Shane gave an approving nod. "I feel exactly the same urge. But it would be inappropriate in the workplace."

Feeling assuaged, Mia returned to her office, where she focused on ordering favors requested by clients for their upcoming events. An hour or so later, Cammie poked her head in. "I booked the production company. You're welcome. I'm clocking out."

"Great, thank you. And it's noon. You've been here, what a couple of hours?"

"Considering I just filled three slow, mid-week blocks of time with a little Hollywood action, I'd say my day was well spent. Off to edit my podcast. If I can figure out how. Bye-yee."

Cammie started out. "Wait," Mia called. "Where's Donny?"

"He and the Brit broad went to lunch. They really hit it off."

Mia's stomach sank. This was not good news. "Do you know what kind of event the production company booked us for?"

"Yeah. A casting call for some show called *The Dons of Ditmars Boulevard.*"

Mia had a terrible feeling this was worse news.

By the next morning, Belle View was a madhouse. The lobby was filled with reality star wannabes, and a line snaked out the door. While Ariadne and her assistants ran the casting call from inside the Marina Ballroom, Giles St. James, CEO of the eponymously named company, worked the crowd waiting for what they hoped would be their big break. A man committed to hiding the fact he was in his late fifties—Mia had stumbled upon his birth date during her Internet search of the company—he had artfully colored sandy hair, a face gently plumped with fillers, and a fit body that was obviously the work of high-paid personal trainers. She watched as he laughed at one aspirant's jokes and placed a comforting hand on the shoulder of a tearful hopeful who'd been rejected. He caught Mia's eye and winked—not for the first time. The man was an incorrigible flirt.

She'd been disappointed to learn that, despite their shared running of the production company, Giles and Ariadne were divorced. Little Donny was respectful enough to eschew any thought of a relationship with a married woman. But no such luck this time, so Mia had spent the previous afternoon distracted from work as Little D sang Ariadne's praises. "She's super smart and sophisticated. I don't think I even knew what that was until I met her," Little D had said this with the dreamy eyes of a tween as he leaned back in his chair.

"Uh huh," Mia had responded, pushing his feet off her desk. "You do know she's gotta be, like, ten years older than you."

"It's awesome. She knows the world. And she's a lady. I mean, she's definitely a lady, but I mean a real one. You know, like royal and stuff."

"Really?" Mia, highly skeptical, had made a mental note to initiate an Internet dive into this claim when she had the time.

But that was then, and this was now. CEO Giles approached, snapping Mia out of her brooding. "Mia, love."

She managed a friendly smile. "Hi. Everything okay?"

"Brilliant." He flashed a mouth of perfectly spaced implants that put to rest all jokes about British dental care. He placed a hand on her arm. "I was wondering if I might trouble you for a cup of coffee. I could use a bit of a pick-me-up."

"Of course," Mia said. She removed her arm from under his hand. "Be right back."

Mia started down the hall to the facility's main kitchen. "And it would be lovely if it was a half caf, half decaf cappuccino with a tiny hint of cinnamon," Giles called after her.

Mia gritted her teeth but gave him a thumbs-up. The minute he turned his back, she stomped into the kitchen, ready to let loose about the handsy producer. Instead, she found the kitchen had been commandeered by Nicky Vestri, Donny and Jamie Boldano's younger cousin, and a few members of his low-rent crew. What Nicky lacked in looks he did not make up for in charm. He'd gone prematurely bald in his early twenties and opted for shaving his head. While this worked for a lot of men, in Nicky's case it highlighted the dents on either side of his head where he'd been pulled out of his mother at birth by forceps. And though his head lacked hair, he sprouted it everywhere else, including on his face, where a unibrow gave the impression of a perpetual frown. But the unibrow was quickly forgotten when he smiled, revealing a gold grill with the initials "NV" in tiny diamonds on his two front teeth. He flashed the grill now at the sight of Mia. "Hey, Mamma Mia."

"*Don't*," she warned.

Nicky held up his hands in mock obeyance. "*Mi scusi.*"

Mia ignored him. "I gotta make a cappuccino for Mister Producer out there," she said to Evans, Guadalupe's sous chef and Belle View's enormously talented pastry and dessert chef.

Evans pulled a tray of croissants from the oven. "I'll get it for you. I need these to cool before I plate them for the crew."

"Thanks so much."

Nicky gestured toward the Marina Ballroom. "This whole casting thing's a joke. Maybe four of those people'll get on the show, and none of 'em if they don't got what they call a 'chemistry read' with me. You know I'm on the show, right? Mia? You heard?" Not wanting to give Nicky any satisfaction, Mia muttered a response. "They say it's an 'ensemble' "—he threw derisive air quotes around the word—"but I'm basically the star. I'm looking at getting some swag—that stands for 'stuff we all get'—with my signature line on it. I been workin' on a couple, but I think I'm gonna go with 'Get outta here!' "

Nicky struck a pose and repeated the line several times, bolstered by his crew's exclamations of *yeah!*, *nice!*, and *good one!* Mia rolled her eyes, to Evans's amusement. She thanked him for the cappuccino and started for the ballroom, stopping at the sight of Nicky reaching for a croissant as Guadalupe emerged from Belle View's walk-in refrigerator with a butcher knife. She got in the miscreant's face and held up the knife. "Touch that and I take off your hand."

Nicky backed off, genuinely terrified, much to Mia's satisfaction.

She managed to avoid additional contact with Nicky and Giles St. James by hunkering down in her office for the next few hours. At the end of the day, there was a light rap on her door and Giles entered without an invitation to do so. "Success!" He threw his arms in the air in a gesture of triumph.

"In a single day, we have found our dons and donettes."

"Yay," Mia responded, thinking of the additional two days the company had booked that would now lie fallow.

"We'll pay for the days we booked," Giles said as if reading her mind. "I'd also like to hire you—"

"I assume by 'you' you mean Belle View—" Given the lecherous vibe she'd picked up from the man, Mia thought it wise to confirm.

"Yes, of course. I'd like to book Belle View to cater a party I'm throwing Friday night to celebrate the completion of pre-pro—that's pre-production. Sorry, sometimes I forget I'm talking with civilians." Mia, who was about to retort that it didn't take a Mensa IQ to figure out what "pre-pro" was short for, managed to restrain herself. "Anyway," Giles continued, "it will be a party for cast, crew, network execs, et cetera. Around fifty people. I'll have my assistant call you to work out the details. Do make it top of the line. I want to impress those executives."

The phrase "top of the line" chased away any annoyance Mia felt toward St. James. "I'll put together a package that will make those execs wish they were picking up two shows from you."

"Glorious, love," Giles said with a laugh. "I look forward to seeing you Friday night. I assume you'll be there to supervise?"

"Of course," said Mia, who had planned to dump the event in Shane's lap. She faked a smile. "See you then, love."

Chapter 4

Mia had to admit that St. James's East Side penthouse was spectacular. She stared out the massive glass windows onto a view that stretched from the East River to JFK and beyond. Friday night had come, and Mia felt a teensy bit of guilt at saddling Shane with drunken college grads while she and her party crew enjoyed the perks of catering to Manhattan's one-percenters.

With dinner completed, Mia tore herself away from the view to supervise the buffet of dessert items her cater-waiters were setting up. She nodded her approval, and they disappeared back into the capacious kitchen. Mia scanned the crowd for Little Donny. To her relief, he was hanging out with a few of the cast members and not Ariadne. She said a silent prayer he'd moved on and then turned her attention back to the dessert display. She moved a platter of mini cannoli front and center, hoping to entice guests with the tasty traditional treat before the crispy shells turned soggy from the ricotta filling.

An attractive woman wandered over to peruse the selection. She sported a haircut within an inch of her scalp and, as opposed to the other female guests, who were dressed like the homepage of the latest fashion blog, she wore cargo pants and a white T-shirt. "This all looks delish," she said, admiring the sweets spread.

Mia picked up a dessert plate and used tongs to add a couple of cannoli to it. She handed the plate to the woman. "Start with these."

"Cannoli? Love them." She took a bite and mmm'd her pleasure. "Homemade. I can tell. You're the caterer?"

"Yes." Mia extended a fist to bump. "Mia Carina. Belle View Banquet Manor."

"I'm Lysette House." She fist-bumped Mia. "The production company unicorn." She noticed Mia's quizzical expression and explained further. "I'm a show business rarity—a camera operator who's female *and* Black. You see? A unicorn."

"Got it. I'm impressed. Now you get a 'you go, girl' fist bump."

Lysette laughed. "I'll take it." The women fist-bumped again. The camerawoman's smile faded. "Not sure I earned that fist bump. I took St. James's crummy contract in exchange for the experience and a credit and eventually a step up to director. Here I am, five years later, in exactly the same position. It's a crazy business—entertainment in general, reality in particular."

"How so?"

The innocuous question triggered an avalanche of unexpected but intriguing gossip from the camerawoman, who seemed in desperate need of an ear. She pointed to a homely scarecrow of a man in his forties who appeared to be fawning over Ariadne. He smoothed his unnaturally dark hair with his hand, and it moved slightly off center, indicating a toupee. "That's Michael Planko. He was a TV drama writer, but his career dried up, and the only place he could get work was in reality TV as a segment producer, which is like being a writer, but we can't say that because reality shows aren't 'written.'" She took a breath, then kept going. "The big, doughy guy next to him is Jason, our 'intern.'"

"Intern?" Mia gazed at the man, who looked to be pushing fifty. "Isn't he a little old for that?"

"I know, right? He always wanted to work in show business, so he quit his job as an accountant making decent money to hire on with Giles as an accounting 'intern' making zero money. Giles promised he'd bump him up to a paid position. Just like he promised to give me a shot at directing and Michael a credit as executive producer. Like any of that will ever happen with that cheap SOB." The bitterness and anger in Lysette's voice took Mia aback.

A brawny twenty-something with tattooed arms approached the dessert table and began loading a plate with desserts. He looked vaguely familiar to Mia. "Hey, Kelvin," Lysette, once again cheerful, greeted him.

"Hey. You think it would be okay if I took some of this stuff home?"

"I'm the caterer," Mia said, "and sure. Ask in the kitchen, they'll make you a to-go box of whatever you want."

"Thanks, I appreciate it."

"Another intern?" Mia whispered to Lysette. "I figure with them not getting paid, they need to scrounge for food."

Lysette shook her head and took Mia's arm to lead her away from the table. "That's Kelvin Williams."

Mia's eyes widened. Williams had played the adorably precocious youngest child of an upwardly mobile Black family on *Say What?!*, a popular sitcom she'd watched religiously growing up. "I knew he looked familiar. Why is he working here? Shouldn't he be acting somewhere?"

"When he stopped being cute, he stopped getting cast. His dream is to move out of reality into documentaries, but no one in Hollywood will take someone seriously who peaked at age eight, especially when his teen years and early twenties were a series of tabloid fiascos. So he's a production assistant, stuck here with the rest of us, pigeonholed in reality TV. It'd take an act of the show business gods to move us out of it and into scripted."

"Or Saint Genesius of Rome."

"Huh?" Lysette gave Mia a blank stare.

"He's the patron saint of actors, comedians, and musicians. We learned about various saints in Catholic school, especially on their feast days. There's one for pretty much everything. Sometimes I look them up for fun."

"*Riiight.*" Lysette said this like she was doing her best to humor a disturbed person. She added a lemon square and brownie to her plate. "Nice talking to you."

She walked away, leaving Mia feeling embarrassed and depressed. She wasn't surprised to hear that "crummy boss" was on Giles St. James's list of smarmy credits. But she hadn't expected to find the business so sordid. Was that true of the entire entertainment industry, or did St. James make a career of hiring people desperate for a break no one would give them—including him? To Mia's mind, it was a business model sure to make the instigator some very angry enemies.

Her cell rang. Seeing the caller was Shane, her mood brightened. "Hi, you."

"Hi yourself. How's everything going?"

"It's going."

"That doesn't sound good."

Mia heard the concern in his voice and hastened to explain. "The party went great. But I had a long conversation with a woman who works for the production company, and all I can say is, I'm glad this is the last we'll see of them."

"I can say the same thing about the graduating class of Bishop Clark High School. If we could use the liquor I confiscated from these kids tonight at other Belle View events, we'd be set for a year."

Mia chuckled. "We should have had the parents give out breathalyzers as favors." She stifled a yawn. "We're about an hour away from heading out."

"Text me when you get home, so I know you're safe."

"Will do."

The call over, Mia took a moment to bask in the glow of her relationship with Shane. *How did I get so lucky*, she thought with a happy sigh.

Feeling the call of nature, Mia went to find a bathroom. The first two were occupied, and a guest directed her to two more down a second hallway, leading Mia to marvel at the fact the apartment not only had a plethora of bathrooms but a second hallway. She went to tap on the door of the third bathroom when she heard what sounded like canoodling coming from within, followed by an "Oh, Nicky. Ohhh . . ."

Ewwwwwwww!

Mia scrunched her face in distaste and scurried away. She continued down the hallway to find the fourth bathroom. It was en suite, which Mia had learned meant adjoining a bedroom, thanks to an explanation from a guest who saw the blank look on her face when he mentioned it.

She located the massive primary bedroom housing bathroom number four and was about to step into the room when she heard someone talking. She peeked in and saw Giles sitting on the room's king-size bed on a cell phone, his back to her. He spoke in a low, angry voice. "Calm down . . . I said, *calm down.* I told you, I'll handle it. Don't say a word to anyone, you hear me? Not one word. We have to be careful, babe. If anything goes wrong, there could be trouble. The kind you don't come back from."

St. James wiped his forehead with the back of his hand. Mia could see he was perspiring. He ended the call and muttered a few profanities. Before Mia could make a getaway, he turned and saw her. "Oh, hello, love," he said, quickly slipping into flirtatious mode.

"Oh, hi." Mia turned back and forth a few times, hoping to pass herself off as a flustered airhead. "I was looking for a restroom. There are so many in this amazing apartment, I got lost. Sorry." She added a bimbo-ish giggle for effect.

Giles rose from the bed and started toward her. "There's one right here in my boudoir."

Chapter 5

Happy to have Giles St. James Productions in the rearview mirror, Mia found herself looking forward to visiting bucolic Connecticut for Jamie and Madison's celebratory barbecue. The Queens contingent, which included Boldano cousin Nicky Vestri and some of his *Dons* costars, arrived at Worthington in a flotilla of Escalades and other giant, high-end black SUVs. Bringing up the rear was the purple Tesla the Boldanos had given to Mia to show their gratitude for her help in solving a murder in which several family members had been implicated as suspects. Preferring her preowned Honda, she'd passed the car on to Shane, who treated it with the love and affection usually lavished on a newborn child. He'd happily ferried her, Elisabetta, and Ravello the hour-plus from Queens to the barbecue.

They stepped out of the car into sweltering heat. "*Eh, che successe?*" Nonna, who wore a top crocheted in a quilt of clashing colors over a black skirt, fanned herself. "What's going on here? I

"Oooh, cool, oh wait, the one down the h
opened up, thanks anyway, bye."

Mia practically ran toward the bathroom
cently inhabited by Nicky and his hookup. O
inside, she locked the door behind her and spra
the room with disinfectant. She heard heavy f
steps and Giles's British accent as he walked p
her hideaway. Once she was sure he was gone, s
whipped out her cell and placed a call to her h
cater-waiter.

"Cody, put any leftover desserts into to-go bo
the guests can take with them. I want us on t
road back home in ten."

"But—"

"I mean it. The sooner we're out of here, t
better."

thought Connecticut had better weather than New York."

"Worthington is only an hour north of us," Mia said. "And I guess the Wythes' house is a little too far inland for a sea breeze. Dad, you might want to take off your sport coat."

"Never."

"Then at least unbutton the top button of your shirt."

"Fine." Her father reluctantly undid a button. "But I don't wanna hear gossip about me being underdressed."

"I wouldn't worry about that," Mia said. She motioned to the Connecticut crowd. Men and women alike were clad in polo shirts, topsiders, and khaki or Bermuda shorts. The women's hair was either pulled back in a ponytail or contained by a headband. And the hair . . . Mia had never seen so much glossy hair in her life. Blond, brunette, red, silver—all of it shimmered and shone in the sunlight.

Mia cursed her fashion choices. Shane had lucked out from her online search for outfits. All she'd been able to find for him was a polo shirt with a tiny anchor embellishment. Except for the fact he was wearing khaki slacks instead of khaki shorts, he fit right in with the local crowd, more so than any of the other Italians. Mia, on the other hand, had gone all in on the nautical theme. She'd found a romper decorated with sailboats that came with the sailor hat now perched on her head. Her feet sported high-heeled thong sandals with the leather shaped like a big anchor. Excited by her finds, she'd considered the look on point. But now . . . "I look like one of the extras in those

1930s movies you watch on TCM," she muttered to her grandmother.

"I told you to wear the cute top I crocheted for you, but would you listen? Nooo."

"I think you look pretty," Shane, ever the gentleman, said.

"I see Donny Senior and Aurora," Ravello said. "We should say hello, Mama. *Andiamo.*"

They departed to pay respects to the parents of the groom, just missing the groom and bride-to-be, Jamie Boldano and Madison Wythe, who were heading toward Mia and Shane. The couples exchanged hugs and kisses. Jamie gave Mia a salute. "Ahoy, matey," he said with a wide grin. "How's things on the Good Ship Lollipop?'

Mia glowered at her friend. "Shut up."

"Jamie, leave her alone," his fiancée chided. "She looks adorable." She pointed at Mia's footwear. "Tory Burch 2021 spring collection. Those are a find."

"So are you, Maddie." Mia stuck her tongue out at Jamie as she hugged Madison. While Mia had once debated rekindling her high school romance with Jamie, she was glad they'd wound up in the friend zone. She'd come to cherish Madison for both her friendship and her amazing connections as the editor of a popular fashion blog.

"Where's your dad?" Jamie asked. "I want to say hi."

Mia indicated Ravello, who was chatting with Donato Boldano Senior and his wife, Aurora. "Over there, talking to your parents."

Jamie looked in the direction she pointed, squinting in the bright, hot sunlight. "He doesn't look so good. Why is he wearing a jacket? The invitation said casual dress."

"You know my dad. That is casual for him. Uh oh."

The others looked to see what generated the "uh oh" and Mia's concern. Little D had sauntered into the party with his date . . . Ariadne St. James. He kept an arm around her waist in a way that seemed less romantic than defiant. Mia noted the expression on his parents' faces, which advertised that they were not fans of their son's new inamorata. Aurora looked stricken, while Donny Senior simmered with rage.

"Is that DJ's new girlfriend?" Given the skeptical tone in Jamie's voice, Mia added Little D's brother to the list of those not on board with the relationship. "She's a lot older than him. I mean, not that that's a bad thing, it's just . . . there's something off . . . I don't know . . ." Unable to articulate, Jamie stopped talking.

"She's supposedly some kind of royalty. A lady or something." Mia watched the couple approach the elder Boldanos, who mustered up tentative smiles. Little D's body language radiated tension. On the other hand, Ariadne, clad in an elegant beige jumpsuit, a straw hat framing her lovely face, gave off a coolly collected charm—which Mia could tell Donny Senior and Aurora weren't buying.

"I know who can confirm whether she's royal," Madison said. "My cousin Pickney. She's an extreme Anglophile. Like, she wishes the US never declared independence from the Brits and hates that George Washington chose to be president and not king."

"Whoa, that *is* extreme," Shane said.

"Picks," Madison called to a young woman dressed in a dull gray A-line shift who looked bored out of her mind. "Come here. I need to ask you something." Madison's cousin wandered over, bringing a sense of apathy with her. "Don't let her see you checking her out, but that woman over there. Do you know who she is?"

Pickney glanced at Ariadne. "Ariadne St. James, born Lady Ariadne Tottenham. Her father was the Earl of Scarborough, mother was Lady Vanessa Barnes, eldest daughter of the Marquess Averbury. She took her married name to separate herself from her OG family and establish her own identity in the entertainment business, much to the horror of her landed gentry relatives. Anything else?" Madison shook her head, and Pickney wandered off.

"Those are some pretty impressive creds," Mia acknowledged reluctantly.

Shane rubbed his chin. "Yeah, but . . . why is she here? And why is she making crappy reality TV shows? You'd think she'd wanna do classier stuff."

"Good questions," Mia said. "Maybe Pickney knows the answers."

"She's leaving the party," Madison said. "She's got an online date with a monarchist in London."

Shane nudged Mia. "I think Mr. Boldano wants to talk to you."

Mia glanced over to see Donny Senior gesturing to her with urgency. "Be right back."

She forged an awkward path toward the Boldanos, her heels sinking into the soft, wet grass with each step. The older couple took turns kissing her on both cheeks, then Donny Senior said,

"Mia, *bellissima,* we need you to do us a favor. We need you to break up Donny and this Arachne—"

"Ariadne. I think Arachne is like a spider."

"That's what she is," Aurora interjected. "A spider. Trying to catch our baby in her web. Saying she's a 'lady' like the queen. Feh."

"She actually is a lady."

"Oh, she's no lady," Aurora said, ire rising. "Even if she is a lady, she's not a lady. A mother knows. And her age. A woman in her forties has a five percent chance or less of giving me grandbabies. I googled it." Aurora held up her cell phone.

"*Basta, cara mia.* Enough." Donny Senior placed a comforting hand on his wife's arm. "I'll take care of this. Mia, you have to break them up and find Junior a new girlfriend. That's the best way to get over a relationship. March straight into a new one."

Mia wasn't surprised by the couple's request to eighty-six their eldest's latest romance. She knew they dreamed of Little Donny settling down with a nice Italian girl—or any nice girl, a vibe Ariadne did not give off. But Mia had to be honest with them, which wasn't easy given Donny Senior's position as the Boldano overlord. "You know I love you all. But Junior is an adult. He's gonna make his own choices. Some will be good, some won't be. Whatever they end up being, they're his to make."

The blast of an air horn interrupted the conversation, engendering startled screams from the Italians. "Minibus to the sailboat! Let's go!" The call to action came from Madison's ruddy-faced older brother, Scooter Wythe.

"I can't swim, so I gotta pass." This came from a

Dons cast member. A couple of others echoed the same demurral. The Queens contingent was not a seafaring lot, or an outdoor lot in general.

Scooter slapped an arm around the shoulder of the guy. "No excuses. Life jackets for all my friends!"

He and several hearty-looking friends steered a nervous group that included Ravello and Donny Senior toward the minibus. "I'll go and keep an eye on the elders," Shane said.

"Can you swim?"

Shane nodded. "And sail. A friend in Italy had a yacht, but he liked to sail, so the power yacht would tow a sailing yacht around the Mediterranean."

He jogged to the minibus and hopped on. The bus took off. And not for the first time, Mia had a flash of insecurity wondering when Shane would bail on event planning at Belle View to return to his former glamorous life.

While the others were out at sea, the guests who remained behind snacked on crackers and cheese cubes, which Mia assumed was the Connecticut version of antipasto. She endured a drunken rant from Madison's maid of honor, Delany, a childhood friend who was now in the middle of a nasty divorce. Mia finally extricated herself with the excuse that Elisabetta needed more cheese cubes. "With all the cheese I'm eating, I'm never gonna make another BM," an unhappy Elisabetta said. "Don't they got nothing else to eat?"

"There's potato chips and onion dip."

Elisabetta reacted with disgust. "*Non è cibo.*"

"It is food, Nonna, just not what you're used to eating. I'll see if I can dig up anything else."

Mia rose from the table. She was on her way to the Wythe kitchen when Ariadne crossed her path. "Mia. Hello. Might I have a word with you? In private?"

"Of course," Mia said, managing to hide her discomfort. She'd found in life that conversations held "in private" tended not to bode well.

Ariadne led them to a stand of trees away from the party. "I've learned from Donato that his parents asked you to break us up."

Mia flushed. "I wouldn't take it personally. You wouldn't be his first girlfriend they didn't li—they had . . . issues . . . with."

"I don't need to tell you he's extremely unhappy about anyone interfering with our relationship."

Mia fumed at the undercurrent of threat in Ariadne's comment. "He doesn't have to worry about me on that score. I told his parents he was an adult and to back off. Let him make his own life choices, good or bad." She put a little spin on the word "bad."

Message sent, Ariadne backed down. "I'm happy to drop names to prove my royal bona fides, should you need them. I left Britain because that world is such a bore. Between us," she adopted a friendly, conspiratorial tone, "I like bad boys. Not the dull, skin covered with spots kind you find in merry old England. The Noo Yawk kind. Like Little D. Who also happens to be a gentleman who knows how to make a woman feel special. The best of both worlds."

"The Boldanos are a very tight family. And they can sniff out if someone is using them. Well, most of them can. Little Donny, not so much."

"I swear to you, I am not using him. We make a

wonderful team." Ariadne grew dreamy-eyed. "I can imagine him taking over the family 'business.' With me at his side."

"That will never happen," Mia said, horrified at the thought of Ariadne as a different kind of lady—a Lady Macbeth, running the sketchy show for her less devious partner. "We're trying to get him out of the Life, not get him in deeper. And what happened to your producing thing? Don't you have a whole company going with your ex, and by the way, what is that about? You two are pretty cozy for a divorced couple."

"I would never give up the production company, which I made sure to garner a good portion of in our settlement. My former husband knows what an asset I am to the company, hence his amiable attitude. We even have apartments in the same building. And I see no reason why Giles St. James Productions can't eventually wind up under the Boldano business umbrella."

Ariadne flashed a sly smile and slithered off. Disturbed by the conversation, Mia retreated to Elisabetta's table. "My stomach's growling," her grandmother complained. "I can't stuff down another cracker. Whatcha got for me?"

"Huh?" Mia responded, still brooding over her contretemps with Ariadne. "Sorry, I couldn't find anything. You'll have to tough it out until they serve lunch."

Elisabetta made an exasperated sound. "No wonder these Connecticut people's so thin. They got nothing good to eat."

An hour or so later, the minibus returned from the sailing excursion, interrupting a spirited argument among the locals about the pros and cons of adding relish to potato salad. The visitors staggered off the bus in various stages of disrepair. A few victims of seasickness were pale or slightly green. "These cost three hundred bucks." Nicky picked up a foot to show Mia his soggy and ruined Italian leather loafers. "That's comin' out of Jamie's wedding money present."

Mia caught up to her father and Shane. "How'd it go? You okay, Dad?"

"Fine," Ravello gasped. "I'm getting water. Regular, not ocean." He headed off with a slightly unsteady gait.

"I couldn't get him to take off his sport coat," Shane said, frustrated. "He wore it over his life vest."

Madison's mother, Betsy, a perky, thirty-years-older version of her daughter, rang a cowbell. "Soup's on!" she trilled. "Everyone, line up."

"Tell me she's not really serving soup," Shane said, appalled. "It's gotta be ninety-five degrees out here."

"I think that's a figure of speech they use here in Connecticut."

A line formed for food. Mia and Shane joined it. The Italians cast wary glances on the mounds of ribs and chicken slathered in sauce and buckets of coleslaw, potato salad—without sweet relish—and macaroni salad. In addition to not being a seafaring or outdoor lot, the Queens crowd wasn't a barbecue lot. But plates were filled, and seats were taken. The meal commenced, followed by slices from a large vanilla sheet cake covered with store-bought vanilla frosting and decorated with strawberries and blueberries arranged to emulate the stars and stripes of an American flag.

Betsy Wythe rang the cowbell again to get everyone's attention. "Hello? Hello, everybody? Can I have your attention?" The crowd quieted. "Good." She held up a red Solo cup of lukewarm beer from one of the party's kegs. "On behalf of the mister here and me—." She gave an affectionate nudge to her husband, Topher, whose beet-red face indicated a lack of sunscreen and an abundance of keg beer, much like son Scooter. Madison's father waved to their guests and motioned for his missus to continue. "We want to thank all of you for coming and offer a toast to our beautiful daughter and her wonderful fiancé, whom we are thrilled we'll soon get to call our son-in-law . . . to Madison and Jamie!"

The guests toasted with a cheer. More toasts followed, some jocular, others weepy. Mia managed to shut down inebriated maid-of-honor Delany, whose toast devolved into a rant about husbands who were too weak to stick out a marriage after discovering their wife installed spyware on their cell phone in case they even *thought* of cheating on her.

The last toast came from Jamie's big brother, Donato Boldano Junior. He stood up and raised a glass of Strega, the Italian liqueur Mia had noticed his group passing each other surreptitiously under the table. "Baby brother, my heart is filled with more love for you than I can say. And now I get to share that love with the special someone I'll soon get to call my sister-in-law." The guests responded with "awwws." Madison wiped a tear from her cheek. Jamie beamed. "We've had our ups and downs, but that's brothers. Am I right?" He said this to the guests, who chuckled. He even got a couple of "you know its" and "*so* rights." Little D resumed his speech. "I know my family worried about me, especially next to Jamie, who I'm proud to say will soon be the therapist you see when your own marriage is falling apart, ha ha."

"Don't laugh, it's true!" Delany cried out. Scooter Wythe ushered her off into the house.

Little Donny addressed his family, all seated together at one table. "Brother . . ." He choked up. "Dad . . . Mama . . . you don't have to worry about me anymore." He cast adoring eyes at Ariadne, who batted her pale gray peepers back at him. "I found my person. And we've got great news to share." He returned to addressing the entire party. "Not only are we in love, but we'll soon be working together. When I . . . wait for it . . . join the cast of *The Dons of Ditmars Boulevard*!"

There was a moment of silence from the Boldanos. And then they let loose.

CHAPTER 6

Big Donny cursed and roared. Aurora wept and wailed. The locals watched in fascination like it was a Fellini film. All they were missing was popcorn.

"Stop infantilizing me," Little D screamed at his parents.

"Fancy words for a kid I had to pay someone to take high school tests for," his father yelled back. "Did you get it from your brother, the shrink?"

"I won't be a shrink, Dad. I'd have to go to medical school for that," Jamie corrected. "And . . . maybe." Caught talking about his parents behind their backs, he added the latter sheepishly.

"I'm thirty-four, and I still live at home. I can't no more, I can't." Mia heard desperation in the Boldanos' prodigal son's voice and felt a spark of compassion for him.

"That's how it works with our people," Aurora said. "Kids live at home until they get married. Sometimes they grow old and die there. It's our way."

"Jamie moved out in his mid-twenties," Little D argued.

"Jamie's . . . different." The way Donny Senior said this implied it wasn't necessarily a positive.

Little D gave an aggravated groan. He ran his hands through his thick dark hair. "I need a life. My own life. Not one where I make you and Mom happy. One where I make *me* happy." He took the hand of his girlfriend, who'd stood by his side watching the fight in silence. "Come on, Ari. Let's get outta here."

"Hey," his cousin Nicky said, outraged. "*Get outta here* is *my* signature line. It's on all my swag."

Donny stomped off with Ariadne in tow. As they passed, Mia swore she heard his producer girlfriend say, "If only we'd filmed that."

"Mia, do something," Donny Senior, beside himself, ordered.

"*Me?*" Mia echoed, startled.

Jamie held up a hand. "Dad, leave Mia out of this. I'll let DJ cool off tonight and call him tomorrow. He's not wrong. He does need a life."

His father let a string of invectives fly from his mouth. Fortunately for the party guests, they were all in Italian. "You want him on that *pazzo* show making our family and our Family look like idiots?"

"Little Donny knows where the line is." Jamie lowered his voice. "If you have to worry about anyone in the family making us look like idiots, it's that guy." He indicated Nicky, who was unintentionally mimicking a cartoon character as he flaunted his biceps for a nonplussed friend of Madison's. "If nothing else, Donny can keep an eye on him when they're making the pilot."

His father responded with a grunt, but Mia could tell Big Donny was slightly placated. Aurora took Jamie's hands in hers. "*Mi dispiace, carino.* I'm sorry your brother had to go ruin your party."

Jamie substituted his mother's hands with Madison's. He gazed into his fiancée's eyes with adoration. "As long as I'm with Madison, nothing can ruin today. Or any day. I want my brother to feel that way about someone someday. Maybe he does right now, with this Ariadne."

Aurora pulled her phone out of her purse. "I got a Google graph about fertility in older women to show you."

Despite Jamie's attempt to extricate Mia from the family drama, she once again found herself in the center of it the next morning. "Did you see the request from Little Donny?" Cammie asked moments after Mia arrived at Belle View.

"You're here early? And checking your work e-mail? Are you okay?" Given Cammie's commitment to coasting on the job, Mia was genuinely concerned.

"I need to futz with my podcast, but it's harder to do than I thought, so I'm tending to other things."

"I see. You're procrastinating by doing your actual job."

"Exactly. Anyway, he and that producer chippie want to film him in action here at Belle View."

Mia reacted with a combination of disbelief and annoyance. "Seriously? You've got to be kidding."

"No joke. He sent the request to both of us.

What should I tell him? I need to know. I've got, like, a hundred e-mails to plow through. I really need to go through them more often. I'll put it in as overtime."

Mia rubbed her temples in an attempt to stave off a Boldano induced headache. "My instant response is a hella no. But I need to check with Donny Senior. I don't want to make any decision about his son without him weighing in."

Cammie gave her a thumbs-up with a mauve-polished nail. "Got it. I'll go through my in-box and then tackle anything else you need me to do."

Mia gaped at her. "Cammie, it sounds like you might be putting in a full day here. Now I'm really worried."

"Don't be. As soon as I nail this podcast thing, it'll be back to my all-four-seasons summer hours." Cammie delivered this as she sashayed out of the office in the suede aqua pumps she'd bought in 1987.

Mia found Little D's e-mail. After perusing it, she placed a call to Donny Senior, who answered on the first ring. She detailed the request to him. "This is what they call pro forma because I know what you're gonna say, but I wanted to keep you in the loop."

"Do it," he instantly responded, to Mia's surprise.

"Really? I was sure you'd say no. I thought you hated Little Donny being in the show."

"I do. But if they're around Belle View, it'll give you a chance to keep an eye on this Ariadne character and maybe dig up dirt I can use to kill the relationship. Don't worry, I mean that as a figure of speech."

"I'm not gonna spy for you, Donny. I'm not comfortable with that."

"Don't think of it as spying. Think of whatever you uncover as, ya know, conversation starters. Small talk. Like, I wonder if it's gonna rain today. And oh, by the way, I found out Little Donny's girlfriend has a rap sheet in jolly old England."

Mia counted to ten, and then said, "I'm okay filming here. But that's it. No spying."

"Fine," Big Donny said, disgruntled. "I'll ask Cammie. I hear she's procrastinating."

He signed off. "Great," Mia muttered. She closed her eyes and dropped her head in her hands. Her instincts sent a Mayday that the situation with Donny and the show was in danger of spinning out of control. Mia needed to talk to someone who could offer insight into exactly how volatile things might get, and she knew exactly who that was.

"They got a new table." Mia ran her hands over the smooth metal table bolted to the floor of the visitors' room at the Triborough Correctional Facility. She sat across from her brother, Positano "Posi" Carina. Older than her by two years, he had been one of Little Donny's closest friends until Posi's penchant for stealing luxury sports cars landed him his most recent stay at the facility.

"Nicer chairs, too." Posi lifted his rump to reveal his sturdy metal chair, which was also bolted to the ground.

"Who's the new guy?" Mia spoke in a whisper, motioning to the guard keeping a watchful eye on them. "Where's Henry?" she asked, referencing the guard her family had come to know so well through various bouts of Posi or Ravello's incarcerations that they considered him a family friend.

"Vacay in Vegas. So, what's up, sis? I'm assuming it has something to do with the show pilot."

"You know about that?"

"Little D paid me a visit this morning. Told me about the show, his new girlfriend. I never pegged him for dating cougars, but the heart wants what it wants."

"His dad wants me to spy on him. I said no."

"Good for you, standing up to him. Little D's in a good place, except for the stupid new nickname. I don't think I ever saw him so excited about anything as he is about this show and this lady friend. The Boldanos need to cut the cord."

"Thanks. I needed a little reassurance. The fact you think everything's okay—"

"Oh, I don't think that at all. I can guarantee there's gonna be trouble at some point." He frowned. "I should be on that show. If there was ever a don of Ditmars Boulevard—"

"Wrinkles," Mia reminded him, pointing to his forehead.

"Right." Posi, who was up-front about his vanity, immediately stopped frowning.

Mia gave her brother a look. "I thank God you're in here. I'm terrified thinking what you might do for attention on TV."

"I'm not the one you should worry about." Posi frowned again, then dropped it. "Little Donny said his cousin Nicky is on the show. He's a snake. There are two guys in here because they got caught up in one of his sketchy 'ventures' and he ratted them out in exchange for probation. Do. Not. Trust. Him."

"Believe me, I don't plan to."

"That's my smart, gorgeous sister. Hey, how's Dad? He called a couple of times, but I haven't seen him in a couple of weeks."

"Good. Kind of. Lin's got him on a health kick—you know, good food, more exercise—but he seems kind of off his game."

Posi chuckled. "I bet. Healthy eating and exercise gotta be a shock to his system."

A bell indicating the last few minutes of the visiting hour rang. "Time to wrap things up," the guard said.

Mia stood up. She blew her brother a kiss. "Love you."

"Love you, too. Hey, keep me posted about the show, will ya?"

Mia noted the plaintive undertone under her brother's attempt at nonchalance and felt for him. "Of course. If a network buys the pilot—listen to me, I'm learning so much about the 'industry,' as they like to call it—maybe you can be on the show when you get out of here."

"Yeah, right. If I live that long."

Posi frowned yet again. And this time, the frown stuck.

Chapter 7

Mia's reluctance to indulge Giles St. James Productions with filming privileges disappeared when Cammie, who had turned into a worker bee, negotiated a contract for Belle View to provide all the company's craft services and catering needs. "Craft services is the snack and drink stuff for between meals," Cammie explained. "Shane can buy in bulk, and then we charge a nice markup for it."

"Okay," Mia said, a bit hesitant. "Is that kosher? Both literally and figuratively?"

"Totally on the figurative. And that reminds me to take note of anyone's special dietary needs. I'll give Ariadne a call."

Mia didn't expect Cammie's burst of industriousness to last, so she made sure to take advantage of it while she could. Having tasks taken off her plate allowed Mia the freedom to nose around the reality show goings-on—not to gather intel for Big Donny, but for her own curiosity.

She learned that following Little D around

Belle View with a camera had proved uneventful—or, as Giles St. James put it, "a soul-crushing bore." But while there was no tension on camera, there was plenty behind the scenes. Camerawoman Lysette grumbled that director Brian, a weary-looking man in his late forties, spent more time on the phone with his agent trying to score other jobs than lining up shots for *The Dons of Ditmars Boulevard,* the show he'd actually been hired for. Segment producer Michael sucked up to his bosses whenever he could, then spread nasty gossip about them behind their backs. And production assistant Kelvin, who'd developed a pitch for a documentary, was gung ho on setting up a meeting with Giles St. James that the company president seemed equally gung ho to avoid. Only middle-aged accounting intern Jason maintained a sunny sense of enthusiasm.

Ratcheting up the tension was an undercurrent of hostility on the part of Little D toward St. James. "Look at him," he said to Mia, his eyes on the executive producer and Ariadne, who were sharing a laugh as they bellied up to the lunch buffet in the Marina Ballroom. "Uh, hello," Little Donny sniped. "She's not your wife anymore, dude. Remember?"

"There are all kinds of divorces," Mia said. "Friendly ones and not so friendly ones, like with Delany, Madison's maid of honor. Transactional ones, like Cammie and Pete's. From what I pick up, Giles and Ariadne have a work partnership, not a romantic relationship. I wouldn't worry about it." Realizing she was encouraging the questionable romance between Little D and Ariadne, she hastily added, "but if you *are* worried, maybe it's best to call things off and move on."

"Never." The Boldano eldest spoke with an intensity Mia had never seen in him before, then strode toward the buffet, where he elbowed his way between Ariadne and St. James, who rolled his eyes.

With the Belle View shoot a wash, production moved to the sole mansion in Astoria. A block of modest two-family homes had been leveled to make room for Casa Giovanni—or as it was known by its less florid translation in English, John's House. The manse was a goombah palace that fulfilled every mobster stereotype, both without and within. Sadly, the John in question only lived in his eponymously named estate for a few months. But if visitors to the home's roof garden squinted and looked in the distance, they could make out the gangster's current home—New York's infamous Riker's Island, where John was currently awaiting sentencing for a myriad of crimes.

Shane helped Mia set up a continental breakfast spread for the *Dons of Ditmars Boulevard* cast and crew in one of the mansion's many massively marbled and gilded rooms. This particular room overlooked the pool, where the next scene was being shot. "I think we're good here," Mia said. "All I have to do set up the craft services table so there are snacks to tide everyone over between breakfast and lunch."

"How much food do these TV people need?"

"An endless amount, apparently."

Shane checked his phone. "I gotta get back to Belle View. Cammie said something about reorganizing the file cabinet in my office, and I forgot to lock the door to keep her out."

"We'll all be better off when she returns to coasting mode," Mia said.

"Amen to that."

Shane glanced around to make sure no one was watching. He gave Mia a quick kiss that turned into a not-so-quick one, then the couple forced themselves to part, and he left for Belle View.

After putting out an array of packaged bars and cookies, along with covered fruit trays, Mia took a break. She put on sunglasses and wandered outside to the mansion's Olympic-size pool, which was flanked by statues of half and fully naked Roman gods and goddesses. Inspired by the dons' general lack of water skills at the Connecticut barbecue, Ariadne had come up with a scene where the young men received swimming lessons. The dons were in the pool house, which doubled as a gym, changing into what Mia hoped against hope weren't Speedos. But the donettes, pretty girls in their late teens and early twenties, were lying prone on lounge chairs, catching rays. "You're blocking my sun," a particularly stunning girl said to Mia in a Queens accent so thick it recalled a line Mia once heard from a comedian: "New York women are beautiful until they open their mouths."

Mia stepped back "She's doing you a favor, Chiara," the girl next to her said. "You never use sunblock. Your skin could use a break. I'm Francesca." She added this by way of introducing herself to Mia.

"Mia." She waited for an introduction from Chiara. None came.

"And this is Chiara," Francesca said with a resigned tone that told Mia she was used to picking up her friend's slack.

"Nice to meet you," Mia responded politely. Beneath her sunglasses, she eyed the girls. Chiara's olive skin glistened with oil under a white bathing suit, which was technically a one-piece, although cut with so many peek-a-boo holes Mia wondered how it stayed on. Francesca, petite but possessing an equally perfect figure, wore a black string bikini that looked almost modest by comparison. "Are you excited about being on the show?"

Francesca made a face. "It's so sexist." She gestured to the row of donettes on their lounge chairs. "We're ornaments. If they think all we're gonna do is get wasted and fight with each other over these idiot guys, I may have to lead a protest."

"Ignore her," Chiara said with a languid stretch. "That's her character. The 'Feminist.'"

Francesca glowered at her. "It's not an act."

Chiara snorted. "I didn't see any girl power last night when you were flirting with Joey, Chief Low-Rent in Charge of Skimming Gasoline from the neighborhood cars."

"You're just jealous because a guy wasn't all over you for a change."

"He was before he moved on to you."

"You wish."

"With Joey?" Chiara made a dismissive arc with a hand sporting neon-green, two-inch press-on nails. "Uh, I don't think so."

Mia, tired of the girls' sniping, changed the subject. "What's your character on the show, Chiara?"

Chiara stuck out her ample chest. "Hot girl who's looking for a guy who's gonna treat me like the ornament I am."

Mia grudgingly admired her moxie. While she didn't know these girls specifically—they were all a good ten years younger than her—she knew their type. She'd grown up with them. The only options that might get them out of the neighborhood were higher education, which wasn't too popular with their crowd, or, these days, a reality show. "Well, good luck to both of you."

Chiara squinted at Mia with her dark brown eyes. "You're the caterer, right? We could use water bottles out here. On ice."

Mia bristled at the girl's preemptory tone. "Please."

"Seriously?"

"Yes."

The women stared each other down. Chiara broke first, as Mia was sure she would. "Fine. *Please.*"

"Coming right up." As Mia headed off to get water bottles, she heard Francesca say to Chiara with much glee in her voice. "Ha! She totally got you," to which the other girl responded with a disgruntled profanity.

Mia returned to the room where she'd set up the food. She was on her knees pulling a twelve-pack of water bottles out from under the table when she heard angry voices. They grew louder until Mia realized the two men arguing were in the room. She crouched low, hidden under the table.

"You can't steal my idea." She recognized the voice of production assistant and former actor Kelvin.

"A where-are-they-now show about former child stars is hardly a new idea, Kelvin."

"Yeah, but one focused only on child stars of color is." Kelvin spit this out with fury. "You can't steal my life for some show I'm not even part of."

"Of course you'll be part of it. We'll need reliable production assistants."

"You son of a—"

"Temper. You have enough trouble getting work in this business. You wouldn't want me to add an assault charge to your sketchy record, would you?"

"I'm gonna talk to Ariadne."

Kelvin stormed off. Mia held her breath. Her left leg was falling asleep, and she adjusted her position. She almost toppled over but managed to regain her balance and not reveal herself. She heard other people enter the room, and more arguing, this time between a man and a woman. "I don't care what you say, I'm not doing it." Mia recognized the infuriated voice of camerawoman Lysette.

"If this pilot's gonna sell, it needs more sex," segment producer Michael responded. "Am I right, Giles?"

"But—" Lysette protested.

"Michael is right and you're wrong, Lysette."

Giles's tone brooked no argument. Still, Lysette shot back, "I'm not going to secretly film the cast members changing out of their bathing suits."

"You absolutely will. They knew what they signed up for. We'll pixilate any inappropriate body parts. If you have a problem with this scenario, find another job. And best wishes for that in a marketplace where unemployment for camera operators is at an all-time high and non-existent for reality camera operators trying to break through to scripted entertainment. Now, since you're still on my payroll, go do your job. Which right now is filming the dons' swim lessons."

From her hideaway, Mia could see Lysette's feet

as she slumped away, leaving Giles alone with Michael. The non-writing writer made a sound that was either a chortle or an allergic reaction. Mia wasn't sure which. "Nice work on my part, huh?" She cringed at the unctuous tone in the segment producer's voice. "Any chance I can get rewarded with an executive producer credit?"

"Not now," Giles said. "Not ever. If there ever is a third executive producer at Giles St. James Productions besides myself or Ariadne, I can guarantee it will not be you. But well done on coming up with the new scene. See if you can come up with more T and A moments like it."

St. James strode off toward the pool. Michael waited until his boss was out of hearing range before letting loose with some choice scatological descriptions of him, then stomped off.

Mia sat tight for a few minutes, then, sure she was alone, backed out of her hiding place and rose to standing. She took a step on her leg that had fallen asleep and toppled over. She gave the leg a vigorous shake, then tried again. Successful this time, she hefted up the water bottles to carry outside. But her mind was on the conversations she'd overheard, not catering chores.

Mia might not know much about the entertainment business, but she knew the dark side of human nature thanks to her upbringing. There was an ugly undercurrent to Giles St. James Productions she was sure would eventually lead to some form of blowup. Mia just hoped that when it happened, Belle View's commitments to the company would be in the rearview mirror.

She carried the water bottles poolside. After placing them in a party bucket, she grabbed a bag of ice from the home's freezer and emptied it on the water bottles to chill them. The dons made their poolside entrance, clad in Speedos, as she feared. There was much muscle flexing on the part of dons trying to gain the attention of donettes. The macho gestures went unnoticed by the girls, who were busy ogling the swim instructor, a former Olympian hoping the reality show would goose sales of his line of designer bathing caps. Only Chiara hung back. She took a water bottle from Mia's bucket. "Not your type?" Mia asked.

Chiara shook her head. "I googled his net worth." She made thumbs-down gestures with both thumbs. "Not interested."

The instructor ushered his charges into the shallow end of the pool. A few of the dons who'd exhibited muscle braggadocio moments earlier now looked trepidatious. St. James and Ariadne climbed into director's chairs parked next to where Mia stood. Little Donny, not needed in the scene yet, planted himself by his girlfriend's side. Ariadne, who wore a sheer top over a brightly colored bra, fanned herself. "It's blistering hot out here."

"Feel free to remove the blouse, love." St. James gave his ex a wink. "I remember the bra you've got on underneath. It could double as a very flattering bikini top."

"HEY!" The shout came from Little Donny, who leapt past Ariadne to throw a fist at St. James. The producer cried out as he toppled backward. Mia's bucket broke his fall, but Donny was on him in an instant. He yanked the producer up by the collar. "You hit on my girlfriend again, I swear, I'll cut you."

"Donny, stop." Mia grabbed one of his arms. Nicky Vestri jumped in to grab the other. Mia didn't attribute this to an act of altruism. She'd seen Lysette turn her camera toward the altercation, and knowing Nicky, Mia assumed he was making sure his cousin didn't get any more screen time than he did. A few other dons caught on to this and ran over, adding to the ruckus. Mia placed two fingers in her mouth and produced an ear-piercing whistle. Little Donny released St. James, and the dons fell back.

Mia let go of Donny, who was led away by his buddies. She hadn't factored the hotheaded Boldano getting fired into the equation but figured it was one way to remove him from Ariadne's grip. But to her surprise, Giles righted his director's chair and sat back down. "Right. Let's get on with the shoot, shall we?"

"He's not being kicked off the show?" Mia asked, bewildered.

"Absolutely not," said Ariadne, who hadn't moved an inch during the entire altercation. She looked after Little Donny with lust in her eyes. "His passion is exactly what this pilot needs."

After the lunch break, Ariadne and her ex-husband both disappeared to tend to other business, she to do a wardrobe check for the next day's shoot, he to take an online meeting regarding the project he may or may not have stolen from Kelvin. While the dons were preparing to go back into the pool, Mia pulled Little Donny aside. "Are you okay? I feel like something's off with you today. I know you can't stand St. James, and you're not alone on that score, but you were out of control this morning."

"I know." Little D stared down at the marble tile, flecked with gold, edging the pool. "I don't know how I'm gonna get through this shoot with him around all the time. I can tell he's still hot for Ariadne. I wish he was out of the picture."

"Let's get going, dons." Director Brian clapped his hands together.

"Where's Nicky?" one of the dons in his clique asked. "Anyone see him?"

The others shook their heads and said no. A few called his name but got no reply. Francesca, who was walking by the pool after retrieving a diet soda and bag of Flaming Hot Cheetos from craft services, glanced down at the pool. She screamed and dropped her snacks. She pointed to the pool and kept screaming.

Mia ran over. Nicky Vestri's body rested at the bottom of the pool. "No!" she cried out.

She made a move to jump into the pool. Suddenly, the body came to life, eliciting startled shrieks from the bystanders. Nicky swam to the surface, where he gasped for air before breaking into a wide grin. "Ha, gotcha. I know how to swim. I was faking that I don't. I even know how to hold my breath a long time."

Mia wanted to throttle the arrogant poser. "You scared us to death, you idiot. Don't ever do that again."

"I won't." He jumped out of the pool and shook himself off, getting her wet in the process. She shoved him away from her. He grabbed a towel and rubbed his shiny, wet bald head with it. "I'll come up with something better. Like the lawsuit I'm gonna slap St. James with for stealing my signature line."

"What are you talking about?"

"The *stronzo* said because I came up with the line on *his* show, he owns it and I have to either give him all my 'Get Outta Here!' swag or toss it." He shook his head "Not gonna happen. Guy's a goner if he tries." Nicky flicked his towel at Mia, then stopped. "'Not gonna happen.' That's another great line. I'm telling you, I got a gift for this."

The shoot proceeded without additional drama. The pool scene wrapped by the end of the afternoon, and the cast headed into the pool house for the infamous scene where they changed out of their bathing suits. Mia had secretly warned the donettes, who responded with what she considered an appalling lack of outrage, even from so-called feminist Francesca. "If the pilot sells and the series gets on the air, we get a shot at being reality stars, and then *we* get to make the rules," she told Mia, who managed not to respond, "Dream on, honey."

Feeling a bit like a mother hen, Mia followed the cast into the pool house. Concerned the donettes might eventually regret their cavalier attitude toward being filmed changing their clothes, Mia decided to keep a watchful eye on things, hanging back enough to stay off camera. Once inside the pool house, the group discovered a DO NOT ENTER sign on the door leading to the women's changing room. "Giles insisted there's better footage if the guys and girls have to negotiate the same space," Lysette, camera resting on her shoulder, whispered to Mia. The women exchanged a look that confirmed their disgust with the situation.

"I'm impressed this place is so big it's got two separate dressing areas," Mia whispered back.

The dressing room manipulation appeared to be the line in the sand for Chiara. "No way am I gonna change in some gross boys area," the stunner declared. She ripped the sign off the door and tried pushing it open. "It's stuck."

"It ain't stuck," Nicky said. "Something's blocking it. Let me."

Nicky gave the door a shove, moving whatever the blockage was out of the way. Chiara stepped into the room. She let out a heart-stopping scream and then, to the shock of all, crumpled to the ground in a faint.

Francesca dropped to the floor to help her friend. Mia stepped over the unconscious girl to see what had caused her traumatic reaction and almost passed out herself. "Oh my God."

"What?" Lysette glanced over Mia's shoulder. She paled. "Oh no."

The blockage behind the door to the woman's changing room was the body of Giles St. James. He lay cold and still, a small pool of darkened blood under his head.

Chapter 8

Chaos followed the discovery of St. James's body. The donettes screamed and wept, as did some of the dons. Fortunately, Mia had Detective Pete Dianopolis on speed dial, thanks to past murders involving Belle View, so she was able to quickly report the potential crime. But before Mia could head her off, Ariadne shoved through the clutch of wailing cast members. She took one look at her ex-husband's body and went white. Ariadne staggered, but Mia managed to keep her from collapsing. "Get her out of here," she instructed Little D, who had materialized by his girlfriend's side. He gave a grim nod and half-carried her out of the room.

"I wanna go home," Chiara, who had come to and was sitting up, cried.

"*Hey!*" The sharp tone in Mia's voice quieted everyone. "Nobody leaves. You got it? Nobody. Lysette, Michael, Kelvin—get everyone into the marble and gold room."

"Which one?" Kelvin asked.

"The biggest."

"They're all big."

"*Pick. One.*" Mia said this through gritted teeth.

Kelvin got the message. He hollered for the cast and crew to follow him, which they did, their caterwauling having transitioned into stunned silence. Lysette brought up the rear, which was when Mia realized the camerawoman had been filming the entire time.

"Huh."

Pete Dianopolis contemplated the body of St. James. After conferring with Pete and his partner, Ryan Hinkle, an NYPD Crime Scene Unit was now working what had been classified as a homicide investigation.

Mia bit her lip, an attempt to stifle any retort to Pete. After years as adversaries, they'd formed an alliance, uneasy though it might be. Pete had finally, if reluctantly, accepted that (a) her father, Ravello, had zero interest in a romantic relationship with Cammie, the ex-wife Pete would do anything to win back, and (b) the Carina family was a bazillion percent committed to running Belle View as a *legitimate* business for the Boldano Family.

After another agonizing minute of Pete's pondering, he spoke. "Hinkle, you and the team start taking statements from everyone who's here. I'm gonna have a little talk with my friend Mia here, then I'll meet up with you."

The pool house emptied, except for the Crime Scene Unit, Mia, and Pete. Perspiration sprouted on Mia's forehead, a result of nerves and a lack of ventilation in the pool house. "Looks like another case for Steve Stianopolis. You're welcome."

Mia's lame attempt at a joke referencing Pete's sideline as a mystery author fell flat. He eyed her with skepticism. "What are you hiding?"

Mia cursed to herself. Pete might lean toward being an arrogant blowhard, but he was a good detective, and he'd picked up on her tells. She'd instantly realized that Little D's status as a Boldano, coupled with his sketchy background and hostility toward Giles St. James, made him a prime suspect in the producer's murder. "Nothing," she said, wincing at the lame response. "I'm upset, okay? It's never fun coming across a dead body. I mean, I know that's what you do for a living, but it's not part of my daily routine."

"It kinda is these days." Pete motioned to a large round sofa upholstered in gold leather, and they both took a seat on it. "So. Talk to me. How'd you come across the late Giles St. James?"

Mia detailed the plans for shooting the pool house changing-room scene. "I was only here because I wanted to make sure the girls weren't taken advantage of. By the way, Michael, the segment producer, was really ticked off Giles wouldn't give him a promotion for coming up with the idea. You should have heard what he said. My ears." Mia covered hers and mimed horror at the language he'd used. "He wasn't the only one who hated the guy. You should have heard the fight between Giles and Kelvin, the production assistant. He's a sweet kid, but wow, was he not happy when he found out Giles had stolen one of his ideas. And Lysette, the camerawoman, was furious about having to film the scene in the changing room. She thought it took advantage of the cast." Mia hated selling out the one person on the crew she considered an ally. It was a desperate move she hoped would protect Little D from getting in Pete's crosshairs. Unfortunately . . .

"After Cammie and I met with the guy who's gonna design the logo for her podcast thing, she let me buy her dinner and mentioned Little Donny's hot and heavy with St. James's ex-wife." Pete shared this without taking his eyes off Mia, who used every ounce of willpower she could muster up not to buckle under his glare. "I saw Donny practically carrying the lady out of here. So now let's stop with all this deflecting and get to what you're hiding about the Boldano's eldest spawn."

"Spawn. That's what Cammie calls him too. You two really do belong together." Pete didn't let up on his glare, and Mia buckled. "Fine. There was a slight altercation between Little D and Giles."

"A reminder that I can bring charges against you for withholding evidence, and seeing as how you and your grandmother are the only Carinas without rap sheets, and only because your grandmother skated when her neighbor wouldn't press charges for stalking—"

"That neighbor, Mr. Agnelli, was stealing Nonna's tomatoes, and she wasn't stalking him, she was trying to catch him in the act—"

"*Anyway,* given the fact you're trying to stay legit, you wouldn't want any stain on your record, so how's about telling me the truth re: this 'slight altercation?'" Pete made air quotes with his fingers for emphasis.

"Fine." Mia sighed, then shared the confrontation between Little D and Giles in detail. "But to reiterate, he said, 'I'll cut you,' not 'I'll kill you.' "

"Uh huh."

Mia hated the gleam she saw in Pete's eyes. "Look, Little Donny is no prize. But he's trying to be a better person. And he's not a killer. He doesn't have it in him to be ruthless. Why do you think Big Donny is steering him away from the family business?"

Pete ran a hand over his thick thatch of salt-and-pepper hair, a habitual act of vanity that focused attention on his most impressive attribute. He might have had middle-aged middling looks and possessed a thickening middle, but his hair never failed him. "Love can make a person do crazy things. Believe me, I know. I just laid out a grand for materials to soundproof Cammie's office for her nutty podcast."

"Wait, what? She's soundproofing her office? At Belle View?" Mia crossed her arms in front of her chest, aggrieved. "News to me. Her *employer* at Belle View."

Pete made a helpless gesture. "What can I say? It's Cammie."

"I'm not sure how well the whole thing is going for her. It's not a good sign that she'd rather do her job than work on the podcast."

"I know, I mean, it was one thing when her hobby was needlepoint, but—" Pete stopped and glowered at Mia. "You're using Cammie to distract me from ID'ing Little Donny as the number-one person of interest here."

His partner Ryan cracked open the door and stuck his head into the room. "Hey, Pete, good news. We got a lot of stuff that happened around here recorded. Some guy named Nicky even said the camera lady shot footage of a fight between Boldano Junior and the vic."

Mia fumed. Leave it to jealous, skeevy Nicky Vestri to point a finger at his own cousin as a way of undercutting the competition for screen time.

Pete stood up. "Good news indeed." He pointed to a set of dumbbells. Mia noticed one ten-pound weight that looked suspiciously cleaner than the others. Pete addressed the Crime Scene Unit. "When you're done working the vic's area, dust all of these for prints. I got a feeling that ten-pounder is our murder weapon. Hinkle, get prints from everyone involved with the production. I'm pretty sure some of the dons are already in the system. A few of those donettes, too. I see a lotta familiar faces out there."

When Pete finally released Mia, she escaped to the mansion in time to hear Ariadne sob to Little D, "The only comfort I have from this whole horrible ordeal is that Lysette assures me she got the discovery of poor Giles's body on camera."

"For the police," Mia said, steaming. "To help solve his murder. Which you'd never want to exploit, right?"

"Of course not." Ariadne did her best to act horrified Mia would even suggest this, but her rudimentary effort made it clear why she was a producer and not a performer.

A couple of hours later, the police wrapped things up with the cast and crew and let everyone go. Exhausted but also wired, Mia headed to Belle

View instead of home. She found Shane waiting for her in the banquet facility kitchen. "Everyone else is gone for the night." He handed her a full glass of chardonnay. "Here. I know you need this. I'll drive you home and pick you up in the morning."

"You're my hero." She took a hefty gulp of wine and closed her eyes. "I don't know where to begin."

"I got a lot of info out of Cammie, who got it out of Pete."

Mia opened her eyes. She pointed to the Belle View grand foyer. "The big delivery clogging up the lobby. Is that the soundproofing for her office?"

Shane nodded. "I was pretty p.o.'d about the delivery, so she tried making it up to me by giving all the deets she could on St. James's murder. She said Pete will move everything tomorrow. Or the guys he'll have to hire—because now he's busy with the case—will do it."

Mia gave an annoyed grunt. "Podcasts, reality shows . . . influencers. All people want to do anymore is to be famous. Or even infamous. They don't care, as long as they're getting attention."

Shane gave a sympathetic nod. "People don't know what we know. What it's like to show up at school the day after the news showed your father being carted off to jail and you crying on the front lawn. The kids avoiding you or feeling sorry for you or thinking you're dirty because your parent is. The playdates canceled because the parents don't want you hanging with their kids anymore, or because they're scared of your family. The worst is kids trying to be your friend because they think the connection is cool."

"Donny Junior's been there himself," Mia said, frustrated. "He knows all this."

"But he doesn't know who he is yet. Or what he wants. Maybe this is a wake-up call for him."

"He's had a lot of those," Mia scoffed. "He never wakes up. He must have that sleep thing—narcowhatever."

"Narcolepsy."

"Right. That."

Mia took another hefty hit of wine. Her cell rang, and she pulled it out of her purse. Mia got a rush of anxiety when she saw who the caller was. She held a hand to her rapidly beating heart and then took the call. "Hi, Mr. B."

Shane's eyes widened. "Big Donny?!" he mouthed.

Mia nodded. Shane made the sign of the cross. "I'm guessing you're calling about the incident at Casa Giovanni today."

"Incident my a—" Donny Boldano Senior stopped himself. "*Mi dispiace.* I shouldn't use vulgarities around a lady."

"That's sexist, but don't worry about it."

"*Grazie,* because I got bigger things to worry about. Like Little Donny being a suspect in this sonuva—this producer man's murder."

"I'm so sorry. You know I'll do whatever I can to help Donny."

"Good, because I want you to figure out who really killed the guy."

"Wha—" Stunned, Mia dropped the phone. She hastily retrieved it. Big Donny was still on the line.

"What's going on?" Shane whispered.

Mia put a finger to her lips to shush him. "Mr. B, when I said I'd do whatever I can to help Donny, I meant it more as moral support. And maybe food. You know, comfort food. He loves Guadalupe's cooking. And my nonna's. I'll have her make him some meatballs. Big ones. The size of a baseball."

"His mother can make him meatballs if that was the answer to this problem. But it ain't. I need you to do whatever it is you do that helps nail perps."

"I don't do anything to 'nail perps,' Mr. B. I got lucky a few times."

"It's not luck. It's you. You're a nosy, pushy person, and I mean this in a good way. All I'm asking is that you work your nosy, pushy magic for my son. Find who really killed this *idiota* St. James. Oh, and I knew your answer would be yes, so I told Little Donny you were on the case. He's at Singles, that low-rent hangout he loves so much, waiting to talk to you. And now I want meatballs."

Big Donny ended the call. Mia stared at her phone. Shane drummed his fingers on the kitchen island. Unable to stand the suspense, he stopped drumming and blurted, "So? What did he want? Do I need to do something? Like, tell him to back off? Because I'll do it. Yeah, he might not like it. And I might get in trouble. Big trouble. But I don't care. You need me to get in his face, I will get in his face."

Mia, touched by Shane's bravado, broke her trance to favor him with a warm smile. "It's okay. You don't have to mix it up with Mr. B. But I could use a ride to Singles."

CHAPTER 9

Mia and Shane found Little Donny hunched over a drink at the restaurant's massive bar. True to its on-the-nose name, Singles' layout was designed for maximum mingling. The dark walnut bar and its environs took up two-thirds of the space, with two-top tables and small booths ringing the perimeter for couples whose pheromones had synced up. The place was as dark as pitch, the better to literally stumble into a potential soul mate. "Dad told me he called you," Little Donny said without looking up from his drink. "I didn't do it. I know the cops think I did, but I didn't."

Mia and Shane pulled up barstools on either side of him. "I—" Mia caught Shane's eye. "*We* don't think you did."

Donny motioned to the bartender, who replaced his empty glass with a full one of what Mia guessed was some kind of scotch on the rocks. The bartender gave her an inquiring look, and she shook her head. Her focus was on helping Little D, and the last thing she wanted was a drink on top of the wine Shane had poured for her at Belle View.

Don swallowed a slug of his drink. "There's a reason my dad is on me to find another line of work. We both know it's not in me to do what sometimes has to be done in his . . . business. That's why the show is good for me. I get to pretend I'm that kinda guy but not really be one."

Mia gave a vigorous nod of agreement. "That's what I told Pete."

The expression on Shane's face indicated Mia may have stepped in it. Donny looked up from his drink. "You told the police I'm a coward? A loser? Thanks, Mia. Thanks a lot."

"No, no," she backtracked. "I didn't use those words." Shane mouthed "not helping," and Mia second-guessed her choice not to order a drink. "I defended you by saying you were working real hard on being a better person and would never, ever do anything as horrible as take a life." Donny seemed mollified by this, so she continued, "But someone else obviously had no problem taking a dumbbell to the back of St. James's head, so we need to figure out who and get you off the hook for his murder."

"I'm all in on saving my—" Donny's cell rang. "It's Ariadne. She needs me. I gotta go." He hopped off his barstool and strode out of the restaurant.

"Beautiful," Mia muttered.

Shane took over Donny's barstool and pulled it closer to Mia. "He makes it hard *not* to want him on top of the NYPD suspect list."

"Tell me about it," Mia said with fervor. "It would make my life so much easier if they nailed him for this. But I know he didn't do it, so the question is, who did?" She squinted her eyes as she thought back to the chaotic moments post-discovery of St. James's body. She recalled Ariadne's comment that at least Lysette filmed the whole thing. "You don't have to be in the TV business to know the murder makes the *Dons of Ditmars Boulevard* pilot more sensational," Mia said, thinking out loud. "Which probably makes it more sellable, so there's one motive. And Giles got on a lot of people's bad side. I can count three on the *Dons* crew alone—the segment producer Michael, production assistant Kelvin, and camerawoman Lysette. I'm sure there are more." Weary, Mia rubbed her forehead. "I'm beat. I gotta get some sleep. Can you do me a favor and run an Internet search on Giles St. James and his production company? See if anything useful comes up, like people suing him. And can you run things at Belle View in the morning?"

"Sure, but what are you gonna do?"

"Get myself back into Giles's apartment and do some snooping."

Mia flashed a sly smile at Shane. She hopped off her barstool, and he followed suit. Shane took her hand and looked deep into her eyes. "Not gonna lie. I'm super hot for you right now."

The couple started for the door, but the bouncer, responding to a sign from the bartender, blocked their path. "Your friend didn't pay for his drinks. 'Fraid you can't leave 'til you settle his bill."

"Effin' Little D," Mia said through clenched teeth as Shane pulled out his wallet.

* * *

On her subway ride into Manhattan the next morning, Mia received the results of Shane's Internet search into Giles St. James, which yielded a long list of aggrieved competitors, former employees, and even a housekeeper suing for back pay. She forwarded the list to Pete, who responded by writing back, "We know this s—t. It's our job." Chastened, Mia focused on her game plan for gaining access to the late producer's penthouse.

Mia trekked down 51st Street toward the East River. She reached St. James's sleek modern building, where a doorman pulled open the double glass doors for her. As before, the lobby was a vision of expensive minimalism. An arrangement of exotic-looking flowers, perched in a black vase on a glass pedestal, gave off a heavenly scent.

Mia approached a security guard manning a check-in area. "Hi, you probably don't remember me." She accompanied this with a self-deprecating smile. "I catered the party in Mr. St. James's apartment the other night, God rest his soul." She made the sign of the cross. "Anyhoo, I only this morning found out that one of my cater-waiters forgot to pack my chef's knife set, and she's losing her mind. Which means until I get that knife set back, I'm out a chef. And my business can't afford that. Is there any way I can get into Mr. James's apartment for a couple of minutes to get the knives? Please?" She worked up a tear or two in her bright blue eyes and added an emotional lip quiver for effect.

The security guard eyed her. Mia had dressed the part of professional caterer, from black pants and simple white top down to her work clogs. He shrugged. "The cops are gone, so the place is just sitting there right now. The guy never met a holiday he tipped on. 'Not my country's culture,' he'd say in that accent of his. You got a key to the place?"

"No," Mia said panicking. *How could I not think of that? Idiota!*

"Not a problem," the guard said, and her heart resumed beating. He reached under the desk and retrieved a key that he handed her. "Lotta people in this building have key apps on their phones, but we keep spares in case the power goes out or their phone needs a charge."

"Thank you so much. You're a lifesaver"—Mia checked his nametag—"Geraldo."

The guard puffed out his chest. "Always happy to help a pretty lady. But don't tell no one I said that. These days, I could get fired. This whole me too thing really cramps my style, lemme tell you."

Mia mimed zipping her lips and turned so he couldn't see her roll her eyes. She hurried to the elevator and pressed the button for St. James's penthouse.

Stepping inside the late producer's apartment, Mia once again admired the view, then set about scouring the place for any clue to his demise. Assuming the police had made off with all the man's electronics, she located his office with the goal of searching his paperwork—of which there was very little. St. James was apparently a man who took the dictum "go paperless" seriously.

She left the office and moved on to the primary bathroom. Mia wasn't surprised to find a half-empty bottle of Viagra in the medicine cabinet. It seemed on par with the lascivious producer. She noticed the prescription had been filled only a few weeks prior, meaning he'd made good use of it in a short period of time. Mia filed this tidbit away and stepped back into the bedroom for a search of the nightstand drawers. Under a slew of sleep masks and used tissues—*Ewwwww!*—she found a framed photo of St. James with his arms wrapped around the waist of a well-endowed blonde with pouty lips whose assets were barely kept in check by a string bikini. Mia guessed St. James was easily twice the girl's age. "That explains the Viagra," she said to the photo.

She contemplated the discovery. Why would St. James hide an image of himself with a piece of arm candy like this girl? If anything, he seemed like the kind of guy who would parade her around like a Mardi Gras float. Mia recalled Ariadne mentioning she lived in Giles's building. Given that the woman had attached herself to Little Donny with her impeccably manicured claws, Mia couldn't imagine Ariadne would be jealous of Giles's hookup and might know the story behind the mysterious photo.

The rest of the apartment search yielded no additional potential clues, so Mia finished and took the elevator down to the lobby. "Got my knives," she said to the security guard, holding up a tote bag in which she'd stuffed a few ancient knives from Elisabetta's kitchen. "I can't thank you enough."

The guard preened. "Happy to help."

"One more question, and I'll leave you in peace. What's the apartment number for Ariadne St. James? She told me, but, duh, I forgot." Mia copped a ditzy expression, cringing at her reflection in the mirror wall behind the guard.

"She's in 5C, but to get there, you need to use another entrance."

Mia gaped at the derogatory spin he put on the last two words. "Are you telling me she uses a poor door?" she asked. "Poor door" was the slang term for a second entrance in a luxury building that led to units reserved for lower-income residents. Public outrage at developers who used the separate entrances to segregate the ninety-nine percent from the one percent had led to a ban on them. "I thought the city doesn't allow those anymore."

"Too late for the one in this building. It's grandfathered in. When you get outside, make a left. It's on the west side. In the shadows."

Mia followed his instructions, which led to a sad, small door facing a brick wall. There was no doorman at the poor door, only a bank of buzzers. She was about to ring 5C when a deliveryman came out of the entrance. He held the door open for her, and she thanked him. "Anytime," he said. "You people here tip better than there." He motioned with his head toward the section of the building that housed rich people, his expression one of disgust.

As opposed to the impressive lobby in Giles's section of the building, this lobby was cramped and dark. One of the two bulbs in a ceiling fixture that looked straight off the shelf of a big box store flickered on and off, creating a strobe effect. Mia pressed the button of the single elevator servicing the apartments of the income-challenged residents, at least by New York's stratospheric rent standards. The button didn't light up, but the clunking sound of gears indicated the elevator worked. But after a wait stretching into five minutes, Mia began to doubt its efficacy. She located the stairs, where an old shoe propped open a door marked EMERGENCY EXIT ONLY, and began the climb to the fifth floor.

Like the lobby, the apartment hallway was dark, lit by a few rudimentary wall sconces. It smelled like a noxious combination of roach spray and vegetable soup. Mia tried her best not to breathe through her nose. She located Ariadne's apartment in the middle of the hallway's west side. It wasn't even a corner unit, which would have given it two sets of windows for gazing out upon the brick walls of other, pricier buildings. She pressed the apartment door's buzzer, which responded with a defeated half beep. No one answered. Mia counted to thirty, then pressed again. She followed this with a knock on the door. Still no answer. "Ariadne?" she called. After a few more minutes of silence, Mia gave up.

She quickly made her way down the stairs, eager to get some fresh air, or what passed for fresh air on a muggy New York summer afternoon. On her way back to the subway, she gave Shane a call and updated him on her sleuthing. "Did you take a picture of the picture?" he asked.

Mia let out a profanity. "Argh. I didn't think of that. But it's hard to forget the girl. I'm pretty sure I'd recognize her if I saw her again. For all we know, she was some contest winner he posed with, like Miss Hawaiian Suntan or something. The thing I can't stop wondering about is how Giles lives versus how Ariadne lives."

"It's New York. Even poor people can't afford a poor door apartment. Some friend of my sister's got an apartment in Hell's Kitchen where the toilet for everyone living on his floor is in the hallway, and he was happy to get the place."

"I know. But . . ."

"But what?"

Mia, deep in thought, joined a group jaywalking across Third Avenue. "I wonder if Giles and Ariadne's relationship was really that cozy? Or were they faking? Or was *she* faking? She's a real lady living like a starving artist in subsidized housing while her ex-husband in the same building lives like a not-real but very rich king. Maybe she couldn't take it anymore. And maybe . . . she lost it and killed him."

Chapter 10

After a morning spent sleuthing, Mia decided she'd earned a break—one that entailed a visit to the closets and drawers of FemmeNYC.com, the fashion and beauty blog where Madison Wythe-soon-to-be-Wythe-Boldano worked as a blogger-editor. The FemmeNYC coffers were always brimming with free products sent by companies wooing the website for publicity, and Mia never left Madison's office without a bag loaded with goodies. She took the subway down to the former beef-packing plant now housing the FemmeNYC workforce and its vegan cafeteria. An industrial elevator took her to the third floor. Mia navigated a maze of cubicles, finally landing on Madison's. To her surprise, she found Jamie's bride-to-be with her head down on the desk, weeping. "Madison! Sweetie, what's wrong?"

Madison lifted her head, revealing tear-stained cheeks. "Mia. Hi. I didn't know you were coming to the city."

"I came in on business," Mia said, choosing to

forgo the specifics of her trip to Manhattan. She hugged Madison. "Talk to me. But please don't say Eviance dropped their line of affordable gold-infused face masks, because I'll bust out crying, too."

"No." Maddie sniffed. "It's my maid of honor, Delany. You know her, right?"

"Oh, yes," Mia said, easily recalling an image of the soused, sour woman.

"She checked into rehab. I mean, we've been wanting her to forever, so it's all good, but now she can't do everything she was supposed to do for me as my maid of honor. My friends shower, the one without my crazy relatives where I can actually relax and have fun, is happening in two days, and now I have to throw it for myself," Madison sobbed. "And my bachelorette party in New Orleans? Jamie can go ahead with his bachelor party there, but I'll have to cancel."

Mia, who had never been to New Orleans and was so excited about the trip that she'd splurged on a long weekend's worth of new outfits for it, literally gasped. "*What?* No. Don't say that. You can't cancel. It *has* to happen."

"I don't have a choice. I can't run everything myself. I don't have time, and besides, who throws their own shower and bachelorette party? It's embarrassing."

"You will not be throwing anything for yourself by yourself," Mia declared. "I'll take over running the shower and bachelorette party."

Madison gazed up at her with puppy-dog eyes. "You will?" Thinking of the slinky red party dress for New Orleans nighttime revelry that had set her back two hundred bucks, Mia gave an emphatic nod. Madison squealed. She jumped up and enveloped Mia in a bear hug. "How can I ever thank you?"

Mia eyed FemmeNYC's largest supply closet, which was so packed with samples the door couldn't close. "No thanks necessary. We're friends, and this is what friends do for each other. But a few items from Rylie Kenner's spring makeup line would be nice. And samples of whatever mascara you're wearing, because you cried buckets and your lashes still look perfect."

She left Madison's workplace with her friend's eternal gratitude and two shopping bags bursting with free products that Cammie instantly descended upon when Mia showed up at Belle View. "Nuh uh," Mia said, pulling the bags out of Cammie's reach. "You've gotta earn these freebies. I need you to do a deep dive into Ariadne's past, especially anything about her divorce from Giles. Was it ugly, did she get a decent settlement, et cetera."

"I know the drill." Cammie cast avaricious eyes on one of the bags. "Do I see an Eviance gold-infused face mask in there?"

"Sorry, that one's mine. But there's plenty of stuff to drool for in here, so *affrettarsi.* Hurry."

Cammie scurried away. Mia dropped the bags in her office, locking the door in case Cammie couldn't resist the urge to explore the bags' contents. She went to Shane's office and was welcomed with an extremely satisfying kiss, inappropriate as it might be. She shared the news about her upgrade from bridesmaid to temporary maid of honor. "Now that I'm in charge, I get to make the schedule, and you best believe I'll be blocking out some quality private time for you and me," she said, her arms around her boyfriend's waist.

"Uh huh."

Mia dropped her arms. "Uh huh? Wow, is that not the reaction I expected. Maybe I should be more specific. By quality private time, I mean—"

"It's okay, *bella*. I know what you mean." He gave a half smile, creating the hint of a dimple in his left cheek. "It's not you—"

Mia froze. "Oh, please don't let your next words be 'it's me.'"

"No, no, nothing like that." Shane waved his hands as if to clear the air and dispel her fears. "It's bachelor parties. I f–ing *hate* them."

The fact that Shane, so careful with profanity, dropped an f-bomb told Mia his hatred ran deep. "How come you didn't tell me this before I laid out two hundred bucks on a sexy dress?"

Shane hung his head. "You were so excited about everyone going to New Orleans. I didn't want to bring you down. But now that the party's almost here—" He closed his eyes and shook his hands. "You know what, forget I said anything. I'll get over it."

Mia eyed him with a combination of annoyance, skepticism, and concern. "I'm getting the feeling there's a bigger story here than hating getting drunk and going to strip clubs."

"Nope, just not my thing. Wow, I love how humidity makes your hair curlier and even sexier."

Shane stroked Mia's hair, then leaned in to kiss her. She knew he was pulling the move to change the subject—and didn't care one bit. Mia bid her trepidations goodbye and went for it.

She tore herself away before their passion escalated into a seriously-not-suitable-for-the-workplace moment. She returned to her office to concentrate on the business of running Belle View. A few hours later, Cammie knocked at the office door. Mia let her in. She deposited herself onto a folding metal chair and picked up one of the FemmeNYC bags. "I come with news. I'm gonna go through this bag for my promised freebies while I deliver it."

"Agreed."

"Giles filed for divorce on the grounds of adultery. Ariadne disputed this, and they wound up in mediation because if there was one thing they could both agree on is why make divorce lawyers rich when they could keep more money for themselves by dissolving their marriage through mediation. Ariadne agreed on less money up front in exchange for half ownership in the production company. She uses her low income to get subsidized housing in Giles's apartment building for her New York stays, but her main base of operations is Los Angeles, where she owns a condo in Beverly Hills. That poor-door apartment is gonna go out the door now that she's got the whole company, but that's not research, just a guess on my part."

"Good work, thanks. Boy, this all seems low-rent for a Brit royal. What about her family's money?"

"I didn't have time to check into that. I've already been here three hours. That's like, three workdays for me." Cammie pulled an item from the bag. "Ooh, a jade roller. Can I?"

Mia nodded. "You can have that whole bag. I split everything into what you'd like and what I'd like."

"You're the best boss *ever*," Cammie said, choking up.

"You may not think so after I give you your next assignment: helping me take over Madison's friends shower and convincing everyone to come here instead of Connecticut. If I have to sit through another potato salad with or without relish debate, I'm gonna have you tie me to one of the Wythe family sailboats, light it on fire, and float me out to sea like a dead Viking."

With Madison's city friends on board with the switch of venue to Belle View, it was only a matter of providing transportation for the Nutmeg State crew. Donny Boldano Senior solved the problem by drafting a few of his own crew onto chauffeur detail. Chefs Guadalupe and Evans, who were invited wedding guests, insisted on providing their services to the party as a present to the bride-to-be, and Cammie actually showed up a half hour early to help set out floral arrangements, albeit with the reminder "The minute the clock strikes seven, I'm gonna Cinderella my way off work and into guest mode."

The party went well. Mia feared a bump when Madison unwrapped Elisabetta's gift, a crocheted neon pink and green nightie with a large lacy pattern that left nothing to the imagination. But Madison loved it. "It's hot!" she exclaimed, holding it up to herself and striking a sexy pose to the hoots and hollers of her friends. Assuming this was not her grandmother's intention, Mia felt bad for her. Then she realized the loudest catcalls were coming from Elisabetta.

Eventually, the party broke into small groups chatting amongst themselves. Mia saw Pickney, Madison's Anglophile cousin, by the dessert station. Pickney picked up a cookie and broke it in pieces. She ate one piece and put the others back on the cookie tray. Mia made her way to her. "Hey there," she said, scooping up the cookie detritus with the goal of pretending to eat it while secretly throwing it away. "Having fun?" Pickney responded with a bored shrug and destroyed another cookie. It occurred to Mia that with the odd woman's royalty obsession, she might be a resource for dirt on Ariadne's aristocratic family. "It's so cool about Donny Junior's girlfriend being an actual 'lady,' isn't it? If they got married, Madison would be related to a genuine royal family."

"One that doesn't even count," Pickney shot back, obviously jealous. Mia considered this a good thing, knowing there was nothing like envy to inspire trashy gossip. "The Tottenhams barely have a pot to pee in. They had to open their manor house to guests, but not as a real B&B—as an AirBnB," she said in a tone so disparaging the hapless manor house might as well have been a cardboard box with doors and windows drawn on by a child with a crayon. "And the rumors about the men in the family are out of control."

"Really? Like what?" Pickney didn't respond. Her focus was on the last chocolate chip cookie. Hoping to save it from the same fate as the other cookies Pickney picked up, Mia positioned herself between Madison's cousin and the dessert spread. "You don't have to be afraid of Ariadne hearing you. She wasn't invited tonight."

Pickney responded with a very unladylike snort.

"I'm not saying anything everyone doesn't know already, even though the Tottenhams insist the rumors aren't true. Ariadne's brother and father were dissolute reprobates." Mia tried and failed to hide a blank look. "Drunk bad guys," Pickney explained. "They gambled, they had affairs. Her brother Thomas even got arrested for selling cocaine, but the charges were dropped. Translation, someone paid off the drug buyer to lie and say it never happened. The worst, though, is that both Ariadne's father and brother died in suspicious deaths. Lord Tottenham fell off his yacht during the last voyage before it was repossessed. And Thomas drowned trying to save his father."

"God, that's awful," Mia said, upset. "I love my dad and brother so much. Ariadne must have been devastated."

Pickney assumed a crafty expression. "You'd think. But the media pointed out she didn't look too broken up about the loss. To this day, no one knows if the lord jumped, fell . . . or was pushed. Same with Tom Tottenham."

Mia's pulse raced. Men who got in Ariadne St. James's way met dire fates. Female serial killers were rare, but they existed. In Ariadne's case, the deaths were transactional. With her ex-husband gone, she inherited a business. With her father and his heir gone . . . "She inherited the Tottenham estate, right? Even if it was almost nothing, it had to be something."

Pickney shook her head. "Nope. Male primogeniture."

Mia didn't bother to try and hide her blank expression this time. "Huh?"

"In the Tottenham line, only a man can inherit

the title and estate. Everything went to the oldest male cousin, now Lord Roland Tottenham. Ariadne got squat. That's why she was never a suspect in her father or brother's death. She had no motive. If anything, she was way better off with them alive."

Pickney swiped the chocolate chip cookie. She broke it into pieces, ate one, and put the others back on the plate. Then she wandered off, leaving a deflated Mia back where she started—nowhere.

The next day was a flurry of tours for prospective customers and putting out fires for current ones. Mia managed to find a pet bakery willing to create an edible sculpture in the shape of a patron's Yorkie for the dog's "Happy Barkday" celebration, the first of its kind for Belle View and Mia hoped the last, at least for this neurotic pet parent.

She was creating a TikTok inspired video invitation for a bat mitzvah girl's celebration when she heard an odd sound coming from her father's office. Mia left her desk to investigate. To her surprise, she found Ravello huffing and puffing away on a state-of-the-art treadmill. "This is new," she said, taking in the image of the usually immaculately clad businessman dressed out of character in a T-shirt and sweatpants. "How did I miss the delivery?"

"Came before you got here." Ravello spoke in a short sentence, breathing heavily between the words.

"I've been on you to exercise for years, and you ignored me. What magic wand did Lin wave to get you on this thing?"

"I hate salad. Couldn't give up fettucine Alfredo.

At Roberto's." Ravello puffed out his favorite meal, one he ate every day at his favorite restaurant to the point of being on the OCD spectrum. "Bought one. For home too. Treadmill. Bought treadmill. Not fettucine. Alfredo."

"Uh huh." Mia eyed Ravello. His face was red from exertion and wet with perspiration. "I'm glad you're balancing your carbs and heavy cream intake with working out, but go easy, Dad. Overdoing it can be just as bad as not doing anything at all."

Ravello grunted a reply, then increased his incline and speed by a notch. Mia muttered her own profane grunt and left him to his trudging. She went to see if Shane could talk some sense into her father, but he wasn't in his office, so she stopped by Cammie. The desk of the extremely part-time event planner was covered with samples from the FemmeNYC goody bag Mia had given her. Cammie's face was covered with a green goop that made her look like the Wicked Witch of the West. "Here's hoping kale works better as a facial ingredient than as a foodstuff," she said, patting her cheek to see if the goop had dried. "You need something? Please don't say it's 'lead a tour' because I got another ten minutes before I can scrape this off."

"I'm looking for Shane. Have you seen him?"

"I heard him on the phone yelling at someone, then he stormed out of his office. I think he went out front."

"Thanks. Hope there's a ranch dressing moisturizer you can put on after the facial."

Cammie tried making a face at Mia, but the tight mask prevented it. "Hardy har har."

Mia walked toward the lobby to find Shane. It was empty, so she stepped outside, just in time to see him peeling out of the parking lot in the Tesla. To see him gun the engine of his pride and joy and drive recklessly concerned her. Mia returned to her office and texted him to make sure everything was okay. After a few minutes, she received a one-word response via voice text: *Yes.* An alarm bell born of instincts honed by years as the daughter of a Mob lieutenant went off. However, she didn't have time to delve deeper.

Another text popped up, this one from Ariadne St. James. She wanted to hire Belle View to cater a memorial service for her late husband, Giles. Ariadne attached an official invitation to the service:

Join us in celebrating the life of Giles St. James
When: Thursday, July 13th, 11 a.m.
Where: at the home of Ariadne St. James
645 East 52nd Street, Penthouse Apartment

"Hmmm," Mia murmured. "Interesting." Giles's own apartment appeared to be Ariadne's new home. Which raised the question . . . how did Ariadne manage a move from poor door to penthouse?

On Thursday, Mia found herself in Giles's magnificent apartment for the third time in a week. She and her crew set up a post-memorial repast in the dining room while guests arrived and mingled in the living room. Mia wandered the room as if in her official capacity as head caterer. But, in reality, her nosiness was on alert, hoping to sniff out potential murder suspects. If Giles's killer came from his inner circle, Mia assumed that, rather than avoid the event, they'd embrace it in an effort to cast off any suspicion. Unfortunately, in twenty minutes of eavesdropping, she only overheard networking, name-dropping, and a couple of conversations about how difficult it was to find good help these days.

Thwarted, Mia returned to the dining room. Ariadne, who'd been busy greeting guests and receiving insincere condolences, strode in to check on the meal's arrangement. "Well done," she said with a nod of approval. She flicked an imaginary speck of dust off her stylish black jumpsuit. "I appreciate the emphasis on finger food. People rarely bother to plate it, which saves the production company on rental costs."

"The production company's paying for this?" The question slipped out before Mia could self-edit. The concept of a memorial being a business proposition was alien to her. In Mia's world, grief was grief and not transactional.

"We're filming the memorial for the show." This came from segment producer Michael Planko, who had followed Ariadne into the dining room. "Giles's murder is gonna jack up interest in the *Dons* pilot from every broadcast and streaming outlet. I bet we're looking at a bidding war." He sounded so enthusiastic, Mia wondered if he'd offed St. James for the juicy storyline.

"I was not on board for capitalizing on my ex-husband's horrible passing." Ariadne's attempt to sound perturbed once again indicated acting was not her strong suit. "But I was outvoted by my staff."

"It's for Giles." This came from fifty-something accounting intern Jason Stern, whose red-rimmed eyelids pegged him as the only crew member who actually mourned his boss's passing. "He would have wanted it this way."

"That is a good point," Ariadne said with a nod of acknowledgment.

"I better check on lighting." Michael palmed two mini-quiches and headed back to the living room.

Ariadne cast a critical eye on a tray of Danish. "Many of our guests are slimming," she said. "That's dieting for you Americans. I think we should quarter all the pastries. My friends wouldn't be caught dead holding a giant sweet."

Given the event, Mia winced at Ariadne's poor choice of words, but the producer didn't seem to notice the wince or the word choice. "Good idea," Mia said. "I'll take care of it myself. Again, I'm sorry about Giles's death. I know you were super close. I mean, he left you this amazing apartment and all." She congratulated herself on a not-too-clunky segue to snooping.

"Yes."

Mia picked up something cagey in Ariadne's tone and jumped on it. "Oh, he didn't leave it to you? My bad. I just thought because of the invitation . . ." She trailed off, leaving an opening she hoped Ariadne took. To her satisfaction, the producer bit.

"Oh, he did," Ariadne hastened to correct her. "There's just a bit of confusion about his will. There's some indication there's a version that supersedes it, and a company called Second's the Charm is somehow involved. But I'm sure it's just a rumor."

No you're not. The "rumor" had Ariadne spooked.

If the woman was responsible for her ex-husband's death, a new will would upend her murderous machinations.

A violinist in the living room began sawing out the opening notes of Pachelbel's Canon. Mia never understood why brides chose to walk down the aisle to the doleful composition. She found it much better suited to an occasion like the current one. "I'm needed out front, as theater actors say." Ariadne gestured to the food. "Ta very much for all of this."

She departed the dining room, expensive spike heels tapping out her exit. Mia instructed one of her cater-waiters to quarter all the Danish, then slipped into the back of the living room to observe the memorial and its attendees. Lysette and alternate camerapersons were filming the proceedings. Ariadne assumed her place behind a podium brought in for the occasion. A movie poster–sized headshot of Giles sat on an easel next to the podium. "Thank you all so much for joining us on this heartbreaking occasion." Ariadne paused to compose herself, and Mia noted the producer was able to drum up a little acting talent when she really needed to. "We're all here for one reason only—to celebrate the life and mourn the death of the extraordinary Giles St. James."

"Who got what he deserved," Donny Junior said loud enough for the entire assemblage to hear.

Idiot! Mia managed not to scream. But she noticed quite a few heads nodding in agreement.

"Great stuff for the show," Michael, who happened to be standing next to her, whispered gleefully.

The memorial continued with a mix of studio

and network executives' bland memories obviously run past company publicists before being shared publicly, desultory comments from past and present crew members, and *Dons* cast members trying to one-up each other with their histrionic displays. The guys took turns vowing to rain down the pain on Giles's killer, while the girls out-sobbed each other to the point where the show's sound mixer had to step in and shut them up.

Mia saw Nicky Vestri sidle up to Ariadne, slide an arm around her waist, and whisper what looked like comforting words in her ear. Donny Junior saw this too. His nostrils flared, and he yanked Nicky's arm off Ariadne. Afraid a fight would break out between the cousins, Mia was about to step in and defuse the situation when the apartment front door flew open, startling everyone. A trashy but very hot twenty-something dressed in an incredibly tight black dress, veiled hat, and sky-high pumps made a dramatic entrance into the living room. Something about her looked familiar to Mia, but she couldn't place what.

"Sorry I'm late," she announced. She spoke with what even Mia recognized as a lower-class British accent. "I had to hire a private plane cuz I couldn't find an airline that would let me bring me own crisps and bev with me in the cabin. Flippin' holdover from the pandemic what's-it. The only thing anyone'd catch from me yummy crisps is wanting more of 'em. Same with me family chard." A fluffy Persian cat peeked out from the woman's giant tote bag. "Like I needed that on top a' all this."

The woman spoke with a quaver as she gestured with a well-manicured hand toward the large photo of Giles. Tears filled her limpid hazel eyes. Ariadne gave her a steely look. "And you are?" she asked, managing to sound both polite and peremptory.

"You hear that, Princess Kate? The old lady wants to know who I am."

Mia choked back a laugh as Ariadne made a gargling sound and turned purple with suppressed rage.

The woman marched to the center of the room and practically hip-checked Ariadne to supplant her at the podium. "Hello, everyone. For those of you who don't know me—which'd be everyone here, wouldn't it?—I'm Violet Kreppy St. James. Yeah, you heard right. St. James. I'm Giles's second wife."

She directed the last line at Ariadne. Violet St. James whipped off her hat, and Mia suddenly knew why she looked familiar. "The woman in the picture. In the drawer."

She was so stunned, she said this out loud. Michael Planko, always on the hunt for a salacious storyline, jumped on it. "What picture? What drawer? Who is she? Tell me!"

What happened next spared Mia from having to answer. Ariadne took a step toward Violet. She released another strangled gurgling sound. Then she collapsed to the floor in a dead faint.

Chapter 11

The room dissolved into chaos. Mia ran to render aid to Ariadne, while guests collided with each other as they tried to make themselves useful or escape the awkward situation. A drone-like buzz of gossip filled the air. Nicky Vestri immediately sidled up to the newcomer with a "Sorry for your loss. I'm the star of the show, and I'm here for you" come-on line. The cat in Violet's purse hissed at him.

Ariadne slowly came to. Mia and Donny Junior helped her sit up. "What happened?" she asked, her voice groggy. "I had a vision of some tart claiming to be Giles's wife, then I blacked out."

Violet snorted. "Tart. Ha. You wish. I may not be Lady La Di Da Tushie-ham or whatever you call yourself, but me dad could buy and sell your bloody lot a billion times over. And yeah, I said *billion.*" Hearing this, all the dons except Donny Junior jostled each other to replace Nicky at her side. He muttered something Mia couldn't hear, but it was enough to get them to back off.

Violet pulled a bag of potato chips from her oversized, luxury-brand tote and dangled it for all to see. The bag featured the cartoon image of a mustached, grinning man holding a sign that read KREPPY KRISPS. A tagline under the image read "Kreppy's got snacking in the bag!"

An executive eyed the bag with longing. "Kreppy's? I love their stuff. It's hard to find in the States."

"Not for long, love," Violet said. "We just closed a deal to import them, so's I'm about to get *richah.*" She sang the last word for emphasis. "And our wine's gonna be at those stores that sell stuff for a dollar or two. Whoo hoo!" She threw her hands in the air in a celebratory gesture. "You're welcome, America."

Ariadne struggled to her feet, batting away Donny and Mia's offers of assistance. She planted her fists on her hips and stared down the interloper with cold fury. "You're lying. Maybe not about the crisps, but about being married to Giles. We may have been divorced, but we were close. He never would have hidden something like that from me."

But, Mia thought, *he did.* She flashed on the secretive phone conversation she walked in on during the party the producer threw for the cast. She closed her eyes to recall what she'd heard him say. Something about him handling things but being very careful because there could be trouble if it went wrong. And he'd called the person on the other end of the line "babe." It wasn't a reach for Mia to assume Violet was the "babe" in question, and judging by Ariadne's reaction at the moment, the trouble would have been her discovering her ex-husband and still-in-business-together production partner had married this "tart" without telling her.

"He was waiting to tell you until we hammered out all the legal details," Violet said, confirming Mia's suspicions. "My lawyers'll get you a copy of the marriage certificate, but here's me and my hubby at our beautiful wedding. We pulled the whole thing off in secret, but that don't mean I weren't gonna dress for it."

Violet pulled a phone from her tote and held a photo up to Ariadne. Mia peered over her shoulder. The bride and groom were Violet and Giles, alright, the bride modeling the most inappropriate wedding gown Mia had ever laid eyes on, which was saying something in Queens. A completely sheer Cinderella gown barely covered what appeared to be a silky white string bikini, if there was enough fabric to even call it that. Nicky took a peek at the picture and whimpered. "Hot *and* rich. Is this what love feels like?"

The second Mrs. St. James pocketed the phone, taking a moment to baby-talk and rub noses with her cat. "The flight here took forevs. I'm knackered and could use a kip. Sorry, that's 'I'm tired and could use a nap' for you Yanks." She spoke slowly and acted out the words as if translating from a foreign language. "Where's the bedroom me and my husband would've shared if he hadn't been offed by someone who's probably . . . you!"

Violet pointed an accusing finger at Ariadne, who gasped and stepped back. The event was beginning to resemble a cheesy soap opera.

"Don't you dare," Ariadne growled. "I never laid a hand on Giles in anything but a loving way. And you can forget about taking a kip in my apartment, which he willed to *me*."

This earned a snort from the competition. "Maybe in some old will written about the time of the Magna Carta, which probably came out 'bout the year you were born."

This time, Ariadne's growl resembled the sound of a bull eyeing a red cape. Mia half-expected her to paw the ground and then charge. She stepped between the women. "Is there a lawyer in the house?" A half-dozen hands went up. "Okay, good. Any advice on how to resolve this?"

A sleekly attired man in his early thirties stepped forward. "Hi, Jay Stures here. Lawyer turned agent, so you can make double the jokes about how sleazy I am, ha ha." He addressed the women. "My advice would be to negotiate a temporary settlement while your own lawyers analyze and determine how to execute Giles's estate plans and final will."

Ariadne closed her eyes and sucked in a breath. When she opened her eyes, she seemed calmer. She drew herself up to her stately height and bestowed a small, regal smile on her nemesis. Mia saw that her game plan was to go with class over crass. "Excellent advice, Jay. I recently vacated my own apartment to move in here. It's available right in this very building and is fully furnished. Violet, you're welcome to stay there for as long as you need to be in New York."

Violet's response was preceded by another snort. "Nice try. "Giles told me all about the whole poor-door sitch, so a hella no on that pitch, love."

Class went out the window as Ariadne spewed invectives at Violet, who ignored her and murmured sweet nothings to her purse cat. A woman who appeared to be the female version of Jay Stures stepped forward. True to form, she was also a lawyer turned agent. *Do they travel in packs?* Mia wondered. "Ladies, here's the deal," the woman said, getting right to it. "If either of you leaves this apartment, it could be construed as giving up rights to it. It's relatively decent-sized—"

"Decent?" a don next to Mia muttered. "You could fit three of my place into this living room."

"My advice," the woman continued, "is to call a truce and both bunk here until your lawyers determine the apartment's rightful owner."

A pause laden with tension followed. "Fine," Ariadne finally muttered through clenched teeth.

Violet shrugged. "Me kitty Princess Kate and me'll muddle through for a few days." The whole room seemed to breathe a sigh of relief. "And I guess we can work out a similar arrangement for the business."

Ariadne made a strangled sound, and Mia clutched her arm, fearful that the woman would go down again. "The business?" The words came out in a squeak.

"Yeah. Giles left his half to me. I'm Second's the Charm Productions." Violet gleefully rubbed her hands together. "I'm so excited. I'm in the telly business."

Donny Junior's face creased with concern. "I think Ariadne's gonna faint again."

"I know," Mia said. "You better grab her other arm."

Chapter 12

The surprise appearance of the second Mrs. Giles St. James put an end to his memorial, although guests seemed in no hurry to leave, preferring to stick around and gossip about the juicy development. As Mia and her crew discreetly began packing up food and equipment, she mused to herself that if Ariadne had murdered her ex to gain control of the company, Violet's appearance could ruin the scheme. However, a brief snippet of conversation Mia overheard while boxing up leftover desserts set her wheels spinning in a different direction.

She was sneaking the remnants of a broken brownie to assuage hunger pangs when camerawoman Lysette appeared at the table to grab a lemon bar. Ariadne sidled up next to her. Over the course of her catering career, Mia had learned guests and clients, particularly wealthy ones, developed a sort of hired-help blindness that could render a cater-waiter standing right next to them invisible. This was the case when Ariadne, oblivious to Mia's presence, asked Lysette if she'd filmed the confrontation between Giles's current and former wives. When the camera woman answered in the affirmative, Ariadne responded, "Send it to me. The pilot could use it." Mia, who'd expected the producer to destroy the footage, was stunned to hear the order.

Ariadne grabbed a bottle of bourbon from the sideboard. She unscrewed the cap, gulped a huge swallow of it, and strode off, bottle in hand. Lysette turned to go and literally bumped into Mia. "Sorry. I didn't know you were there."

"No worries." Mia paused and then said, "I heard what Ariadne said about using what just happened in the pilot. I mean, the new Mrs. St. James accused her of murder. You'd think Ariadne would want to bury that."

Lysette responded with a look of bewilderment. "Seriously? No way. It's great drama. You can't make this stuff up. Although"—she winked at Mia—"to be totally honest, a lot of the time we do." She took another lemon bar and headed off.

Mia pondered this as she carried boxed sweets into the kitchen. *Maybe Violet showing up wasn't such a surprise to Ariadne. Maybe she planned the whole thing for the shock value. If she already knew about Giles's new wife, then it makes her less of a murder suspect because she knew she'd be sharing ownership of the company. Unless . . . Ariadne and Violet are in on it together! And all their hating each other is an act! If it's "great stuff," as Lysette said, maybe they planned the whole thing to make the pilot even more sellable. Which would mean they already knew each other. Could they be a couple of black widows who plotted behind Giles's back?*

Finding a link between the two women would

require research. Mia groaned. There was only one person she knew who had the skills and connections to take the needed deep dive into both women's pasts—annoying *Triborough Tribune* reporter Teri Fuoco, whom Mia had reluctantly come to accept as a frenemy, especially since she was sort of dating Belle View's very own Evans.

A guest walked right into Mia, who managed to keep the top box on her stack from toppling onto the floor. "I'm so sorry," the woman apologized. "I didn't see you."

"Happens all the time," Mia said with a resigned smile.

"Well, hello there. If it isn't my Boldano bestie, Mia Carina."

Mia, who'd put in a call to Teri from her car on the way back to Astoria, gritted her teeth and swallowed an acidic response to the reporter's amused tone. Teri knew Mia only called when she needed something. Thus the reporter milked every interaction for whatever she could get from it. "Working for the Boldanos doesn't make me a Boldano." Mia didn't bother to hide how grumpy she felt.

"In the figurative sense, it kinda does. So, what up, girlfriend?"

Mia shared the details of Violet's appearance and her theory about it being planned and not impromptu. "I wondered if you could use your reporter mojo to see if you can dig up any prior connection between Ariadne and Violet."

"And possibly expose them as a deadly duo who got rid of the guy standing between them and fame and fortune? Sure."

"Great, thanks."

"And in return—"

This time Mia couldn't suppress the groan. "Ugh, why is everything with you transactional?"

"And in return," Teri repeated, "you officially invite me to Madison's bachelorette party in New Orleans."

Mia took a hand off the steering wheel and slapped her forehead. "Ugh, the party. I forgot all about that."

"It's a good thing I reminded you because you're in charge, and we leave tomorrow."

"How did you find out I'm in charge?"

"Delany, the world's worst maid of honor. I tried hitting her up for an invite, and she wrote back she traded current wedding duties for a stint in rehab and I should check with you. Boy, when I propose to Evans and make you *my* maid of honor, you better not pull any of this crap on me."

"Gross." Mia recoiled at the image of Evans and Teri plighting their troth, as well as the thought of spending an entire weekend in New Orleans dodging the pugnacious journalist's company. "It's too late to buy a plane ticket," she said, grabbing at a possible out.

"Not a problem. Once Giles St. James got offed and Donny Junior got tagged as suspect numero uno, I knew you'd need my help eventually and I'd be able to leverage that into a shower invitation, so I bought a ticket on your flight. See you at LaGuardia in the a.m. *Laissez les bons temps rouler.* Let the good times roll!" Teri signed off with a whoop and a chortle, missing some choice words Mia threw her way.

Mia exited Grand Central Parkway into the

parking lot Belle View shared with Flushing's World's Fair Marina. She got out of the car, wrinkling her noise at the smell wrought by Flushing Bay's meetup with the humid July heat. Mia hurried through the lot into the cool climes of Belle View, where her first stop was Cammie's office. She stuck her head in and was happily surprised to see the event planner was actually there, although judging by the recording equipment and new soundproofing, her focus wasn't on Belle View tasks. "I forgot I'm now in charge of Madison's bachelorette party," Mia said to Cammie. "I was gonna use the fact I'm trying to save Donny Junior from jail or marriage to Ariadne as an excuse to bail, but now I can't. I need you to cover for me this weekend."

Cammie lifted what looked like very expensive headphones off her head. "I'll do my best, but it's not ideal with a wedding and two graduation parties booked. More importantly, I've got Guadalupe's podcast to debut."

Shane stepped out of his office into the hallway. He reflexively bent down to kiss Mia, then stopped himself and snapped back up. "Hello," he said stiffly. "How was the memorial?"

"Very, very interesting. I'll fill you in later. Right now, I've got to find someone to help Cammie manage the fort here this weekend. Even with *postponing her podcast launch*"—Cammie responded to the heavy emphasis with an eye roll—"it's a lot. I have to make a few calls."

"I'll do it."

"Huh?" Mia said, taken aback. "You can't. You're going to New Orleans with me. Jamie's bachelor party. Remember?"

"Making sure our guests have the event of their lifetimes is way more important than watching drunk guys barf on Bourbon Street. Because you know with Donny Junior and Nicky and the whole crew, that's gonna happen."

"Probably," Mia acknowledged. "But still—"

"Evans is going; he can provide backup if you need it. Meanwhile, I'll manage things here."

"What about my dad?" Mia was growing annoyed. "He works here too, you know."

"And *you* know he's useless after ten p.m."

Unable to deny this, Mia responded with a stubborn sulk.

Shane folded his arms in front of his cut chest. "You can't tell me some bachelor party is more important than five-star reviews for Belle View on event websites."

"No, but—"

"Then it's settled." He addressed Cammie. "Looks like it's you and me this weekend. Partyin' Belle View style."

Shane shot Cammie a double thumbs-up and disappeared back into his office. The two women stared after him. "That was weird," the fledgling podcaster said.

Mia pursed her lips. "Very. He told me he hates bachelor parties. I had no idea just how much until now."

She retreated to her own office, where she forced herself not to brood about Shane's odd behavior, instead focusing on tying up loose ends for the weekend's events. However, once she finished, worrisome questions wormed their way back into her psyche. Why was Shane so quick—and eager—to bail on a weekend in New Orleans? One where she'd promised to build romantic alone time for the two of them into the schedule? And what exactly *was* his problem with bachelor parties? While she respected his reluctance to indulge in the bacchanalian pursuits associated with the celebration, it was obvious that in this case, there was a larger issue at play.

Mia pulled her phone from her purse and called up a selfie she and Shane had taken in her living room. The photo showed the couple laughing while Mia held a bored-looking Doorstop and Pizzazz perched on Shane's shoulder. "You're holding something back, Shane Cambrazzo," she said to his dimpled, green-eyed visage. "And as soon as I get back from New Orleans, I'm gonna find out what."

Chapter 13

Traffic into LaGuardia Airport was its usual hellscape, which slowed down Mia's arrival. She hurried to security and straight into a drama involving some of the party guests. A few dons and donettes who'd never bothered to upgrade their driver's licenses to Real ID had forgotten their passports, a non-starter for the TSA. Being denied entry to the airplane and thus the bachelor and bachelorette parties prompted the kind of wailing usually only seen at Italian funerals. "I reminded them every day to bring their passports," Mia told Michael. "Did anyone from the show do the same?"

He responded with a derisive snort and a gesture to Lysette, who had her camera trained on the scene. "And risk missing great moments like this? No way."

Airport police ushered the disappointed guests out of the line, and the TSA resumed work. Once Mia made it through security, she grabbed a to-go coffee from a kiosk and hastened to the flight gate. Most of the other guests were already there, chatting with excitement among themselves. Donny Junior stood protectively by Ariadne's side, moving everywhere she moved. Jamie and Madison's "civilian" friends mingled with the show's dons and donettes. Having finished shooting footage at security, Lysette now hovered at the gate. To gain access to the parties, the crew had to abide by Jamie's strict ground rules: Keep filming to a minimum, and no putting him or Madison on camera. Mia had echoed them for herself, issuing a strict order to all concerned that if the camera caught a mere corner of her face, be prepared to face the consequences.

Madison saw Mia and came to her, and the women exchanged air kisses. Jamie's fiancée wore a glittery "Bride-to-be" sash over her flowered boho peasant top. Mia noticed the bachelorette had eschewed her usual light touch with makeup, opting for a much heavier hand, and her stick-straight blond hair had been forced into sultry waves. "Is that a new lipstick and . . . everything?" She gestured to Madison's face.

The bachelorette shrugged. "It's just in case, you know, I accidentally end up on camera or something. I mean, that wouldn't be the worst thing, right? But shhh. Don't tell Jamie."

She put her finger to her lips. Mia responded with a nod, making a mental note to sound an alarm with Madison's future husband.

"Whoo hoo!" The hoot came from Teri Fuoco as she approached the gate. "Whassup, party people? Ready to pass a good time? It's what they say in N'Awlins. I researched it."

Mia winced at Teri's outfit. The reporter had

traded her usual polo shirt and chino togs for too-tight leggings striped purple, green, and gold, and an oversize top with "Party 'til the Check Liver Light Comes On" spelled out in colored rhinestones. She'd pulled her brown, frizzy hair into a ponytail and topped off the look with a baseball cap decorated with a sequined jester.

"Hello." Not wanting to encourage Teri's urge to fraternize with her, Mia delivered the single word in the coldest tone possible.

Teri glanced around the gate area. "Where's the guy you're not dating who you're secretly dating?"

"Not coming."

"Really?"

Her tone irked Mia. "Something came up."

"Really?" Teri repeated, not bothering to hide her skepticism.

Mia released a frustrated grunt. While Teri's reporter instincts often came handy, they were far less welcome when they sniffed out a story in Mia's personal life.

The gate official announced boarding had begun, and the travelers lined up. Ariadne, who'd quickly traded mourning for a return to producing, took a head count. "We're still missing a few people."

Mia scanned the group. "I don't see Violet."

"She won't be here. Her kitty had digestive issues."

Ariadne delivered the update with a British take on the word *issues* that made it sound like "tissues" and an evil smirk that sent a chill through Mia. She looked away and saw Nicky Vestri saunter up to the gate, a few members of his posse in tow. "He had to make an entrance," Donny Junior muttered darkly.

"Excuse me?"

Mia wasn't sure if Ariadne genuinely didn't hear him or was tossing out one of those "Did you just say what I *think* you said?" excuse me's. Apparently, Little D wasn't sure either, because he backed off. "Nothing," he responded, glowering at his cousin's arrival. "I didn't say nothing."

Mia watched Nicky claim center stage, up-topping dons and civilians alike, and flirting with any pretty partygoer whose eye he caught. He wore baggy pants and a purple T-shirt emblazoned with the image of his face and a dialogue bubble that read "Get Outta Here!" *Which,* Mia thought to herself as she watched Teri tug her leggings out of her derriere, *is surprisingly not the worst outfit here.*

A thought occurred to Mia. With Giles gone, so was the threat to Nicky's precious "signature line" and accompanying swag. She couldn't see elegant and titled Ariadne wanting to claim credit for it. She crunched her face, trying to remember what Nicky had said when he revealed Giles was gunning for his goodies. *Something threatening. What was it?*

The gate agent announced the party's group number, and everyone slowly filed forward. Nicky got in line behind Mia. "You seriously think you're getting the aisle seat, Anthony?" she heard him tell his chief hanger-on. "Sorry, my friend. Not gonna happen."

"That's it!" Mia cried out, recalling what Nicky said. Everyone turned to her, and she cringed. "Sorry. I was playing Wordle in my head." To Mia's relief, this was deemed an acceptable explanation, and people lost interest in her.

As she marched down the jetway, Nicky's other, more inflammatory, declaration came back to her—the threat that Giles was a "goner" if he came after the don's line and accompanying line of swag. *Chalk up another suspect besides Donny Junior for NYPD,* she thought with satisfaction. She felt his hand on her derriere and reached back to swat it away. *And a suspect I will happily narc on.*

The flight to New Orleans proved uneventful to the point where Mia, exhausted by the arduous combination of a full-time job, maid of honor duties, and amateur sleuthing, dozed off. A painful jab in the ribs from her unwelcome seatmate, Teri, alerted her to their arrival in the Big Easy. "Wakey, *chere.* That's French for 'dear.' "

"I know what *chere* means," Mia said, glaring at Teri as she rubbed her side. "Why didn't you sit with Evans?"

"He's up in first class. My boyfriend's *rich.*" Teri mimed making it rain. The sous chef came from a wealthy Upper East Side family, a connection he adamantly refused to take advantage of—except, apparently, when it came to flying.

"I love Evans, but a guy who flies first and lets the woman he's supposedly dating fly coach can't be called a boyfriend. Show yourself some respect."

"And respect myself right out of our almost-relationship? Pass."

Mia frowned. "When all this is over, we need to have a long talk about your self-esteem."

"I have plenty of self esteem. Sex, not so much."

"*Ugh.* TMI."

The two retrieved their carry-on luggage from the overhead bin and deplaned with the others. Evans helped Mia by rounding up the bachelor party, while she focused on the women. "How was first class?" she couldn't resist teasing him.

Evans shrugged. "Same as always."

Mia sighed. "Oh, for the day when I can put 'first class' and 'same as always' in a sentence." This got a grin from the laconic chef.

The partygoers piled into cabs lined up outside the airport terminal and headed for the French Quarter. The high pitch of excited chatter in her cab made Mia's head ache, and she welcomed the driver's announcement they'd arrived at their Bourbon Street hotel. To provide at least a degree of separation for the two parties, Jamie and his guests were staying at a hotel a few blocks down the street. Madison and her crew tumbled out of the cabs and made their way into the hotel singing Taylor Swift songs at the top of their lungs. "They're not even drunk yet," Mia muttered to no one in particular.

She took advantage of keyless check-in to score her room and practically raced to the fifth-floor double. Once inside, she tossed her luggage to the side and did a face plant onto one of the beds.

She was about to doze off when she heard someone jiggling the door handle. She bolted up just as Teri entered the room wheeling her carry-on bag. She wore a goldfish bowl around her neck but instead of fish, it was filled with what Mia assumed was New Orleans's famous daquiris. Teri gave a cheery wave. "Hi, roomie." She inhaled a large gulp of drink through a straw.

"What are you doing here?!"

"I couldn't afford my own room, and Evans said you told him you got a double at a good rate, so . . ."

Teri plopped down on the edge of Mia's bed. Mia cursed and shoved her off. "The room has two beds. Get off this one."

"Actually, this is the one I need. If I'm not near a fan of some kind, I perspire profusely."

"ARGH!"

Mia jumped off the bed by the window and took two angry strides to the room's second bed. She did another face plant. "There. Now leave me *alone.* I'm tired and need a nap before tonight's festivities."

"Okay." Teri inhaled another swig of daquiri. "But before you pass out, who do you think killed St. James?"

Mia whimpered in frustration. She rolled over onto her back. Donny Boldano Senior had begged her to help clear his first-born of any suspicion in the producer's murder, and so far she hadn't been much help. Much as Teri drove her crazy, she was sharp and had proved herself helpful in the past. Running a few theories past her wasn't a bad idea.

She fluffed up the two large pillows behind her, then threaded her fingers behind her head and leaned back. "According to Cammie, who wheedled the info out of Pete, with all the endless footage the camera crew shot at Casa Giovanni, there was nothing trained on the pool house until the dons and donettes went there to change. They don't even have film showing anyone going in that direction. So pretty much everyone who was there when Giles was offed could be a suspect because any one of us could have could have snuck off to the pool house, bonked him on the head with the weight, and snuck back to whatever was going on during the time period. And there was zero security because Giles didn't think they needed it, so pretty much anyone could have snuck onto the property and taken him out."

"So, means and opportunity, meet wide net." Teri pulled a flat candy wrapped in plastic out of her fanny pack. She unwrapped it and took a bite. "Oh man, pralines are delish. Pure sugar."

"Don't make crumbs. We don't wanna attract roaches. I read they have flying ones the size of a fist down here, God help us."

"Noted. Moving on to motive."

"That narrows things down at least a little. Ariadne certainly benefited from Giles's death, at least until Violet showed up. I had the thought that they could be in on it together, especially if they end up sharing control of the production company. Does that sound crazy?"

"We're talking reality show people. The only thing crazy is how some of these shows get on the air. Ariadne and Violet are on the list. Who else?"

"That I know of? That's another wide net, at least when it comes to his employees. Michael, the segment producer, was ticked off because Giles wouldn't promote him. Lysette hated some of the scenes he forced her to film. And poor Kelvin, the production assistant. I overheard him go ballistic when he found out St. James stole his idea for a show."

"What about Jason, the money guy?"

Mia wrinkled her brow. "I forgot about him. He's the only one in the company who seems genuinely sad Giles is dead."

"Which makes me suspicious. Especially since he's working for free. Who does that? Give up a good job to do the same thing for no money? And probably worse hours."

"People who want to get into the entertainment business, I guess. If you're gonna crunch numbers, it's a lot sexier to do it for a TV show or movie than for some boring couple from the boroughs who need their taxes done. But good point. The quiet ones can be the most dangerous. Not that as an Italian, I know anyone who's quiet. Speaking of Italians, there's also Nicky Vestri." Mia made a face. "He's such a *cafone*, hitting on all the girls and bragging like he's the star of the show. St. James was gonna market Nicky's stupid line himself—you know, 'Get Outta Here!'—and Nicky got all threaten-y about it when he told me."

"Do you think he's got the testes to follow through on it?"

Mia debated for a minute. "My first instinct would be no. But this show is incredibly important to him, so make that a maybe."

Teri finished her praline. She brushed crumbs from her lap onto the floor, earning an outraged scolding from Mia she ignored. "You left out another Italian."

"Who?" Mia asked, knowing exactly who she meant.

Teri gave her a look. "I know you know, but I'll say it anyway. Donny Junior. The most likely suspect of all."

"Come on. You know it's not him."

"No, I don't. Neither do Pete Dianopolis and the NYPD. Donny Junior is a not-so-bright hothead. Conking someone with a barbell is totally in his wheelhouse."

Mia glowered at Teri. "You just want it to be him because you're out to get the Boldanos. Be quiet and clean up your sugar crumbs. If I see one roach in this room, you'll be sleeping in the hallway."

"Noted. One last question. Any word from your he's-not-my-boyfriend?"

"Yes," Mia lied. "Why are you even asking that? It's none of your business."

"I'm asking as a friend." Teri's tone lacked her usual affable arrogance. "I can tell you're upset. Something's been bothering you this whole trip."

"I'm fine. It's nothing." Mia paused, then overcome with the need to talk to someone, she blurted, "He's hiding something from me, I know he is. It's making me nuts."

"I'm sorry."

Mia backed off her urge to share. "It's okay. I'm making way too big a deal of the whole thing. It's the lack of sleep talking."

She turned away from Teri and closed her eyes. She was about to fall asleep when her phone buzzed. She uttered an annoyed exclamation and turned off the ringer. Teri's phone beeped a text alert. "It's your nonna," she said, checking it. "Call her, it's important."

"Ugh, I will never get any peace. And how does she have your number?"

"I'm reporter, I give it to everyone. You never know where you'll get your next story."

Giving up on her dream of taking a nap, Mia sat up and FaceTimed her grandmother. A corner of Elisabetta's face appeared on the phone screen. The octogenarian had yet to nail the finer points of a video call. "Nonna, hi. Are you okay? What's wrong?" She flashed on her father and his recent exertions. "Is it Dad? Did something happen?"

"No, no. He's fine. I'm fine. Are you wearing the top I made you?"

"What?!" Mia exclaimed, swallowing a more scatological response. "That's why you're calling? No, I'm not wearing it." The top in question being a hideous and ill-fitting crocheted number in a blinding color combination of fuchsia, bright orange, and neon yellow that Mia made a show of loving for Elisabetta and then planned to sneak out of her suitcase into the far recesses of a dresser drawer as soon as her grandmother left the room. She'd forgotten to do the latter.

"Why not?" Elisabetta pressed.

"Because . . ." Mia searched for a reason. "I didn't want to get plane smell on it."

"Ah. Makes sense."

Mia's moment of congratulating herself for shutting down the issue lasted not even that long.

"Put it on," Elisabetta ordered. "I can see you're off the plane and at the hotel. You can wear it now."

"Sure. I'll put it on as soon as we get off the phone."

"Put down the phone. I want to see it on you."

Trapped, Mia uttered a weak, "Okay."

She rested the phone on the bed and went to her suitcase, where the offending garment sat rolled up like a crocheted sausage. She switched out her T-shirt for the top, earning a snort from Teri. The reporter mouthed "Hideous!" and Mia mouthed back, "Shut up, I know!"

She picked up the phone. "Here you go, Nonna," she said, modeling the top.

Elisabetta's face lit up. "*Che bella.* You look lit."

There was the sudden sound of hoots and screams from outside. Teri ran to the French doors leading onto a small balcony and stepped outside. The acrid scent of beer mixed with throw-up wafted up from Bourbon Street into the room. "It's the bachelorette party," Teri called back to Mia. "I think they're flashing people on the street."

"Oh no!" Mia said, panicking. "Madison better not be one of them. If anything winds up on the Internet, the Boldanos will not be happy. Her job won't be, either. Nonna, I gotta go."

"Have fun," her grandmother chirped. "*Ciao, bambina.* I'm expecting lotsa pictures of you in that top all over New Orleans. Lots of 'em."

Mia ended the call and hurried to change. Her hoop earring caught on the crocheted top as she pulled it over her head, and she stumbled around the room, unable to see. "Help, help!"

Teri ran to her and worked to disengage the earring from the top. "Thanks," Mia said, once the task was complete. "Give me a sec to get out of this monstrosity."

"You don't have time. They started singing 'I'm a Slave 4 U.' Who knows where that could lead?"

Mia grabbed her purse. "Ugh. This is gonna be one long weekend." She and Teri ran to the door. "Wait, my phone.'

Mia ran back and grabbed her phone off the bed just as it pinged a text. She saw the sender was Shane and paused. Then she shoved the phone in her purse and took off with Teri. When Shane was ready to tell her the real reason he'd thrown her solo under the bus that was the bachelor and bachelorette party, she'd talk to him.

Until then, all he'd get was radio silence.

Chapter 14

Much to the disappointment of the enthusiastic crowd on the street below, Mia and Teri managed to corral the bachelorette party before any body parts were exposed. Considering some of the girls were already a little, if not a lot, drunk, Mia commended herself for booking an early dinner reservation at one of the more casual French Quarter eateries instead of the city's famed landmark restaurants.

The group of around a dozen walked a few blocks and piled into Jambalaya's, a trendy eatery on St. Peter Street. They deposited themselves onto benches set around a long, distressed wood table toward the back of the room. Black-and-white photographs of past Mardi Gras celebrations decorated the exposed brick walls, and mood lighting came courtesy of faux gas lamps on every table. To avoid the complication of a dozen different food orders, Mia had arranged a pre-set menu with the restaurant, including a round of champagne for the table. She tapped her glass to get everyone's attention, then raised it. "To Madison, and a lifetime of happiness with one of the best guys out there."

"To Madison," the others chorused.

They drained their glasses, which were instantly replenished by the eager waitstaff. Everyone seemed to be having a good but not a raucous time, so Mia took a break to call Jamie and check in. "Hey. How's it going on your end?"

"Drunk guys at a strip club. Your typical bachelor party. How about you?"

"I was worried at the hotel that things might be getting out of hand, but the girls seem to have calmed down."

"Good. To be honest, I was nervous about Madison hanging out with the donettes. Most are okay, but keep your eye on Chiara. She's a little too into this whole show thing."

"Oh, believe me, I am on it."

Mia returned to the table, where she saw the champagne glasses were again full. As the meal segued from hors d'oeuvres to appetizers, so did the women's state of inebriation, to Mia's concern. She flagged their headwaiter. "Just an FYI that I didn't put bottomless champagne on the menu for this event."

"Oh, we know. Don't worry, you're not paying for it. She is."

The waiter pointed to a table in a dark corner at the other end of the room. Mia fumed to see Ariadne ensconced at the table, her chin resting on her palm as she studied the party guests. "It's so cool to have a reality show shooting here," the waiter enthused. He leaned down and whispered,

"I heard her tell the camera lady that the party's boring, and they might have to use 'frankenbiting' to liven things ups."

"Frankenbiting?" Mia repeated, confused.

"Yeah. You never heard of it? They cut dialog from different scenes and add it to a boring scene to make it better. Reality shows do it all the time."

"Not on my watch."

Furious, Mia stood up and marched toward Ariadne. She passed Lysette hiding behind a pole, her video camera resting on her shoulder. Mia glared at the camerawoman, who responded with an apologetic shrug. Upon reaching Ariadne, Mia set her fists on the table and leaned toward the producer. "I know what you're doing. You're getting the girls drunk so they do stupid stuff. Stop it. And stop filming."

"Relax, love," Ariadne responded, unfazed. "I promise you won't be in any of the shots. I can't imagine showing off that awful, crocheted bit you're wearing in my pilot. It would chase away potential buyers."

"It's not about my top, although—never mind that. I repeat, stop. Filming. Let Madison enjoy her bachelorette party in peace."

Ariadne smirked, or at least attempted to, given how little movement was left in her face thanks to Botox shots and fillers. "Your bride-to-be friend is the one who gave permission to film. So your issue is with her, not me."

Thwarted, Mia stomped back to the party table, pulling aside the headwaiter on the way. "Not one more drop of booze here." She gestured to Ariadne. "She may be the one paying the bar bill, but I'm the one tipping on everything else. So it's goodbye drinks and hello, big glasses of water. You got it?"

"Yes, ma'am." Cowed, the waiter ran off to follow Mia's order, leaving her to steam that on top of everything else, she'd just been addressed as "ma'am" instead of "miss" for the first time ever.

Knowing the evening was still young enough for much more partying, Mia made sure dessert was liquor-free. "Pace yourselves," she instructed the girls after putting the kibosh on a round of Café Brûlots, a famed New Orleans brandy-spiked coffee drink. She glared at Ariadne, who'd tried a stealth delivery of the boozy beverage. Mia wondered how much the producer bribed the waiter to insist it was "just coffee." She said a silent prayer that evidence would soon prove Ariadne to be her ex-husband's killer, if only to rid her from Mia's life.

The meal ended, and Mia realized she hadn't seen Teri since the main course. *The least that party crasher could have done was help me babysit the bachelorettes,* Mia thought, annoyed.

She managed to corral all the girls yet again and usher them out of the restaurant without Teri's help. She also got in a quick stop at the hotel, where she changed out of Fashion by Nonna into the sexy red number she'd bought to wear on a romantic New Orleans evening with Shane. *Your loss, buddy,* she thought, vengefully adjusting the dress for maximum cleavage display.

As she and the bachelorettes strolled the scenic streets of the French Quarter to the bar where they'd rendezvous with the bachelors, Mia breathed a sigh of relief. So far, so good on circumventing any potential disaster. She'd even garnered enough admiring hoots and whistles to bolster her shaky self-esteem.

Her phone sang out "New York State of Mind," and she pulled it out of her purse. Seeing Cammie's number, she took the call.

"Hey," said the familiar and annoyingly sexy male voice of Shane.

"Why can't certain people like *you* take the hint I don't want to talk to them instead of sneaking to reach me through someone else's phone?" Without Shane's perfect features staring back at her, Mia found it much easier to grouse at him.

"I'm sorry," Shane said, sounding abashed. "It's just we booked an event that's so cute I had to tell you about it. A funeral—for three goldfish. Small luncheon, just the immediate family, but the parents told me their kid was so attached to the fish that this little send-off would help him get through it. Sweet, huh? I wanna be a parent like that someday."

Hearing these words made Mia's heart clutch. She'd had a daydream or two herself about becoming a parent—with Shane cast as the father in the daydreams. "Very sweet," she said, softening.

"Mia . . . I know there's stuff I haven't told you. And I want to. It's just . . . complicated."

Complicated. The relationship doomsday word. Mia hardened again. "When you're ready to uncomplicate things, lemme know. Until then—"

She ended the call and had a sudden pang of remorse. Was she truly responding to red flags with Shane or had her marital disaster made her hypersensitive? Mia brooded over this question as the bachelorette party made a right onto Bourbon Street. She landed on the old saw "Better safe than sorry," especially when it came to protecting her previously broken heart.

Once on tourist-heavy Bourbon Street, Mia briefly lost sight of her charges in the crowd of revelers. She found them just in time to see Madison, who hadn't drunk enough coffee to totally sober up, stumble. She grabbed a stranger's arm, sending his large go-cup cocktail flying. Madison gasped. "Oh, I'm so sorry." Mia wasn't happy to hear the apology come out slurred.

Before the man could respond, his date, who'd easily answer to the description of "tough-looking broad," stepped in front him and confronted Madison. "You need to watch where you're going. He just bought that drink. It was full. You owe him a new one."

"Yes. Of course." Madison fumbled through her purse and pulled out her phone. "I don't have cash, but I can Venmo you the money."

The woman waved away the phone. "And steal our identity? I don't *think* so."

"Babe, it's okay," her boyfriend said.

"No, it's not," his girlfriend said, literally pushing him aside. "Don't worry, I'm handling this." She took a step closer to Madison. "Pay up. In cash."

Mia shoved aside a few dawdling tourists and made it to Madison's side. "I'm her friend, and I've got cash. I'll pay."

"Thank you, Mia, but no." As Mia feared, dinner's steady pour of champagne had loosened

Madison's inhibitions. The bride-to-be took a step toward the other woman. "This is between us."

The other bachelorettes had circled around the pair, watching the standoff with a combination of fascination and glee. The man Madison knocked into had given up trying to call off his girlfriend and was taking in the show with the others.

"Madison—" Mia didn't get to finish her sentence. The tough broad pushed her out of the way.

"Hey!" Madison shouted. "That's not cool! Apologize to my friend."

"Make me."

Madison, incensed by now, took another step closer. The warring women were literally nose to nose. "My ancestors came over on the Mayflower. My five times great-grandfather signed the Declaration of Independence. Show our founding fathers some respect."

"I wouldn't have gone with a Declaration of Independence thing here," Mia heard one donette whisper to another, who nodded agreement.

"Ya think that makes you better than me?" Madison's nemesis hissed at her.

"Yeah." Mia had never heard Madison sound so arrogant. Or drunk. "I do."

"You know what, speaking of early Americans, this whole thing can be settled with an Andrew Jackson," Mia said, trying to keep the argument from escalating.

She pulled a twenty-dollar bill from her purse and waved it in the air. The woman grabbed it, knocking Madison out of her way and to the ground in the process. "Sorry, not sorry," she said in a sing-songy voice, showing off the money.

"You're the one who's gonna be sorry." Madison jumped to her feet and shoved the woman, who stumbled. She regained her balance and returned the shove. Before Mia could stop it, a melee broke out. The bachelorettes jumped in to defend Madison. They were matched by a group of the tough broad's friends who suddenly materialized. "No, stop!" Mia screamed. "Do something!" she yelled at the man whose drink started the imbroglio.

"I never had chicks fighting over me before," he responded, watching with delight.

Mia was in the thick of the battle, trying to pull Madison's hair out of the hand of a Team Tough Broad member when a feral roar froze the action. Chiara, who until that moment had been watching the action from the sidelines, stepped into the middle of the fight circle. She let out another roar and released a fist into the tough broad's face. The woman staggered, then collapsed to the ground in an unconscious heap.

Chiara turned to Lysette and spoke straight into the video camera. "And that's how you do it." She reached down, picked up Mia's twenty, which lay on the ground next to the woman, and sashayed off.

The crowd, now quiet, dispersed. The tough broad came to and sat up. Her friends and boyfriend helped the groggy victim to her feet, while the bachelorettes huddled around Madison, who seemed shocked into sobriety. Mia stood frozen in place next to Lysette, who was equally still. "I've been shooting stuff for ten years," Lysette finally said, using a more profane word for "stuff." "Before I got into reality TV, I worked for a news station. I've filmed everything from shoot-outs to wrestling matches to freeway pileups And I have to say that watching that Chiara girl in action may well be the scariest thing I've ever seen."

"I hear you," Mia responded. She saw Chiara, now sipping a frozen daquiri from a giant go-cup, saunter back to the bachelorettes. Mia had pegged the donette as ruthlessly ambitious, willing to do whatever it took to make the transition from reality player to show star.

She now wondered if Chiara's career game plan could also include murder.

Chapter 15

The bachelor and bachelorette parties met up at Lafitte's Blacksmith Shop, one of New Orleans's most legendary bars. Little Donny approached Mia, who had an arm around Madison's waist. Whether it was due to the champagne or the street fight, the bride-to-be was unsteady on her feet. "Is Ariadne with you?" Donny asked, anxiously scanning the crowd.

"Hopefully not," Mia said.

Donny's expression lightened. "Ah, I see her. She's here."

"Of course she is." Mia said this through gritted teeth. "That woman is the human equivalent of a herpes sore. A painful, annoying embarrassment."

She didn't have to worry about Little Donny hearing her. He was already in a lip lock with his paramour.

"Madison!" Jamie pushed aside a few drunk tourists to reach his fiancée. "Are you okay?"

"I'm fine," she responded with a toss of her

blond hair. She staggered slightly. "Ooh, that made me dizzy."

Jamie substituted his arm for Mia's around Madison's waist. "We saw the fight but couldn't get through the crowd to stop it."

"She's gonna feel it tomorrow," Mia said. "It got rough. Punches, scratching, hair pulling."

"It was hot," declared Vincent Moltisani. He was one of the few dons not from Astoria, but that didn't stop him from fitting the mold.

"Chicks fighting is always hot," Nicky seconded, to Mia's outrage.

She glowered at both of them. "You are truly a bunch of Neanderthals, who would probably be insulted that I grouped you with them, so my apologies to Neanderthals."

Nicky responded with a cocky smile, then put his fingers in his mouth and emitted an ear-splitting whistle. "A round of Purple Drank on me for all the bachelors and bachelorettes!" He winked at two blondes who'd managed to claim seats at the bar. "And for you gorgeous ladies, too."

The girls simpered and giggled, and Mia managed to restrain the urge to add the contents of her stomach to what tourists had already deposited in the street outside the bar. "What exactly is the Purple Drank?" she asked the busy bartender.

"Our Voodoo Daquiri," he called over his shoulder as he mixed drinks.

"What's in it?"

"Grape juice, bourbon, Everclear—"

"Pure grain alcohol?" Mia said, horrified. "Do me a favor and use something less strong in the drinks that guy just ordered."

"Sure. I'll substitute vodka."

"Not sure that's a big improvement, but I'll take what I can get."

Mia turned and saw Evans enter the bar, followed by a glum-looking Teri. Mia threaded her way through the throngs of drinkers and confronted the reporter. "Where have you been? You bailed on me at the restaurant."

"Someone gave me a coupon for a discount at an escape room on Decatur, and I thought it would be a great chance to get Evans alone for an hour in a dark room."

"And?" Mia asked, curious about the potential romantic interlude in spite of herself "What happened?"

"He tried to escape," Teri said, bummed.

"That's generally what you do in an escape room."

"Yeah, but I was hoping he wouldn't take it so literally. Did I miss anything?"

"Uh, a *little.*" Mia filled Teri in on the altercation and Chiara's cold-cocking of the woman challenging Madison.

"Wow," Teri said, eyebrows raised. "Should we add Chiara to our list of suspects?"

"*I* already added her to *my* suspect list."

Mia yelled this to be heard over the bar din. The bar piano player had launched into Billy Joel's song "Piano Man," and the drunken crowd was loudly singing along with him. They finished the song and immediately launched into Journey's "Don't Stop Believin'," which they sang even louder. Mia rubbed her temples. The noise and stress of the evening, along with the unsatisfying phone call from Shane, were creating the perfect storm for a migraine.

Teri handed her a purple concoction. "Here. Someone gave me two."

"Sure," Mia said, tired of her role as party den mother. "When in Rome, with actual Romans . . ." She gestured to a cluster of dons and donettes and took a belt of the drink. Her eyes widened and she gasped. "Oh my God. This is the drink with vodka instead of pure grain? My blood alcohol level must be three times the legal limit from just that one sip."

"These should make for an interesting walk back to the hotel," Teri said, sipping her own drink, "because Nicky Vestri just ordered a second round for the whole party."

The boozy weeping. The cookie-tossing. The bachelorettes passing out every few blocks. The details of getting the girls back to the hotel would be buried in the deepest recesses of Mia's mind, to emerge as a recovered memory in future sweaty nightmares. But with Teri finally stepping up to help, the two women managed to deposit all the guests in the safety of their rooms. Mia plunged herself into a hot bath, followed by a hot shower, followed by a second hot bath. When she emerged from the bathroom an hour-plus later, she held up the red dress she'd been wearing to Teri. At least it had been red when she set out for the evening. Now it sported large splotches of grime, and stains Mia was scared to identify. "I don't think I'll ever get the smells of tonight out of this dress. I'll have to burn it." In response, she got a snore from the sleeping reporter.

Mia tucked herself under the cool, clean hotel sheets. *Going to bed never felt this good,* she thought, contented. With no bachelorette morning activity on the agenda, she looked forward to a morning spent sleeping in.

Alas, that was not to be.

At 7 a.m., she woke up to gasps and chortles from her unwelcome roommate. "Be quiet," Mia scolded Teri, "I'm trying to sleep."

She pulled a pillow over her head and responded with an angry yelp when Teri pulled it off her. "You have to see this. But warning: If you're trying to go back to sleep, it won't help."

Teri thrust her cell phone in Mia's face. A bystander had filmed Madison's dustup with the bad-news drunk broad and uploaded it to social media. It was Mia's turn to gasp, but in horror. "Oh no. Madison will die when she sees this. Maybe really, if Donny Boldano Senior hears about it. Is it anywhere else?"

"It's everywhere else." Teri went from site to site, showing each to Mia. "This guy added background music and quotes from the movie *Fight Club.* It's pretty cool."

"It's not cool, it's terrible. But social media posts have a short tail. We need to do something that replaces this. I know!" Mia threw off the covers and jumped out of bed. "I'll dangle you off the balcony by your ankles. That'll get some attention."

"That would be a no. And while you're correct on the social media shelf life, news stories stick around longer. Take it from someone who knows."

Teri opened a local news app. Below a headline

reading MAYFLOWER MAYHEM IN FRENCH QUARTER, the screen filled with an image of Madison about to head-butt her enemy's stomach. Mia groaned. She covered her eyes with her hands. "Take that away. I can't look at it anymore."

Teri took her phone and sank down in the room's corner chair. She put her feet up on its matching ottoman. "All we can hope—"

"I hate when you say 'we'—"

"Is that the AP doesn't pick up this story. Say a prayer for a weather disaster in some sad part of the country."

Mia bent down and pulled a pair of jeans and a purple tank top from her carry-on. "I better see if I can do any kind of damage control."

Teri leaned back in the cushy chair. "One other thing I thought of. Do you know if the show filmed the fight?"

Mia snapped straight up. "They did. I talked to Lysette afterward. She's the one who put a light on how scary Chiara is."

"Uh oh. You better see what's happening with whatever they shot. A catfight is perfect for a sizzle reel."

"A what reel?"

"A *sizzle* reel. That's the video producers make to try and sell a project. They put together the best clips from a show or, in this case, the worst clips, which would be the best. The dishier and more salacious the better. Think of commercials you see for shows like *The Bachelor*. When isn't there a nasty fight or big-time makeout session?"

Mia dropped her head in her hands. "Frankenbites. Sizzle reels. I *hate* show business." Her cell phone buzzed. She lifted her head and retrieved the phone from the nightstand, where she'd left it the night before. "Oh boy."

"What?"

"We're not the only ones up early. So is Madison." She held the phone up to reveal the screen. It displayed the single word HELP, followed by a screenful of exclamation marks.

Trusting she was clean from the bath and double-shower of the night before, Mia got dressed and hurried out of the hotel room, texting Madison to meet her in the hotel coffee shop. She skipped the elevator, choosing the faster route of running down the stairs.

She found Madison sitting at one of the shop's café tables, looking every inch a woman who'd been in a street fight and was now nursing a massive hangover. She'd obviously slept in her clothes, and her hair, in need of a wash, hung in lank chunks. Mascara streaked her gray, tear-stained face.

Mia took a seat at the table. She examined Madison, then picked up a paper napkin and dunked it in the girl's glass of water. "Here," she said, handing it her. "Wipe your face. A little cold water will go a long way in your recovery from last night."

"Thanks." Madison took the napkin and wiped her face. "I don't think I'm cut out to be a donette," she said, her lower lip quivering.

"That's good, because if you were, Jamie wouldn't be marrying you."

"He may not marry me anyway." Tears spilled over Madison's lower lids. She took a shuddering breath. "Have-have-have you seen the Internet?"

"Yes, and you're all over it. But the good news is, no one knows your name, only that your ancestors came over on the Mayflower. Which apparently a bazillion people did. That boat must have been the size of a cruise ship. Back to the videos: Given the punches you were throwing and the hair pulling, your face is blocked for most of them."

"Jamie is still going to be mad at me. You know his friends are going to tease him about this whole thing."

"He'll be upset, but he'll get over it. The attention won't last long. My big concern is with the production company footage."

Madison's face wrinkled with distress. "When Jamie finds out I gave that woman permission to film me . . ." Unable to finish the sentence, she began weeping.

"I'll handle Jamie. If he doesn't get it already, I'll make it clear to him it's not your fault his idiot friends and relatives sucked you down their dysfunctional rabbit hole." Out of the corner of her eye, she saw Ariadne saunter away from the shop barista holding a café latte. "I'll handle that show biz witch, too. Don't let yesterday ruin today. But, Madison . . ." Mia gave a furtive glance around the room to make sure no one was nearby, then spoke in a whisper. "Be careful. Aside from all the reality show red flags here, remember that the owner of the production company was murdered. There's a really good chance his killer was someone in the pilot's crew or cast."

A worried Madison chewed on a fingernail. "I didn't think of that."

"That's why I'm telling you. Now, go upstairs and get some sleep. Be prepared to have some genuine fun the rest of our time here, 'kay?"

" 'Kay." Madison managed a weak smile. "Mia . . .

I know we started off badly. You liked Jamie, and I was in the way. But I'm so glad we got through that. Because I don't know what I'd do without you as a friend."

"Awww. All I ask is you continue to thank me with those free samples and mad discounts." Touched, Mia got up and went to hug the fashion blogger. She wrinkled her nose. "Make sure to add a nice, long shower to your schedule."

Madison left for her room, making sure to avoid Ariadne's table, which Mia strolled over to. "Mornin'," she said, taking a seat across from the producer.

"I don't remember inviting anyone to join me."

"You didn't."

Mia's bright blue eyes held a stare with the producer's cold gray orbs. Ariadne finally broke the contest to take a sip of coffee. Her face was fully made up, and her lustrous dark brown hair was piled in a bun atop her head, revealing the faintest glimmer of gray roots. She wore a snug black tank top, and flowing black pants covered her long legs. She crossed one over the other, revealing blood-red nail polish on her sandaled, perfectly pedicured toes.

"You look rested," Mia commented.

Ariadne gave a snort. "I hardly call what Donato and I did last night 'resting,' love."

Mia quelled her revulsion, along with a strong urge to start a catfight of her own with the noxious cougar. "Here's the sitch." She kept her tone calm but added a layer of threat to it. "I make it a rule never to play the 'Family' card. But, unfortunately, I find myself in a position where I am forced to break that rule."

Ariadne didn't flinch. She took another sip of coffee. "Meaning?"

"If any footage you shot of Madison ever sees the light of day anywhere, I will make sure you are very, *very* sorry that ever happened."

Ariadne narrowed her eyes. "Are you threatening me?"

"You betcha."

"I wonder what my boyfriend would have to say about that." Ariadne gave her a defiant look.

Mia removed her phone from a front jeans pocket and spoke to it. "Siri, what's the best poker hand you can get?"

"The best poker hand is a royal flush," Siri's robotic voice responded.

She put the phone back in her pocket. "A royal flush," she repeated. "That's your boyfriend's father, Donny Boldano Senior. Trust me on this: If you get on his bad side, Little D or not, you will be 'royally' screwed." She rose from the table. "Have a nice day, *love*."

Mia walked away. But not before enjoying the satisfaction of seeing Ariadne blink.

Chapter 16

Having hopefully nipped any further humiliation for Madison in the bud, Mia entrusted the care and feeding of the bachelorettes to Teri. She checked in with Jamie and Evans, who were rooming together. They promised to keep an eye on the bachelors, who were itching to start their own street fight, given the attention the ladies scored with theirs.

Somewhat regretfully, Mia traded an afternoon of sightseeing for sleuthing. Being in New Orleans provided Little Donny a break from being the primary suspect in Giles St. James's murder, but Mia knew he'd be back in the NYPD's crosshairs as soon as their return flight touched down at LaGuardia. It was time to keep her promise to his parents and do whatever she could to remove him from suspicion once and for all.

Her plan was to engage production crew members in casual conversations that might point a finger at a killer in their ranks. She'd start with the most approachable of them and work her way up from there. The goal was made easier when she glanced out her hotel room window and saw Lysette heading out onto the street.

Mia dashed down the stairs, continuing straight out the door. "Lysette," she called, out of breath. The camerawoman turned around. "Are you heading to Café du Monde?" Mia asked, making an educated guess since Lysette was headed in that direction. She was rewarded with a head nod. "Can I come? I've always wanted to go there."

"Sure. It'd be nice to have company."

The women walked past Jackson Square, making small talk about the beauty of the park and surrounding buildings. After a short wait in line, they were seated at one of the café's iconic round metal tables and were quickly served two orders of beignets, along with chicory coffee.

"Watch out for the powdered sugar," Lysette warned. "It gets everywhere."

"You've been here before?"

"My family's from New Orleans. I still have relatives here."

Mia held her beignet over the plate and bit into it. Her tastebuds were overwhelmed with a blast of doughy, sugary goodness. She made quick work of the beignet, following with a few swigs of coffee. "OMG, I'm in love. Why did your family ever leave this town?"

Lysette smiled. "Same reason everyone leaves a place. To find better opportunities in a new place. For us, that was Los Angeles. No way would I have the career I have now if my family had stayed here."

Seeing an opening, Mia used flattery as a transition to the topic of Giles's murder. "I'm so impressed. I don't know Hollywood at all, but it doesn't take an insider to figure there are a ton of people who wish they had your career. Although . . . it sucks Giles wouldn't give you a shot at directing."

"That was Giles. He loved making promises he had no intention of keeping."

Mia was surprised to hear Lysette sound wistful instead of bitter. His death seemed to have genuinely affected her. "Do you think that's what got him killed?"

"*No,*" Lysette said, appalled. "Absolutely not. I can't imagine anyone on the crew or in the company going to that extreme. It's obvious who his killer is: Ariadne's latest boy toy. Your friend Donny Boldano Junior."

Mia groaned inwardly. "I've known Little Donny my entire life. He's a lot of things—stubborn, obnoxious, self-centered, hotheaded, annoying. I could go on and on, but the one thing I would never add to that list is killer."

"I could say the same thing about everyone I work with."

"Really? You know them that well?"

"Well enough to know they'd never kill anyone. So, if you joined up with me to see if you could get me to 'finger' one of my coworkers, you can remove yourself to an empty table or out of the café entirely."

Caught, Mia stammered an apology. "I'm sorry. I'm only trying to help a friend."

Lysette fixed a look on her. "One who happens to be a hothead from a family with a history of illegal activity. Good luck to you."

Realizing they'd reached an impasse, Mia reached for another beignet. It came with a shower of powdered sugar that covered her lap. "You're right, this does get all over. But, boy, is it worth it. *Yum.*"

Mia's embrace of beignets seemed to relax Lysette. The women resumed small talk, with Lysette sharing a bit of history on the historic buildings bordering the square behind them. Mia responded with the appropriate reactions. But her mind was elsewhere. Mia was an avowed show business neophyte, but it didn't take an expert to recognize it was a cutthroat business where people often schemed and clawed their way to the top. This made her doubt Lysette's adamant assertion that none of her coworkers would ever resort to murder. But after two cups of coffee, three beignets, and a shower of powdered sugar, Mia was no closer to figuring out who among them it might be.

After the Café du Monde indulgence, Mia set out for a walk, hoping exercise coupled with the city's searing, sweaty heat would melt off a few of the fried donut calories. She caught an investigative break when she saw segment producer Michael on the street ahead of her. He walked in a purposeful way, then suddenly stopped and hid in a doorway. Having tailed a few murder suspects in past amateur-sleuthing endeavors, it occurred to Mia he was following someone. She strained to see who and noticed a man and woman examining various buildings on the street, stopping to take pictures and type on an iPad. Each time they stopped, Michael also stopped and ducked out of sight. He walked when they did.

Mia followed his pattern until he suddenly switched gears. She hid in one of the doorways he'd abandoned and watched him fake a casual walk up the block to the twosome and then surprise at seeing them. They reluctantly engaged in conversation with the segment producer, their desire to keep the interaction short—and Michael's to keep it going—obvious. The woman finally brought things to an end by receiving a phone call. Whether it was real or faked, Mia couldn't tell, but Michael took the hint and left. As soon as he was gone, the woman lowered her phone and exchanged an eye roll with her companion. *Fake call,* Mia decided.

She left her own hiding place and walked to the couple. "Hi," she said, opting for a bold approach. "It looked like that man was bothering you, and I wanted to make sure you were okay."

"Oh," the woman responded, taken aback but not wary. "Thank you for your concern, but we're fine. I know him."

"You do?"

Mia had assumed this, but her manufactured surprise worked to engender a further explanation. "I'm a writer," the woman said. "So is he. Well, was. We once worked together on a show."

"Jana's too modest to toot her own horn," her companion said, "She's more than a writer. She's a full-on showrunner. We're from Los Angeles. We're in town scouting locations for a drama she wrote that got a series order."

"Oh. Cool. Let me guess. Mi—" Mia caught herself before she said Michael's name and revealed herself as knowing him. "*Myyy* guess is that guy was hitting you up for a writing job."

"Good one," the woman said, smiling. "That's exactly what he was doing. But it's never going to happen. He has a reputation for coming on to the younger actresses on shows. One took out a restraining order on him, and that killed his career, at least in scripted. I heard he's doing reality now. Ugh." The showrunner practically pinched her nose to ward off the stink of the despised TV format. "Anyway, thanks for checking on us. You know, I've read there's a version of a New Orleans accent that sounds like a New York one. But I never heard it until now with you."

Mia gave a sheepish shrug. "Like we locals say down here, *laissez les bons temps rouler.*"

She left the showrunner and coworker to their scouting and returned to the hotel, where she was unable to find any other crew members to stalk. Ready for a break, she headed out yet again, this time to relax and enjoy an early lunch at Napoleon House, one of the city's oldest eateries. She was tucking into a bowl of jambalaya when Teri suddenly materialized in front of her. "What are you doing here," she asked, annoyed. "Wait, how did you even find me?"

Teri held up her cell phone. "Find My Friend. I set it up on your phone while you were sleeping."

"You hacked my phone?" Mia, furious, yelled this, garnering looks from patrons at other tables. Embarrassed, she mouthed "sorry" to them.

"Of course not," Teri said, offended. "I would never do something so illegal and sneaky. I figured out your password. Which, by the way, I recommend you change. 'Doorstop and Pizzazz exclamation mark' is pretty much a 'duh' for anyone who knows you."

"What do you want?" The reporter had gone beyond testing Mia's patience.

Teri parked herself at Mia's table. She flagged a waiter. "Two bourbons, neat, please."

Mia held up a glass. "I have a Pimm's Cup. It's delicious."

"You're gonna need something stronger."

The look on Teri's face was one Mia had never seen before—a combination of pity and compassion. It scared her. Appetite gone, she pushed aside her plate. "What is it?" Her heart clutched. "Is it Dad? *No*. He hasn't looked good lately. I should never have—"

Teri held up a hand. "Your dad is fine. It's not that."

"Then what?" Her heart clutched again. "Nonna?"

"No. All family members are fine. Although I should tell you that your nonna secretly texted me to document you wearing everything she made you. I deleted the text."

"Thank you. But if everyone is fine, what's the problem?"

The waiter dropped off their drinks. Teri took a belt of hers, then spoke. "Here's the deal. I had a lazy morning, nothing on the agenda, so I decided to poke around Shane's background."

"Cammie already did that. He was a model and party boy in Rome. Nothing new there."

"Actually, there is." She hesitated, worsening Mia's fears. "Cammie can't take the deep dive into the Internet that I can. She doesn't have the connections or skills to dig up stuff people think is gone. Anyone who thinks 'delete' means 'delete' on the Internet is kidding themselves. It just means 'stuff you can't see anymore.' Anyway, I went to one of my industrial-strength reporter search engines and used the specific search words 'Shane Gambrazzo' and 'bachelor party.'"

Mia relaxed. "That's what this is about? You found bachelor party dirt on him? Oh no! Whatever will I do?!" She mimed shock, then chuckled and resumed eating her jambalaya.

"He got into a lot of trouble at one. There was a knife fight."

"Par for the course with our gang."

"He spent time in jail. In Italy."

"Again, par for the course, given his past."

"There's this. After another bachelor party."

Teri handed her phone to Mia. An old tabloid headline blared a headline in Italian that Mia translated in her head to GORGEOUS MODELS MARRY! Underneath the headline was a photo of a clearly drunk Shane and a spectacularly beautiful redhead Mia recognized from fashion magazines.

Mia's appetite disappeared again, replaced by a sick feeling in the pit of her stomach. She checked the date on the article. "This is from ten years ago." She scanned it. "Okay, so now I know why he hates bachelor parties. He made a stupid mistake at one once. This is like with Britney Spears, when she married that childhood friend in Vegas and got it annulled a day later. I'm not one to judge, with my own stupid marriage in the rearview mirror. It's old news. Not like creepy Giles, hiding a second wife from his ex."

"Uh . . . about that . . ." Teri took her phone back. "I'm not so sure this marriage is in the past."

"What are you saying?"

"There's no record of a divorce."

"What?"

"No record. Anywhere. Believe me, I looked. I even had my hacker, who I would never, ever use on you, look."

"That's crazy, there has to be," Mia insisted. "Otherwise, that would mean—"

"Shane is still married. To a rich, gorgeous, extremely hot model."

CHAPTER 17

Mia gaped at Teri. "You're pranking me."

"I'm not. I'm sorry."

"Then Ariadne got to you." Mia spit out the name. "Where's Lysette? Where are the cameras for that foul show?" Mia spun around, searching. "What did they give you? Money? A job with the company?"

"Mia, I would never, ever do that to you," Teri said, hurt. "You're my closest friend."

"If that's true, God help you." Mia took a slug of bourbon. It burned going down, and she coughed. "Maybe you didn't dive deep enough."

"Oh, I dove. And Torgev—he's my personal hacker—he dove to the center of the Internet earth. Nuthin'. Even when he hacked into New York, Las Vegas, and even Rome's records databases. Torgev came up with some other juicy stories I look forward to pursuing. But no divorce for Shane. I'm sorry."

Mia took another slug of bourbon. This one went down easier. "Fine. So what? Why should I care?" She made a dismissive gesture with her hand. "It's not like we're in a relationship."

Teri barked a laugh. "Oh, please. Everyone knows you've been hooking up for months. It's the worst-kept secret since—since—I can't think of a good analogy, but you get the idea."

"It's not serious, we're just, you know, coworkers with benefits, if that—I mean, it's been a while, at least for me . . ." Mia trailed off. She crumpled. Tears dribbled down her cheeks. "How could Shane not tell me he's *married*? Who does that? Oh, right, Giles. Who was murdered. Very possibly by his ticked-off ex-wife. Who he at least had the decency to divorce. Unlike *some* people I know."

Mia drained her glass. Not used to day-drinking, her head spun. She chugged a glass of water to help compensate for the liquor. "And sidebar: You could've left 'gorgeous and extremely hot' out of your description of Shane's—" Mia couldn't bring herself to say the word "wife."

"I wanted to stress the seriousness of the situation."

A thought occurred to Mia, and she brightened. "This was ten, almost eleven years ago. Maybe she hasn't aged well."

Teri sighed. She tapped on her phone and showed Mia a photo. Mia's brighter outlook instantly evaporated. "I thought models were supposed to have short careers. How can she have gotten even more beautiful than she was ten years ago? This is so not fair."

"She was only eighteen when they marr—you know."

"Which makes her twenty-eight. Three years *younger* than me. More good news." She held up a hand to flag their waiter and motioned to her empty glass. "Would you mind getting me a refill? And is there a way to make bourbon stronger?"

Teri put her hand over the glass and shook her head. "We're good." The waiter departed with a sympathetic nod, and she turned back to Mia. "I'm so sorry about this. It sucks. I can't even begin to think how I'd feel if I found out Evans was secretly married."

"Does Evans even know you two are dating yet?"

"He's starting to get it. But even with my enormous attraction to him, I took the deepest of deep dives into his background. He's squeaky clean. I wish I could say the same for your guy."

"I wish you could, too." Mia inhaled a shuddery breath. She blew it out, then stood up. She swayed and reached for the wall. "Whoa. A little too fast there." She finished her water and gave her head a shake to sober up.

"What are you going to do?" Teri asked, concerned.

"Pay the bill and pee."

"About *Shane.*"

"That's a much harder question to answer."

Teri, who was proving to be a genuine friend, understood when Mia told her she needed some time alone. The reporter even insisted on picking up her small lunch tab. Mia left the Napoleon House. She took a slow trudge toward the path that ran along the edge of the Mississippi River, brooding the whole way, vacillating between going full Italian operatic screaming at Shane or ghosting him. Considering they worked together, neither option was viable.

The bells of St. Louis Cathedral rang, and

guests poured out of the edifice, followed by a wedding party. The bride and groom emerged last, to cheers. Mia noted and approved of the environmentally correct rose petals the guests tossed at the newlyweds. But the sight of the happy couple brought tears to her eyes. She'd never admit it to anyone, but she'd imagined this happy moment for herself and Shane, except at St. Patrick's Cathedral in New York. Now she couldn't imagine being in the same room with him.

Mia made a U-turn, passing up a depressed walk along the river for the confines of her hotel room. Once inside, she threw herself on the bed for a good cry, her dreams of the future replaced by what felt like a bottomless void.

The chirping alarm of her cell phone woke her up a few hours later. She slowly pulled herself to sitting. Teri was parked in front of the room's full-length mirror, doing the rarest of tasks for her: putting on makeup. Mia rubbed her eyes. "I guess I fell asleep."

"You did indeed."

"What time is it?"

"Four. We're all due downstairs for the second line before pre-gaming."

Mia wrinkled her brow, confused. "Translation, please."

"A second line is this thing they do here where everyone parades behind a brass band and waves handkerchiefs. Like this." Teri strutted around the room waving a white hankie. She tossed one to Mia. "Ariadne set up the whole thing and had these made. They say MADISON'S BACHELORETTE

PARTY and the date. The guys' hankies are black and say, JAMIE'S BACHELOR PARTY. It's the only nice thing that chick's done for them."

"It's transactional. You know she wants something in return. Argh, I'm so sick of having to police that woman." Mia sat up. "This second line thing is an interesting tradition."

"It started with funerals."

Mia made a face. "Given my current circumstances, that couldn't be more perfect." She rose from the bed. "I'm gonna clean up. I'll meet you downstairs."

" 'Kay. Mia . . . you and Shane will get through this. I know you will."

"No, you don't."

Teri groaned. "Ugh, I'm the worst liar. Sorry. Well . . . I hope you get through this. And if not, you've got a few more years of pretty left. You'll find someone else. Not anyone who looks like Shane, of course. He's like one of those comets that only passes Earth every thousand years on that score. But he's also so nice, which usually doesn't come as part of his package. He's sharp, too, and—"

Mia strode to the door and pulled it open. "Out. *Now.*"

"Right. Pep talk over."

Teri scurried out. Mia pushed the door shut. She closed her eyes, sucked in a breath, and slowly released it. She left the bedroom for the bathroom to wash her face and prepare for any potential battle with producer Ariadne.

Partygoers had already assembled on the street outside the hotel when Mia showed up for the second line. A handful of participants had colorfully decorated umbrellas in addition to their handkerchiefs. The afternoon sun beat down on the crowd, helping to justify the scanty tops and butt-cheek-revealing miniskirts and short-shorts of the donettes. Mia wore shorts herself, but of a more demure fabric and design. There was a lot of leather among the don and donette crews, not ideal for the sweltering heat. An informal head count showed that Madison's Connecticut friends had chosen to skip the second line and hunker down in the air-conditioned comfort of their hotel rooms. However, Madison had shown up. She watched from the sidelines, with Jamie hovering over her like a bodyguard. His bride-to-be, still slightly green, clung to him.

Mia glanced around and noticed Kelvin standing to the side of the cast, holding the handle of a cooler on wheels with one hand. His other held a bottle of water. They exchanged hellos. "You want some water?" he asked. "I can pour you a cup. We're being stingy with the bottles now. Our flats of them keep disappearing. Among other stuff."

"I'm good. And glad you used local businesses instead of me for craft services. I am *not* in the mood." She checked out the assemblage. "I thought there was supposed to be a brass band with one of these lines."

"There is. Ariadne decided to economize and only hired a trumpeter." He pointed to a middle-aged man holding a trumpet. He wore black pants with red suspenders over a crisp white shirt, and a cap that looked like something a boat captain might wear. He caught Mia looking at him and doffed the cap with an amiable wink.

"It seems odd to get budget-conscious this far into shooting the pilot," Mia commented.

"Fine by me," Kelvin said with a smug grin. "Instead of the money going to a bunch of band people we'll never see again, Ariadne gave me a dollar-an-hour raise and a title bump. Assistant producer."

"Isn't that pretty much production assistant with the words reversed?"

"*No.*" Kelvin scowled at her. "It's most definitely not. Production and producer are two very different—you know what, I don't have time to explain the business to a civilian."

He yanked his cooler to the opposite side of the second liners. "I *really* hate being called a civilian," Mia said through gritted teeth.

A camera problem delayed the second line's start. The cast members grew restless as Lysette tried to correct the problem, then gave up and sent her assistant, an eager recent film-school graduate named Cindy Silberblatt, as a replacement. Whether it was the heat or the hangovers, Mia picked up a general undercurrent of discontent.

"Let's do this already." This came from a cranky Chiara, clad in a skin-tight black leather miniskirt that Mia estimated added an extra ten degrees to the already-high temperature. "It's hot." She put the f-word between "it's" and "hot." More than a few castmates muttered agreement.

"And I'm starving," her frenemy Francesca whined.

"I told you that if you ate lunch, you'd have a tummy pooch," Ariadne responded. She patted her brow with an already damp handkerchief.

"Ya didn't tell *me* that," Vincent said. "You just said if I ate anything besides craft services, I'd have to pay for it myself. And all the craft services junk is funky or melted." He motioned to a folding table with a variety of snack and granola bars in questionable shape strewn across it.

"A bit more patience, please," Ariadne said, sounding irritated. "There will be an early dinner once the second line ends." Even her usual cool Brit confidence seemed to be taking a hit. "Ah, there's Lysette now."

The camerawoman assumed a position at the head of the line. Director Brian, who had managed the Herculean feat of maintaining a low profile amid the chaos of production and Giles's death, yelled, "Action!"

The trumpeter played a loud riff that almost drowned out the screeching voice of a newcomer. "Wait!"

Violet Kreppy St. James hurried to the group, impressively navigating the old street's pockmarks and potholes in her purple spike heels, which matched her mini tank dress. She pulled an expensive-looking carry-on bag with spinner wheels alongside her. Princess Kate's furry head stuck out of the widow's omnipresent tote bag.

Ariadne's face darkened with anger. "Ignore her," she ordered the crew and cast. "*Go!*"

The second line commenced. Not sure exactly what to do, the dons and donettes hesitantly waved their handkerchiefs. The girls with umbrellas bobbed them up and down. Mia stuck to the sidewalk, along with the other non-participants, putting her next to Ariadne when Violet grabbed her arm and screamed, "You tried to kill my kitty!"

Ariadne yanked her arm away. "Let go of me, you scheming piece of low-class trash!"

Violet gasped. Her eyes narrowed. She raised her spiked heel and stomped it on Ariadne's instep. The producer let out a yowl. She hauled to slap Violet, but the other woman stepped out of her way. Ariadne lost her balance and tumbled to the ground, landing on her derriere. Donny Junior turned and, seeing his girlfriend on the ground, ran to help her. She pushed him off and rose to her feet. The second line ground to a halt, all attention focused on the dueling Brits. "You better not have filmed that," Ariadne growled at Lysette.

"Brian told me to," the camerawoman said with the helpless sense of being caught in the middle.

"It's true," don Nicky said, looking to stir the pot and garner additional attention. "I heard him."

Ariadne turned her anger on the director. "You're fired."

"Fine by me," Brian shot back. "I'll probably make more on unemployment, anyway."

He stormed off. Cast feminist Francesca confronted Ariadne. "Oh, so it's okay to film *us* getting into fights, but not you? Talk about dishing it out but not taking it. Hypocrite."

"She doesn't want the camera to catch her being accused of murder," Violet piped in. "If she was willing to take the life of an innocent kitty, it'd be easy peasy for her to take whatever she took to me hubby's head."

"Liar!" Ariadne spit this out at her. "I didn't kill Giles. I loved him, first as a man, then as a friend and partner. As to your other false premise, we already have footage of you accusing me of murder on the day you showed up, so ha to that."

"Then you just don't want people seeing you take a tumble onto your boney arse."

"Enough," Little Donny yelled. He swung around, pointing a threatening finger at everyone. "Back off, all of yous."

"What's the problem, Little D?" his cousin Nicky asked with a smirk. "Afraid she'll drag you down with her? Maybe you were in on it together."

"Excuse me," the trumpeter said, "should I keep playing? You only booked me for half an hour."

The cast and crew devolved into a cacophony of screaming, accusations, and loud complaints. "This is not how I envisioned my bachelorette party," Madison said, weepy.

"I know." Mia laid a comforting hand on her shoulder and addressed Jamie. "We're not far from Café du Monde. Take her for beignets and coffee. Lots of coffee."

Jamie nodded and ushered Madison off. Chiara, dripping with perspiration, strode past Mia. "I can't take this heat anymore."

She grabbed a bottle of water out of Kelvin's hand, taking him by surprise. "Hey."

He reached to take the bottle back and Chiara stepped out of range. "Sorry, not sorry," she responded, inserting another eff-bomb between the last two words. She guzzled the water. "Ah," she sighed. "Better." She took a step away, then staggered. Her face went from pale to pure white. "I don't feel so good."

The donette clutched her stomach with one hand and reached out to Mia with the other. Then she collapsed to the ground, unconscious.

Chapter 18

Mia's screams for help ended the infighting. Ariadne and segment producer Michael ran to Chiara. Ariadne fell to her knees next to the prostrate reality performer, and he followed suit. "Chiara. Chiara!" Ariadne slapped the girl's face to no avail. "Mia, what in God's name happened?"

"I don't know. She took a sip of water and collapsed."

Michael tried raising Chiara to sitting, but she crumpled in his arms. "Where's the bottle? The one she drank from?"

"There." Mia pointed to the errant bottle lying on the street. Michael went to grab it, but she pulled him back. "Don't touch it! It's evidence."

The blare of sirens indicated help arriving in the form of an ambulance and a phalanx of police officers from the police station, only blocks away on Royal Street. The EMTs rushed to Chiara, quickly loading her into the ambulance. Ariadne and Michael hopped in the back to ride with her. The ambulance roared off, as much as any vehicle could roar on the Quarter's old, narrow streets. Police officers swarmed the site, roping it off with police tape.

Mia noticed Lysette watching the action with fascination. She went to her. "Poor Chiara. This is horrible."

"It is," Lysette acknowledged. "It's also great stuff."

Mia looked at her askance, her opinion of the camerawoman taking a nosedive. She pursed her lips. "Too bad you're not filming it," she said dryly.

"I'm not. My assistant is. She's the camerawoman now. And now that Brian's been fired, I am finally the director."

Lysette delivered this with a smugness that rubbed Mia the wrong way. The newly minted director went to confer with the police. She gathered the cast and crew, who were wandering in a sort of aimless shock, and matched them with officers for possible statements. Watching Lysette revel in her newfound authority, Mia couldn't help wondering how far the woman would go to secure her desperately desired promotion.

A man whose air of authority led Mia to immediately peg him as a detective approached her. He proved the assumption correct by introducing himself as Detective Jon Burnette. Mia returned the introduction. "You were with Ms. Donatelli when she collapsed," the detective said. "Can you walk me through what happened?"

Mia nodded. "She complained about how hot it was. Then she grabbed a bottle of water from Kelvin's hand—"

"Grabbed," the detective repeated with a hint of skepticism. "You're sure he didn't hand her the bottle?"

"No. In fact, he tried to take it back."

The detective took this in. "Kelvin is the production assistant, correct? What was his relationship with . . . ?" He looked at a notepad in his hand. "Ariadne St. James."

"Ariadne? The producer?"

"And his boss."

Burnette's implication dawned on Mia. "Was the water bottle meant for her?"

"Their relationship?" he prompted, ignoring her question.

"Right. Um . . . good. Very good. She gave him a raise and a promotion. Kelvin's a great guy. If anyone was taking advantage of him, it was his old boss Giles, not Ariadne."

"Giles St. James. Who was murdered."

Mia mentally kicked herself for hurting, not helping, poor Kelvin's case. "If you're looking for someone with a grudge against Ariadne, you should be talking to Violet St. James, Giles's secret second wife. She and Ariadne had a huge blowout right before Chiara drank the water. Violet accused Ariadne of trying to kill her cat and then basically accused her of Giles's murder. Oh, and it's on film or tape or whatever they record with. Ariadne was really angry about that."

This got the detective's attention. "Interesting. Can you point out Violet St. James to me?"

"Sure, she's—"

Mia looked toward the last place she'd seen

Violet. She was no longer there. She carefully scoured the street, checking each cluster of cast, crew, and even bystanders, as well as every doorway. "Violet's not here. She's gone."

With Lysette's superiors Ariadne and Michael at the hospital, she took it upon herself to release everyone for the evening once the police finished their interviews. But first the now-director shared an update from the hospital with the rest of the cast and crew. "Chiara's going to be okay. Apparently there was something either wrong with the water or something in it that made her sick. But they pumped her stomach at the hospital, and the doctors are keeping her overnight for observation. We've bumped back our departure tomorrow by a few hours in case the police need to talk to any of us again."

The group exchanged nervous looks, then headed back to the hotel, talking among themselves in clusters of small groups. Mia noticed Donny Junior keeping to himself, walking with his head down and his hands in his pants pockets. She increased her pace until she was side by side with him. "Hey."

"Hey." He looked and sounded despondent.

"You okay?"

He shook his head. "Kelvin told me the water bottle was specifically marked for Ariadne. He was holding it to hand to her when Chiara grabbed it from him. That means someone wanted to make her sick. Maybe even kill her."

"Well, now there are two police departments looking into it," Mia said, trying to offer comfort.

"You know that New Orleans will be talking to New York. They have to assume there's a connection to Giles's murder."

"I guess." The two walked in silence for a moment. "When I went to help Ariadne, she pushed me away."

"The fall disoriented her. She was probably embarrassed, too."

"Maybe." Donny didn't sound remotely convinced. They reached the hotel. "I'm beginning to think being in *The Dons of Ditmars Boulevard* wasn't such a great idea."

Mia squelched the urge to come back with an acerbic, "*Ya think*?!" Instead, she gave Donny Junior a hug and the generic response of "Don't worry, everything will work itself out."

He slumped off. Mia made sure he was gone, then texted Teri, Jamie, Madison, and Evans to meet her at the hotel bar. Jamie texted back that he and Madison were enjoying a romantic dinner at Brennan's Restaurant, and she gave the message a heart. She got an "On our way" from Teri.

Mia went to the bar and ordered a glass of chardonnay, telling the bartender, "There's a nice tip if you make it a big pour." He delivered, and so did she. She took her drink to the farthest corner of the room, keeping an eye on the door for Teri, who she assumed had dragged Evans off for a hoped-for assignation. Moments later, they appeared at the bar's entryway. Mia waved a hand to flag them, and they approached. Mia noticed both were covered with powdered sugar. "Beignets?"

They nodded. Evans got a dreamy look in his eyes. "Powdery pillows of heaven. You best believe I'll be adding them to event menus."

"I support you a thousand percent in that goal. But I have news."

Teri eagerly plopped down in one of the table's tufted teal chairs. Evans grabbed another one. "Do tell," the reporter said, rubbing her hands together with anticipation.

Mia shared every detail of the second-line fiasco and Chiara's possible poisoning. "Wow," Evans said, sitting back in his chair. "That is a lot."

"So this Violet character was gone when you went to point her out to the detective?" Teri furrowed her brow. "Disappeared?"

Mia nodded. "Never to be seen again. At least so far today."

"She sure seems like the most likely suspect," Evans said.

"Yes. And also no. It looked like she just arrived in New Orleans. She had a carry-on and her tote bag with her. When would she have had time to doctor a bottle of water?"

"So you don't think it was her?" he asked, confused.

Mia threw up her hands. "Who knows?"

"Hmmm . . . Thinking this whole thing through . . ." Teri tapped her lip with her index finger, then stopped. "Wild thought here."

"All are welcome," Mia said. "None of this takes the heat off Little Donny, which is the number-one goal handed to me by his father."

Teri took a furtive look around the room, then leaned in and spoke in a low voice. "What if Chiara did this to herself?" The others stared at her in disbelief. "Hear me out. Was it filmed?"

Mia nodded. "Did everything else stop and the attention go totally to her?" Mia nodded again.

"You've said she wants to be a reality star. What better way than to claim focus on the pilot?"

"Oooh," Mia said. "Good one."

"You won't know for sure until the tests come back on the water she drank," Evans cautioned. "But it's not that farfetched."

Teri batted her eyes at him. "Are you impressed?" she asked in cutesy voice that made Mia cringe. Teri flirting wasn't a pretty sight.

"I'm more impressed by how you got us around the tour bus unloading at Café du Monde and straight to a table." Evans stood up. "Let's go back. I wanna watch how they mix the dough."

"Whatever you say, my love."

Evans flashed Mia an amused look. He took Teri's hand and led her out of the bar. She watched them go with a heavy heart. While she was happy they seemed to be inching closer to an actual relationship, when it came to her own romance with Shane, she couldn't escape the feeling she was plummeting out of one.

Chapter 19

The next day, Mia arrived at the New Orleans airport, both eager to get home and dreading what the return might bring. Her friends hadn't rebooked their flights for a later departure, so it would be her and the *Dons of Ditmars Boulevard* contingent.

She was thrilled to see a Café du Monde outpost and enjoyed a last hurrah order of beignets and chicory coffee. She dawdled in an airport gift shop, picking up pralines for her grandmother, a money clip decorated with a fleur de lis for her father, a T-shirt emblazoned with Mardi Gras images for Posi to wear if he ever got out of jail, and two plush alligators for the young kids of her neighbors Philip and Finn, who had become close friends. She bought nothing for Shane.

She arrived at the flight gate fifteen minutes prior to boarding and found a somber mood among the *Dons* folk. Whether this was due to hangovers or being brought down to earth by the previous day's events, Mia didn't know or care. She was just happy no one was interested in making small talk with her. She saw Donny, head close to Ariadne's; she had apparently welcomed him back to her side. Still, even she didn't display her usual superior sangfroid.

Nicky Vestri appeared to be the only missing cast member. Mia saw an empty seat beside Lysette, who was making notes on an iPad. She took it and exchanged hellos. "I don't see Nicky anywhere," Mia said. "Did he take the earlier flight?"

Lysette shook her head. "He left last night with Violet on her private plane."

"Really. That's a turn I didn't see coming."

"She's a hot, rich widow. Not really a shocker."

"No," Mia acknowledged. "But she was MIA when Chiara collapsed. I guess the police tracked her down and she alibi'd out."

"She better not cause any more trouble. Now that I finally got my shot at directing, no one is gonna get in my way."

The vehemence in Lysette's voice discomfited Mia. To avoid further conversation, she retrieved her phone from her purse and began thumbing through work e-mails. A buzz among the dons and donettes caught her attention, and she looked up. Chiara, escorted by segment producer Michael on one side and Kelvin on the other, came toward them. The donette looked a little weak, but her full face of makeup said "camera-ready." Lysette elbowed her assistant, who'd dozed off in the seat on the other side of her. "Start filming. *Now.* Go!"

The assistant jumped and placed the camera on her shoulder, capturing the scene as the other dons and donettes surrounded Chiara, asking questions and offering support. "Did they find out what was in the water?" she heard Francesca ask.

Chiara shook her head. "Not yet. It was awful. I could have *died.*"

She clutched Michael's hand and emphasized the last word with a dramatic shudder, making sure the camera had her in full frame. Watching, Mia recalled Teri's supposition that the whole event had been staged by the ambitious cast member. The segment producer helped Chiara into a seat, murmuring what appeared to be comforting words to the star donette. As the group moved toward her, Michael practically tripped over himself in an effort to be solicitous to the pretty donette, while Kelvin's behavior was more pro forma.

Mia glanced over at Ariadne and saw her watching Chiara with an expression she couldn't read. She wondered if the producer was thinking the same thing. If Chiara had manufactured an attempted poisoning, it would make for great moments in the show pilot. But if she hadn't... then someone wanted Ariadne dead.

When the flight landed, Mia grabbed a cab home to drop off her suitcase and change before heading to Belle View. As she got out of the cab, she saw her neighbor Philip on the landing outside her home's front door. He gave Elisabetta a hug, then hurried down the steps, turning back once to call, "Thanks again," before reaching the street. The minute he turned away from her, his smile disappeared. He carried an armful of crocheted somethings, all in an array of indescribable colors.

Mia waved to him, and he came to her. "Welcome home. I'd hug you, but—" He held up the bundle in his arms.

"Uh oh. Nonna's been on a crochet jag."

"Oh, yes. Toddler clothes. A dress for Eliza, a sweater for Justin." He held each up. Mia couldn't contain a wince. "Finn will die when he sees these. I don't want to hurt that wonderful woman's feelings, so the kids *have* to wear them."

"And you'll *have* to take pictures for her."

Philip released a strangled whimper. "I know. I just hope Finn doesn't burn them. Or divorce me."

Mia placed a sympathetic hand on his arm, then pulled out the bag with the plush alligators. She handed it to him. "Maybe these will make the outfits go down easier."

Philip peeked into the bag. "These are adorable. Thank you so much. I'll give them to the kids right after I put them in the outfits. It'll distract them." He rolled his eyes. "Too bad there isn't one for Finn."

He left for his house down the block. Mia scurried up the stairs, where Elisabetta was waiting—and watching. Mia kissed her grandmother on both cheeks. "*Benvenuto a casa, cara bambina.* I missed you."

"I missed you, too."

"I hope not. It'd mean you weren't having no fun. Did Philip show you what I made?"

"He did. Those outfits. They're so"—Mia held up her hands—"wow!"

Elisabetta nodded with satisfaction. "I can't wait to see the pictures. I made you something, too." She pulled items Mia couldn't define from the pocket of her apron. "Slippers."

"Ahh," Mia said, managing to stop herself from adding, *So that's what they are. I had no idea.* She examined them. "There's a seam inside. Down the middle."

"It's a new pattern. Try them on. I wanna make sure they fit."

"Sure." Mia managed a weak smile. She traded her designer sandals for the slippers. She took a tentative step, feeling like an ice skater whose blade was on the inside of her skate instead of the outside.

"So cute," Elisabetta said, brimming with pride. "You love them?"

"Of course. Anything you make for me is special because *you* made it."

Mia kissed her grandmother again, then headed upstairs to her apartment, one unsteady step at a time.

After washing up and changing out of travel into work clothes, Mia still didn't feel ready to face Shane at Belle View. "This is what they're talking about when they tell you not to dip your pen in company ink," she said to Doorstop, who ignored her, preferring to focus on the "I'm back" treats she'd laid out for him. Pizzazz was occupied with bird activities, so Mia procrastinated by FaceTiming her father. Ravello answered from his home treadmill. He greeted by blowing kisses between huffs and puffs of exercise. "How did Jamie and Madison's parties go?"

"They went. How about everything at Belle View?"

"Terrific. Cammie stepped up for a change. And that Shane. What a find."

"Isn't he." The response came out more sarcastic than Mia intended, but Ravello was too focused on his workout to notice. "Dad, you look really red. I think you're overdoing it."

"I'm . . . fine."

"You need to drink water. Lots of it."

"I will."

Mia frowned at him. "Translation, you won't. Drink some now. So I can see."

Ravello grumbled something unflattering, then held a bottle of water up to the camera. He took a few gulps of it. "Happy?"

"Happier. By the way, don't ever drink out of a bottle someone hands you."

"Huh?"

"Long story." She checked the ancient living room wall clock, which hung over a photo of the latest pope. Both had been inherited from a neighbor who moved into assisted living. "I better get to Belle View. Love you."

"Love . . . you . . . too."

The call over, Mia peeled herself off the plastic covering the red velvet couch, also inherited from the former neighbor. Then she girded herself for a return to Belle View.

Cammie accosted Mia the minute she stepped over the Belle View threshold. "Evans told us all about what happened in New Orleans. Madison's street fight—which we'd already all seen on the Internet. Chiara being poisoned, but it was really meant for Ariadne. Did you learn anything else before you left? Did the police share any updates?"

"I—" Mia stopped. "Are you recording me for your podcast?"

"Nooooo."

Mia folded her arms in front of her chest and gave Cammie the side-eye. "Show me what's in your hand. The one behind your back."

Cammie hesitated. Then she brought her hand forwarded and opened it, revealing a small digital recorder. "I haven't turned it on yet, I swear."

"Good. Keep it that way, or the only thing you'll be recording with me is the sound of a hammer being taken to that thing."

Cammie groaned. "I need a new way to spend Pete's money. This one's a lotta work."

Mia heard Shane's voice coming from the Marina Ballroom, where a crew was cleaning up the detritus from a high school prom held the previous night. Her heart pounded. "I gotta get to work."

She literally ran to her office, leaving behind a bewildered Cammie. Mia slammed the door behind her and collapsed into her office chair. She closed her eyes and took a few calming breaths. A knock on the door startled her, then the door swung open, and Shane stepped into the room. He closed the door behind him and stared at her with the smoldering eyes of a romance novel cover boy. "You're back. God, I missed you. I know we said no romance at work, but I gotta tell you, I'm having a hard time restraining myself right now."

He took a step toward her. Mia almost flew into his arms. Then she remembered the article Teri had printed out for her at the hotel. "I'm not."

She pulled the reprint of the GORGEOUS MODELS MARRY writeup out of her purse and held it up to Shane. He took a quick look and deflated. "Oh."

"*Oh*?!" Furious, Mia mimicked him. "That's the

best you can do? There's no evidence of you getting a divorce. Even Teri's personal hacker couldn't find it. Are you divorced?" Shane didn't respond. "Great, just great." Mia slammed down the article. "I've been sleeping with a married man. Something I swore to my parents, my *nonna*, and God himself I would never, ever do."

"It's not like that," Shane protested.

"It's not? Then what *is* it like? And does your wife—gorgeous, famous Petra Vilsni—know? Because that's what she is, Shane. Your *wife*."

Shane dropped into the chair where potential clients sat. He rubbed his eyes. "Here's what happened. I went to a bachelor party. In Vegas. And whatever happens at your average bachelor party happens a hundred times that at a Vegas batch."

"I can imagine."

"The groom was a model's agent, and a lot of his clients came. His fiancée was a model, and her friends came. And . . . a bunch of us got married."

Mia stared at him in disbelief. "What are you talking about? How did a bunch of you get married? How many *is* a bunch?"

"I dunno. Five? Six? Everyone but us got divorced right after. Petra and I kind of dated for a while."

"You kind of dated your wife. After you married her."

Shane ran his hands through his hair. "I know it sounds crazy."

"A *little*."

"But I was a different person then. Way different. We broke up, and I sent her divorce papers, but she never signed them. I kept asking, and she kept ignoring me, and I finally gave up. Her people wiped the marriage off the Internet because she's huge in Europe, and they didn't want to mess up her career by feeding the paparazzi a tabloid story. I didn't really care until now."

Shane pulled his phone from his back pocket. He called up an e-mail and handed the phone to Mia. She read the e-mail—a passionate plea for Petra to finally grant him a divorce. She handed the phone back to him. "You're an excellent writer."

"When I want something, I am."

"And you want this divorce?"

Once again, his smoldering romance-cover-boy eyes bored into hers. "More than anything in the world."

"Get me Petra's contact information. I'll talk to her woman to woman and see if I can get her to come around."

Relief flooded Shane's face. "Awesome."

He jumped up and made a reflexive move to kiss her, then stopped himself. He gave an awkward nod and made a quick exit.

Mia started her computer and opened the file of active events. But she was unable to concentrate. Two magical words kept running through her head.

Until now.

Chapter 20

It took some doing, but Mia finally managed to shelve both her romantic life and amateur sleuthing and focus on Belle View business. She was completing an order for personalized jar-opener party favors for a client who owned a local grocery store when Pete Dianopolis stuck his head in. "Hi, Pete," she greeted him. "You taking Cammie to dinner?"

"Yes, but first I gotta talk to you about that business in New Orleans." He came in and took a seat. "NOPD thinks there's a connection between the doctored water bottle intended for Ariadne St. James and her ex-husband's murder. They're working with NYPD on the case, hence my visit."

"So the water *was* doctored. What was in it?"

"You know I can't reveal that."

"I'll tell Cammie you look like you've been working out."

"Arsenic, just enough to make someone sick with a few gulps, probably deadly if they drank the whole bottle." Pete, always eager to get in Cammie's good graces, blurted this. "You were there. Walk me through what you saw and what happened."

"I don't think you'll need your notepad because I've been over this a bunch in my head and, for the life of me, can't land on anything useful." Mia repeated everything she'd shared with NOPD detective Burnette. "The most suspicious person there—well, aside from everyone, because if you're tying this to Giles's murder, which makes total sense, he had *molto* enemies—was Violet. But she seemed to fly back here with no problem from NOPD, so I guess she had an alibi."

"Airtight. Her hired limo driver pinpointed the minute she left the car for the second line to yell at Ariadne. There was zero time for her to sneak a water bottle and poison it."

"Oh," Mia said, disappointed. Proving Violet to be a black widow who bumped off her older husband and his ex-wife to gain control of their production company would have been a great way to get Donny Junior off the hook. "I'm really sorry I can't be more helpful."

"It's okay. You have been in the past. And I'd put money on you being helpful in the future. Hopefully with this case. You got an eye, Mia. What's it you say? You understand the criminal mind—"

"Because I grew up with it." Mia smiled ruefully. "I would've traded my 'eye' for not growing up with it in a heartbeat."

"I'm sure." Pete stood up. "For the record, I mean 'put money on it' in the figurative sense. Every dime I have is going toward getting Cammie back. Does your eye have any update for me on that score?"

Annoying as Pete could be, hearing the insecurity in his voice evoked sympathy from Mia. "My finely honed instincts tell me you're making progress. Slow and steady—"

"And expensive," Pete interrupted with a groan.

"But still, progress."

Pete closed his eyes. He exhaled, then opened them. "Alrighty then. Thanks. If anything comes to mind on either situation, lemme know."

"Will do."

Pete departed, leaving Mia with more questions than answers about pretty much every aspect of her life.

While waiting for Shane to track down contact information for his technically legal missus, Mia focused on her latest assignment from the *Dons of Ditmars Boulevard* production company. Filming had been suspending for a few days due to "Ariadne being totes freaked out about the whole poison-water thing," as Little Donny explained in his most "civilian" way. The producer still had enough of her wits about her to come up with the notion of staging a prom for the show's dons and donettes. Mia grudgingly admitted the idea was a good one, especially considering that a lot of the guys—and a few of the girls—had missed their proms due to various school suspensions, juvenile facility incarcerations, or failure to even attend high school.

At the moment, Mia was in the middle of an office sit-down with the producer, mulling over prom themes. "What about Casino Night?" Ariadne suggested.

Mia gave her head a vigorous shake no. "There's

no way your dons won't turn pretend gambling into the real thing, which is illegal in New York."

"I'll second that," said Pete, who happened to be passing Mia's office on the way to delivering additional expensive equipment Cammie needed for her podcast. "I've already arrested half the guys around here for illegal gambling. Including her father." He gave Mia a jovial wink and continued on to Cammie's office.

"Ravello has such an interesting past," Ariadne said, with a gleam in her eye Mia didn't appreciate.

"My father's got a girlfriend, and you supposedly have a boyfriend." Mia said, shutting her down. "And 'past' is the operative word here. He's gone straight, and we operate Belle View as a completely legitimate business. Back to a prom theme. I have an idea. How about an eighties theme? Lots of color. Strappy, poofy dresses. Big hair—on the girls *and* the guys."

Ariadne only took a moment to deliberate. "I like it. Eighties theme it is."

"Excellent," Mia responded. "Or as they said in the eighties, rad."

She flashed a smile, along with an inward sigh of relief. An eighties theme wasn't just in Cammie's wheelhouse, it *was* her wheelhouse. The minute Ariadne left, Mia e-mailed the news to her fellow event planner and could hear her squeals of joy from down the hall. "This one's mine!" Cammie yelled from her office.

"You got it," Mia yelled back, freeing up her schedule to tackle an onerous task.

Armed with the contact information for Petra Vilsni that Shane had passed on to her, Mia reached out and scheduled a one-on-one with the model. Vilsni agreed to the meeting with the caveat it must occur that very afternoon. She was leaving first thing in the morning for a fashion shoot in Europe, where she planned to spend at least a few months. Which is why, shortly after sending Ariadne on her way, Mia was on the subway to Manhattan.

As the train rattled under the East River and Midtown, Mia entertained herself by revisiting the trifecta of ID'ing murder suspects: means, motive, and opportunity. Since she had no way of pinpointing who might have had the opportunity to avail themselves of arsenic and deposit it in a water bottle marked for Ariadne, Mia focused on motive.

While she considered the dons and at least a few of the donettes capable of anything, as in every conversation or thought about possible suspects, she circled back to the core crew and cast of *The Dons of Ditmars Boulevard*. She closed her eyes and ran through every moment leading up to the delivery of Ariadne's poisoned water to Chiara, and every moment after, envisioning Kelvin, Lysette, Michael, Jason, Nicky, Violet, and even Chiara, who Mia could still envision taking a swig of poison water if it would help her reach the heights of reality stardom. On the other hand, Kelvin's resistance to handing the water bottle over could have stemmed from knowing what was in it. But in addition to his recent promotion, thanks to Ariadne, which put her in good favor with him, he seemed much too bright to hand over a lethal tainted liquid.

Mia's eyes popped open as a realization hit her. Would Ariadne be above poisoning herself if it would help create drama that would sell the pilot? Especially if she could implicate archrival Violet? She pulled her phone from her purse and texted this new avenue of investigation to Pete, noting he might have already thought of it. Pete could be sensitive when his skills were questioned. Originally determined to bust Ravello and close down Belle View, Pete had reluctantly come around to trusting the Carina family, and Mia was careful not to do anything that might undermine the fragile relationship.

Mia exited the subway at the Wall Street station and hiked over to Pine Street. A few blocks later, she entered yet another elegant Manhattan lobby, this one in a spectacular Art Deco building bordering Tribeca and the Financial District. Once home to a stodgy insurance company, the impressive edifice had been transformed into luxury condos. *No poor door for Petra,* Mia thought, handing her license to a security guard manning a bank of computer screens that looked like they belonged in a political thriller and not in a phantasmagoria of undulating marble walls and original silver Deco fixtures. After what Mia assumed was a personal identification verification and possibly even a credit check, he granted her permission to continue on.

She boarded an elevator that soared up to the twenty-fifth floor. The elevator door opened to reveal a tall, lithe, redheaded vision of a human being. "Juan Carlos told me you were on your way up," Petra Vilsni said, the sentence laced with an accent Mia could only define as Eastern European. "Come."

Mia followed Petra down an airy hallway to the model's "New York base," as she'd described in their e-mail exchange, leading Mia to assume the international fashion star had bases in an array of international metropolises. Given that the stunning woman's exotic lifestyle also came with men falling at her feet in every city where she parked them, Mia wondered why she still refused to divorce Shane. She soon had an extremely unsatisfying answer.

"It's a matter of principle," Petra declared, throwing one tiny item of designer clothing into a suitcase after another. She'd informed Mia she had to pack while they talked; hence they were in the model's bedroom, which was decorated in a style Mia would describe as "incredibly expensive high-end hotel I can only dream of staying at someday."

Mia forced her attention away from the suitcase. "But it's been ten years. You've both moved on with your lives. And you're one of the most famous faces in the world." Given Petra's lifestyle and magazine spreads, this was a fact, not flattery.

"I really liked him when we married. Our relationship wasn't a joke to me. I wanted it to work."

"I'm sorry if that's how you feel he treated your relationship. I'd be ticked off, too. But you were both young. Shane owns up to being an idiot during a lot of his twenties. Not with you, of course," Mia hastened to add, sensing her blunder. "He was nuts about you. Just too much of a mess to have a mature relationship."

Petra made a sound indicating she didn't buy this. She continued to pack, tossing in filmy, sexy lingerie. Mia eyed her surreptitiously. Her eyes were a deep, soulful brown rimmed with the longest of thick, frustratingly natural lashes. Her bone structure was the stuff of marble sculptures, as was her elegant build. *My sturdy Italian peasant roots are showing,* Mia thought, catching an unflattering glimpse of her not-quite 5'5" in Petra's full-length mirror. "I know Shane feels terrible about how he acted back then. He has so much respect for you and what you've accomplished."

This earned an un-model-like snort from Petra. "So much respect he offered to buy me out of the marriage?"

This was news to Mia. "I'm sorry . . . what?"

Petra stopped packing and faced Mia with a smirk that made her look a whole lot less gorgeous. "He didn't mention this to you? That he offered me ten thousand dollars to sign the divorce papers? To quote a brilliant model, that's not enough money to get me out of bed."

"I don't think that's exactly how Linda Evangelista said it, but the thought's the same," Mia said, stalling for time as her mind reeled. Angry as she was at Shane for neglecting to mention he'd tried to bribe Petra, she was losing patience with the model's intransigency. "You know, there's such a thing as a contested divorce. Shane hasn't wanted to take that step because he knows it would bring you a lot of unwanted publicity."

Petra shrugged. "So, let him. I've had friends who've gone through them. They cost a fortune and drag on for years." She examined Mia from head to toe. "If you want to have babies, that would be a problem."

"I'm a whopping three years older than you, honey." Mia fumed. Remembering her mission, she quelled her anger. "Shane was truly a different person when you two married. He's changed. He has a responsible job. He's sending his little sister to college. He's been through rehab since you were together. *Twice.*"

"I know all about the drugs and alcohol. But did he ever tell you about his other addiction?" Petra shuddered. "So freakish."

"Yes, he told me," Mia flat out lied. "And it doesn't bother me at all."

Petra looked at her with disdain. "It doesn't? Ugh. Then you two deserve each other."

"We do?" Mia hopes rose. "You'll grant the divorce?"

"Of course not. That was a turn of phrase." Petra left the bedroom for the living room. Mia followed. "My limo will be here any minute." The model opened her front door. "You need to go."

"Happily," Mia sniped. "But this isn't over."

Petra shot back something in a Slavic language that Mia assumed loosely translated as "You wish," and slammed the door.

Furious, Mia kicked the steel door. "Ow!" She gave a yelp and grabbed her foot to massage away the pain. She hopped, then limped to the elevator door, where she gave the lobby button a hard punch, eliciting another yelp of pain. Tears stung her eyes, but they weren't prompted by her injuries. Mia's visit to Petra had solved nothing. In fact, it had made things worse.

Bribery. A freakish addiction.

What else was Shane hiding from her?

Chapter 21

Cammie pursed her pink-frosted lips. "So this Petra piece of work absolutely refuses to divorce Shane."

Mia nodded. The two women were sitting outside in the Belle View gazebo. Much as Mia loved Cammie, she opted to share details of her conversation with Petra in a neutral zone devoid of any podcast recoding equipment. She'd also made her friend-coworker prove that no digital recording devices were hidden in her hands or the pockets of the pale-yellow polyester parachute pants Cammie had lovingly cared for and worn since the mid-1980s.

The only conversational detail Mia withheld was the revelation that Shane had a mysterious addiction, which thrust Mia into a quandary. She didn't want to talk about the addiction until she knew exactly what it was. But afraid of what it might be, she'd yet to bring it up to Shane. Instead, she devoted her energy to analyzing his marital situation. She gazed over the marina, where a plane was taking off from LaGuardia. "I wish I was on that plane. I don't care where it's headed. Anywhere is better than here right now."

"Don't be dramatic. There's already too much of that going around with the *Dons* cast and crew."

Mia faced Cammie. "Why am I so upset about this? Marriage is only an issue if we want to get married ourselves, and that's so not on the table. We're not even in a serious relationship."

Cammie patted Mia's knee. "Right. Keep telling yourself that. Have you talked to him since you got back from Chez Petra?" Mia shook her head. "I think it would help if you did. Whatever the next step is, you need to figure it out together." She stood up. "Oh, by the way, now can we drop this whole farce about you two pretending you're not dating? It's taking up way too much bandwidth for me."

"Sure. Nothing like admitting we're dating right before we break up."

"That is not going to happen. When the two of you are in a room together, the temperature shoots up twenty degrees. It's gonna take more than some pain in the you-know-what cover-girl mannequin to put out that fire."

Cammie hugged Mia, then went inside. Mia stayed behind, working up the courage to face Shane. A small plane took off from LaGuardia. "The 3:05 to Buffalo," she said to a bird stopping to rest on the gazebo banister. "Another plane I wish I was on."

Mia left the bird to groom itself. She took a slow walk into Belle View, up the stairs to its capacious second-floor Bay Ballroom. The ballroom was a frenzy of the activity required to set up for a prom with a "Hey, Remember the Eighties" theme.

Ariadne and Cammie were alternating between shouting conflicting orders at the combined crew of show and banquet facility employees and arguing with each other. Shane hurried by with life-size cutout figures of Simon LeBon and John Taylor from Duran Duran. He stopped when he saw Mia. "Hi," he said. Mia could tell he was nervous. "How did it go with Petra?"

She shrugged. Shane's face fell. "No go," Mia said. "She did mention you tried to bribe your way out of the marriage. What were you thinking?"

Shane set his jaw. "That I'll do anything to get out of this insane situation, even if it means emptying my bank account. Wait, a loan. I'll take out a loan. I'll make her an offer—"

Mia held up a hand. "If you say, 'she can't refuse,' I will end whatever's going on between us and leave you to Petra. Don't take out a loan. We'll find another way."

"Shane!" Cammie barked. "Simon, John, *now.* We need the rest of Duran Duran. And where's Boy George? People, do I have to do everything *myself?*"

Mia decided to abandon the chaos for her office. She needed a quiet place to think. She headed down the travertine stairs to the Belle View lobby, almost colliding with Little Donny, who was making his way up the circular staircase. "Hey," she greeted him. "Where have you been? Wherever it is, I'm guessing it beats the crazy goings-on up there." She pointed to the Bay Ballroom.

"I spent two hours being grilled by Pete Dianopolis." Little Donny delivered this disheartening news with a wry expression. "He still thinks I'm the most likely person to have killed Giles St. James.

Now he's trying to find a reason I'd want to poison Ariadne, the love of my life. So whatever's going on up there wins."

He trudged up the stairs with his head down. Mia felt for him. Arrogant irritant that he'd been growing up, he deserved better than a ridiculous reality show pilot, a cougar girlfriend he refused to see was using him, and a potential arrest for a crime he didn't commit. She reached her office, where she called up the show's production schedule to confirm the start time for the evening's prom shoot. Figuring out how to extricate Petra from Shane's life would have to wait. Mia had a murder to solve.

Even to a "civilian" like Mia, it was obvious the prom shoot was teetering on the edge of being a crashing bore. The dons and donettes certainly looked the part of the eighties theme as they milled around in their eighties attire, the hair of both sexes appropriately teased and moussed. But they seemed to have adopted the personas of insecure, awkward high school students. Mia wandered through, hoping to pick up conversational clues to the recent criminal events or perhaps even the covert hatching of a new plan on behalf of whoever might benefit from getting rid of Giles and Ariadne. But all she overheard were stiff exchanges between couples that reminded her of how much she'd hated her own prom.

"I love you like a mix tape, woman; Walkman walk my way," Sammy Starr sang for the ninetieth time from a small stage to recorded background music. The production company had splurged on hiring the bona fide eighties pop singer for the prom. Unfortunately, they could only afford to pay for the rights to one of his songs, a lesser hit titled "Walkman Walk My Way." It had been released at the tail end of the decade, when both he and Walkmans were falling out of favor. The repetitive drone of the song added to the malaise of the filming.

"Something needs to happen," she heard Lysette, who sounded increasingly desperate, say to segment producer Michael.

"I've tried everything," he replied, equally panicked. He pointed to donette Francesca. "You! Spill your drink on that girl's dress."

"Why another girl?" Francesca demanded, committing to her role as show "feminist." "We women should be lifting each other up, not dragging each other down."

"Besides, the costumes are rented." This came from Kelvin, who Mia could tell was getting on the crew's nerves by using his minor promotion to boss them around. "We have to return them back like we got them. Which means stain-free."

Michael groaned. "Fine. Don't throw anything. If Ariadne had let me start a small fire at Casa Giovanni, we'd have something interesting to shoot instead of this dreck. Why am I cursed with producers who are dumber than me?!"

He stormed off. Lysette glanced around. "Where are all the dons? The only one I see is Little Donny, who refuses to dance with anyone because it would be 'cheating' on Ariadne."

"I'll go look for the guys," Mia said, finally able to make herself useful. She left the ballroom and scoured the upstairs lounges for the male cast members. Having no luck, she went downstairs, where a check of the ballroom and adjoining lounges also came up empty. She was puzzling over where the dons might have disappeared to when she heard muffled conversation coming from down the hall. She moved quietly, putting an ear to each door until she located the source. Mia threw open the door of the small staff lounge to reveal a poker game in progress, with Cammie at the helm. The dons and Cammie froze in the middle of their hand. "What are you doing?!" Mia yelled at them. "You're supposed to be at your prom."

"It's boring up there," Nicky complained.

"Too bad. There's no gambling here, ever. That's the whole reason we didn't do a casino theme. Cammie, you at least should know better."

"What I know is I'm winning." The event planner used an arm to rake a pile of chips her way.

Mia fixed her with a glare. "I'm reporting this game to the police, and your connection to Pete will mean he'll get in trouble for not breaking it up, which means he'll be fired and he won't be able to spend bank wooing you back."

"Game's over," Cammie said, pushing away the chips. "Everyone back upstairs."

The dons protested, but Mia and Cammie ushered them out of the room. "I'm gonna kill you," Mia whispered to Cammie under her breath.

"Will you forgive me if I tell you I learned Nicky Vestri has some kind of side con going on?"

"Maybe. What?"

"I don't know the details. Everyone's being very cagey about it. But if Giles found out, Nicky could have offed him to keep him quiet."

"What about Ariadne and the poisoned water?"

"She could have found out and threatened to use it in the show. That's all she cares about. Remember, Nicky rode home with Violet. He might have brought her in on whatever scheme he's got going. Her showing up could have given him the distraction he needed to add arsenic to Ariadne's water bottle."

"Could be," Mia acknowledged. "Although Nicky's also hit on Chiara and even Francesca. He's on any woman who doesn't move fast enough to get out of his eyeline. But he could be hooking up with Violet for reasons in addition to sex. Like money. And power." The women headed upstairs. "I'm still mad at you."

"Why?" Cammie asked.

"Because this is good stuff and I didn't come up with it."

The women arrived at the ballroom, where the *Dons* higher-ups were gathered in a huddle, apparently being castigated by Ariadne. "You're all useless. Where's the bomb? I want a bomb, I don't care what kind, and I want it *now.*"

"Whoa." Mia waved her hands at them to shut down the direction of the conversation. "No bombs of any kind. Stink, cherry, smoke—"

"For goodness sake, I'm not talking about real bombs." Ariadne delivered this in a tone that was equal parts exasperation and condescension. "I'm talking about a story bomb that will make a plot explode."

"Oh," Mia said, embarrassed, feeling her civilian-ness. "Sorry, can't help you there."

Commotion at the ballroom's entryway stole the focus away from Mia, to her relief.

"What's going on over there?" Lysette craned her neck to try to make out a new arrival surrounded by dons who seemed happy to see whoever it was.

Given the giggling on the part of the donettes, coupled with a salacious "Who's the hottie?" from Chiara, Mia felt safe assuming the person in question was male. "No idea," she said, also craning to see.

The crowd parted, revealing the newcomer. Mia gasped and clapped a hand over her mouth. "Chiara's not wrong," Ariadne said, her tone matching Chiara's in sexual innuendo. "He is quite hot. Do you know him, Mia?"

Mia dropped her hand. "*A little.* He's my brother." She hurried to him. "Posi, what the—what are you doing out of jail?"

"And there's the bomb!" Ariadne said triumphantly.

Chapter 22

Posi pushed a lock of curly hair that had fallen over his eye back in place and flashed a dimpled grin. "Hey, sis. Dad dropped by the facility today and mentioned the prom thing." He struck a pose and flashed two thumbs-up. "Awesome. That's eighties, right?"

"Stop it," Mia ordered a couple of giggling donettes. "Don't encourage him. I repeat, Posi, what are you doing here?"

He gestured to his orange vest and then to the window. "Monitored work release." Mia looked out the window and down to the marina, where she saw a group of Posi's fellow inmates picking up trash under the supervision of two guards. "Henry not back at work yet?" The guard and family friend never would have let Posi talk him into an escapade like this.

"Another trip. He won a few thou at Foxwoods casino and took the grandkids to Disney World. The substitute guards thought cleaning up the borough's beloved marina was a great idea." Posi winked at her.

Mia gave him the side-eye. "Do they know you're on the lam from your cleaning duties right now?"

"Nope. They don't know any of us well enough to know who's there and who isn't." He glanced around the room. "So where's the camera?"

Mia cursed the reality show and the destructive effect it seemed to have on everyone who came into contact with it. "Posi, go back to the work detail. You're gonna get in big trouble. This stupid show isn't worth it."

Posi ignored his sister, instead focusing his gaze on Sammy, who was adjusting the volume on his speaker, which looked like it dated back to the beginning of his career. "Oh man, is that Sammy Starr? I loved him."

Sammy launched into "Walkman Walk My Way" yet again. Posi grabbed Chiara's hand and led her to the dance floor. "Hey!" Nicky bellowed.

He followed them and grabbed Chiara's other hand. "Let go of me, you idiot." She shook him off.

"The guy's a criminal," Nicky said, scowling at Posi.

"Like you haven't done time," Mia's brother shot back.

Nicky growled and pushed Posi away from Chiara. Posi pushed back, and before anyone could say "Walkman walk my way," a fight broke out. Dons threw punches, and donettes egged them on, while Mia yelled at her brother to stop the melee to no avail. She sent a frantic text to Shane, who was supervising a real prom in the Marina Ballroom below.

Seconds later, Shane strode into the room. "This ends *now*," he announced.

Using all of his sculpted 6'3" physique and strength, he yanked the dons off each other and tossed them aside until only Posi, only a little worse for wear, was left standing in the middle of the ballroom. "You gotta be Shane, my sister's boyfriend. Nice to meet you."

He extended a hand just as one of the work-release guards burst into the room. He cuffed Posi and led him toward the exit. "This is gonna be your last outing for a while, Carina," the annoyed prison guard told him.

"YOLO, my friend. You only live once." The guard walked Posi past Mia. "See you at the facility, sis," Posi said. He blew her a kiss the best he could, considering his hands were cuffed behind his back. "Check on Dad. He didn't look so hot when he came to visit."

Posi and the guard disappeared. The cast made a beeline for the prom bar. Shane approached Mia. "You want me to stick around?"

She shook her head. "I can handle things from here. Go babysit the high schoolers."

Shane hesitated a moment, then left. Mia, in need of a drink herself, went behind the bar and filled a wineglass to the brim. "Did you get all that on tape?" she heard Ariadne, who was standing with her crew near the bar, ask Lysette.

"Every single minute of it. Right, Cindy?" Lysette's assistant, who was now manning the main video camera, gave a nod, earning a pat on the shoulder and a self-satisfied grin from the director.

"Brilliant," Ariadne said. "Lysette, you are making quite the rapid climb up the ladder to executive producer."

Lysette preened. Mia put a pin in her goal of making sure the footage featuring her prodigal brother never saw the light of day. Instead, her attention rotated to Michael, whose reality career seemed to have stalled at segment producer. She was curious about his reaction to Lysette outpacing him. The expression on his face telegraphed unhappiness. He reinforced this by declaring he needed a drink.

Michael ordered a scotch on the rocks at the bar. "I'll get it for him," Mia told the bartender. She went behind the bar and removed a tumbler from the glass crate. She dropped ice cubes into it and poured scotch almost to the glass's rim. "You okay?" she asked, handing Michael the glass.

"Been better. But what about you? That was some show your brother put on. I only wish I'd thought of it myself." He took a glum sip of scotch.

"I wish I could say I was shocked, but to be honest, it was very on brand for my brother. Take a big risk and don't think about the consequences." Mia recalibrated from the detour to her brother. She leaned over the bar. "Lysette's really scoring points with Ariadne. I'm only a 'civilian,' but it doesn't seem fair to me." She delivered this in what she hoped sounded like a conspiratorial tone.

Michael gave his coworkers a furtive glance. "It's not that. I heard something. It really concerns me."

"What?" Mia leaned over even farther, praying she didn't topple the bar over.

Michael didn't immediately respond. Mia could tell he was struggling with an internal debate. "I need to talk to someone," he finally said. "But I can't talk about it here. I need somewhere private." He met Mia's eyes. "Do you know Little Island? In Manhattan, in the Hudson off 14th Street?"

"I've read about it, but I haven't been there yet."

"Meet me there at ten a.m. tomorrow. Northwest Overlook."

"See you then."

Screeching feedback from Sammy Starr's equipment forced everyone to cover their ears. "Sorry about that," the singer said. "Alright, everybody, Walkman walk my way with me one last time." He flashed a smile revealing a mouth of capped teeth, gave his bleached-blond mullet a toss, and launched into the song. "I love you like a mix tape, woman. Walkman walk my way . . ."

Little Island, the latest addition to New York City's myriad of wonders, sat in the Hudson River atop what was left of the pier where the ocean liner *Carpathia* deposited the survivors of the ill-fated *Titanic* in 1912. The man-made park was an undulating landscape built on pilings that resembled cement champagne cups. Mia arrived early to take a quick wander before learning whatever clues Michael might deliver. She strolled past flowering gardens and a verdant lawn where visitors lounged, stopping to take in the view west to New Jersey and south to the Financial District skyline—that view only slightly marred by the sight of the majestic Art Deco building that was home to model and thorn-in-her-side Petra Vilsni.

She circled around the island's amphitheater and made her way up the stairs to the assigned meeting place at the Northwest Overlook. Michael was already there, pacing nervously. They exchanged greetings. "This place . . ." Mia held up her hands to indicate she couldn't find words to describe it.

"Uh huh. I only have a few minutes."

"Sure. So—" She looked over his shoulder and gasped.

"What?!" Michael instinctively ducked to hide himself.

"Is that the Empire State Building?" Mia gazed at the iconic landmark in awe.

The segment producer stood up. "Do you want to talk or not?" he asked, annoyed.

"I'm so sorry. I don't get into Manhattan as much as I'd like." She forced herself to focus on the *Dons* crew member, trying to ignore the sleek, double-masted sailboat gliding past on the Hudson. "So, what did you hear that upset you?"

Michael gazed out over the water. He appeared distressed. "It was right before the prom. I saw Lysette pull Kelvin aside, into the hallway off the Belle View lobby. They couldn't see me, but I could hear them. She told him everything was going according to plan and he should be patient. Soon the two of them would be running the whole company."

Mia took this in. She liked Lysette, but she'd seen for herself how much the former camerawoman longed to move up the chain of production command. Mia admired and respected ambition, particularly in fellow women. But not if it came at the expense of someone's morals—and possibly led them to kill for it.

Michael winced. He rubbed his eyes. "I don't

like telling you this. Or thinking what I'm thinking about Lysette and Kelvin. I like them both a lot. We've basically been each other's support systems when it came to dealing with Giles or Ariadne. But they've both changed since their promotions. I'm not gonna lie. I resent the fact they got them and I didn't. But that's my problem to deal with. The bigger issue is, what did they do to get those promotions? And what might they be doing to move ahead even more? That's what bothers me."

Recalling the Boldano family creed, "Trust no one," Mia asked a hard question. "I'm guessing you're telling me all this because it's obvious I have an in with the police *and* the Boldano family. Which means I might be able to move them up the list of suspects. But if Lysette doesn't get promoted to executive producer, doesn't that improve *your* chances for snagging the job?"

"It would if I planned on staying at St. James Productions," the segment producer said. "But I have feelers out all over the place for a new job. You saw how toxic the relationship is between Ariadne and Giles's second wife. That's going to doom the company. I plan on being long gone by then. I've given up on scripted work. But I've got enough credits to land a better job in reality."

Before Mia could respond, two young men in Naval midshipmen uniforms approached. "Excuse me," one of them said with a thick Southern twang. "We're here visiting from the Naval Academy in Annapolis. Would y'all mind taking our picture with the Empire State Building in the background?"

Mia smiled. "Of course not."

"Thank you, miss."

He handed her his phone, then posed with his

buddy. Mia shot a few photos and handed back the phone. "There you go."

The midshipman gestured to her and Michael. "Y'all want me to take your picture?"

"We're not together."

Michael eyed her balefully. "Say it a little faster, why don't you?"

"Sorry. I appreciate the offer." Mia gave the young man a small salute. "Thank you for your service to our country. And for calling me miss instead of ma'am."

The midshipmen returned the salute and took off. Michael checked the time on his phone. "I gotta go. I have to meet with Ariadne and come up with scenarios for the rest of the week. We need more bombs."

"I hope the whole thing bombs," Mia muttered.

"Excuse me?"

"Nothing. Before you go, did you hear anything else from Lysette, Kelvin, or anyone else that didn't sit right with you?"

"Aside from general threats and 'I'll ruin him or hers,' which is pretty much an everyday thing in our business, no."

"Okay then, I guess we're done."

Mia started to step away from the railing. Michael stopped her. "No leaving together. We can't risk it. I'll leave. Give me five or ten minutes, then you go."

He hurried away. Happy to dawdle, Mia took a few selfies of herself with the Empire State Building. She sauntered past the lawn, inhaling the intoxicating aroma of newly mowed grass. The postage stamp front and back yards of Astoria didn't allow for the delicious scent to waft through the neighborhood air. She was about to take a picture of herself with the FiDi skyline and Verrazano-Narrows Bridge in the far distance when she heard cries of alarm coming from the park's edge below. "Help! Someone's in the water!"

Mia looked down and let out an alarmed cry of her own. A black toupee bobbed in the water.

The someone was segment producer Michael.

Chapter 23

Mia raced out of the park to the railing along the edge of the entry path. She hoisted herself up onto the railing and was about to jump into the water when the midshipmen she'd photographed swan-dived into the drink. They emerged each holding one side of an unconscious Michael under an arm. The sound of sirens filled the air as police cars and an ambulance converged on the scene.

Mia ran to the pier's edge, where bystanders were helping the midshipmen and their heavy load out of the river. "Is he alive?" an anxious Mia asked one of her dripping-wet heroic new friends while EMT workers swarmed around Michael.

"Yes, miss." The midshipman spit out water and made a face. "I know they cleaned up that river, but it could use a little more work."

"Make sure you and your friend get checked for parasites or whatever might be in there. And thank you *so* much. If they give medals for saving average citizens, let me know and I'll write a letter." The midshipman didn't hear her. He and his fellow hero were already posing for photos Mia was sure would go viral.

Mia noticed a handful of twenty-something bystanders pointing to the water and chattering among themselves. She went to them. "Did you see what happened? How the man ended up in the water?"

A guy who appeared about twenty began speaking rapidly in a foreign language. "Hold up," Mia said. "Are you German?"

"*Ja.*"

"Not a problem." Mia extracted her cell phone from her fake designer fanny pack. She swiped to open an app. "I use this translation app at work with clients who speak English as a second language. And I bet you didn't understand any of that. Speak into this."

She said the last sentence to the phone, which responded with a written translation she held up to the young tourist. He read it, nodded, and slowly spoke into the phone in German. After a minute or two, he stopped. Mia read back the translation of what he said: *It was weird. He was standing here and then I heard "Ow!" and a thud and he was in the water. Do you know where we can get good New York pizza near here? We are hungry.*

Mia spoke into the translation app. "I wish I could help you on the pizza, but I don't know the neighborhood. But pretty much every pizzeria in New York has decent pizza."

She showed the young visitor the translation. He nodded thanks and gave her a thumbs-up.

The EMTs finished triage on Michael. They strapped an oxygen mask over his mouth and nose and placed him onto a gurney they wheeled toward the ambulance. "Is he going to be okay?" Mia asked, running alongside them.

"Hard to say," an EMT responded. "Looks like he took a pretty serious blow to the back of his head."

"Another head injury?!"

The EMT shot her a strange look. "Another?"

"Because . . . there are so many these days." *Great save, Mia, as in* not *a great save.* "Where are you taking him?"

New York Presbyterian Lower Manhattan."

The EMTs loaded Michael into the ambulance. They jumped in and pulled the door shut after them. The siren let out its piercing cry, and the ambulance took off. Mia saw an empty cab on West Street and jumped up and down, yelling, to hail it. The cab cut across two lanes of traffic, earning infuriated honks from other drivers, and screeched into the Little Island access road. Mia hopped in. "New York Prez Lower Manhattan, please. As fast as you can get there without breaking laws or running anyone down."

The cab took Mia's request to heart, delivering her to the hospital at what would best be described as New York taxi supersonic speed. She used the short trip to text the news about Michael to Ariadne, following this up with an alert to Pete Dianopolis. Once deposited at New York Presbyterian, Mia located the emergency room on Gold Street and hurried inside. "Hi, I'm here for Michael Planko," she told the woman manning the admissions desk. "I was with him when he had his accident."

"I'll let his doctor know you're here," the woman said. "You can take a seat in the waiting room."

Mia found a seat in the chilly, antiseptic environment that ticked off all the boxes of a hospital waiting room. She tried to ignore her fellow inhabitants, who were in various states of misery, if waiting for care, or anxiety, if waiting for news of a loved one. She castigated herself for paying more attention to the lush environs of Little Island than to Michael. She opened the photos on her phone to the one she took of herself with the Empire State Building in the background. *Stupid selfie. If I hadn't been taking it, I might have seen whoever pushed him.* Mia went to delete the photo, then stopped. *It* is *a good one. And it's not the picture's fault I was distracted.* She put the phone away.

A doctor came through the double doors leading to the ER. He conferred with the admissions employee, who pointed to Mia. He came to her. "You're Mr. Planko's friend? I'm Dr. Kapoor."

"Nice to meet you. Is that right? It sounds weird here. Sorry. How is he?"

"He has a pretty serious concussion. We won't know until the X-rays are back, but I suspect a skull fracture. If this is verified, we might have to place him in a medically induced coma to reduce the chance of bleeding on the brain."

The graphic details made Mia wince. "Is there any way of confirming someone pushed him into the water?"

The doctor gave her a look similar to the one she got from the EMT. "Pushed? Deliberately?"

"It's New York. It happens." She was growing impatient with medical professionals responding as if she was incriminating herself. "People get pushed onto the subway tracks. Why not into the water?"

"I see. That is a possibility. It's also possible

Mr. Planko fell and hit his head on one of abandoned pier pilings in the water. I have no way of proving either happened, though. That's for the police."

"Mia," someone called.

Mia glanced toward the entrance and saw Ariadne coming toward her at a quick clip. To Mia's shock, Violet followed the producer into the waiting room. "Hi, Ariadne. Violet?" She couldn't keep the question mark off the end of the sentence.

"Hello, love. Surprise!" Violet struck a pose. A meow came from her ever-present tote bag.

"Violet and I had a very productive heart-to-heart talk," Ariadne said. "Tears were shed—"

"All hers." Mia saw a mischievous glint in Violet's eyes. "I promised to stop accusing her of murdering my Giles, and not to bring charges in the attempted poisoning—"

"*Accidental* poisoning," Ariadne interjected.

"—of my Princess Kate here, if Ariadne stopped shutting me out of the company and instead treated me like the full partner I am. Right, Ari?"

The nickname caused Ariadne to scrunch up her face as if someone had passed gas. She quickly regained her composure. "You are right . . . Vi."

"I should see if Mr. Planko's X-rays have come back," Dr. Kapoor said.

"You're Michael's doctor?" Ariadne addressed Mia. "Thank you for your help. I'll—"

"We'll—" Violet corrected.

"Take it from here."

Ariadne led Dr. Kapoor away to discuss Michael's case. Instead of following, Violet lingered. She eyed Mia. "So . . . you and Mr. Planko were at Little Island. Seems an odd place to meet up on a weekday morning."

Mia forced herself not to flush an incriminating red. "We both had the time off," she said with a casual air. "I've always wanted to go. Michael's been, so he said he'd show me."

"Uh huh. Still . . . interesting."

Violet gave her a shrewd look. She then went to join Ariadne and the doctor, leaving Mia to realize there was a lot more to the second Mrs. Giles St. James than she let meet the eye.

CHAPTER 24

Mia left the hospital eager to ditch Manhattan for the comforts of her beloved Queens. Standing on the subway platform— a safe distance from the tracks—she mulled over the twist of Ariadne and Violet striking up a genuine partnership. It was one she didn't see coming, especially after the latter accused the former of outright murder. It certainly undercut Michael's assumption that the toxic relationship between the women would destroy Giles St. James Productions.

Speaking of toxic, there's a lot of poisoning going around. Mia pondered the fact both Princess Kate and Chiara had been on the receiving end of it. If they were dosed with the same toxin, it had to come from the same source. She took out her phone and texted Pete the possibility. **We looked into this,** he wrote back. **Cat got a diuretic. Not arsenic. Which would've put her in a kitty cemetery.**

Discouraged, Mia put her phone away. Two preternaturally hip thirty-somethings deep in conversation joined Mia and the other New Yorkers waiting for the train. "So I told him, I'm sorry, but I'm not impressed," she said to her friend. "A few million doesn't cut it anymore."

"He is such a swipe-left," the friend said, and the women giggled.

Rich people, Mia thought with disdain. She mused how money was at the root of everything. If *The Dons of Ditmars Boulevard* was a hit, it would mean fame and money for the cast, promotions and money for the crew. The goal of making money united archrivals Ariadne and Violet. Was covering up a murder on the part of one of them part of the deal? Mia flashed on the theory she'd posed to Teri back in New Orleans that the two women staged their rivalry to cover up a joint plot to kill Giles. Given the women's current relationship, it seemed far less farfetched.

Mia glanced up the track to see if a train was coming. Her eyes landed on a poster for a new sparkling water. Holding a can to her lips in a highly suggestive pose was a gorgeous model—Petra. *How perfect that the one person I wish needed money doesn't*, Mia moped. The model's existing wealth made her impervious to Shane's offer of a marital buyout. *If she needed the cash*, Mia thought, *it would be a very different story.*

Mia texted Pete the unexpected development in Ariadne and Violet's relationship, as well as her supposition their animosity might have been staged. Pete wrote back: **Congrats! When were u bumped up from nosy citizen with zero police training to lead detective on the case?**

Mia sent back a sheepish shrug emoji. She could only push Pete so far.

* * *

By the time she got off the N train, Mia was feeling the emotional and physical toll of the morning's traumatic events. She confirmed with her father they'd be fine without her for the day at Belle View and made a pit stop at La Guli Pasticceria to pick up a few cannoli, biscotti, and tricolor cookies to share with her grandmother. She walked the mile from the pastry shop to her home, enjoying the late-afternoon summer warmth.

She found Elisabetta in her kitchen placing a crocheted cup warmer of various clashing colors around an old mug. "You finally crocheted something useful."

"*Che dici?*" her grandmother said, affronted. "Everything I make is useful."

"Of course," Mia backtracked, then quickly changed the subject. "Is that tea? I could use some."

"*Sì.*"

Elisabetta handed Mia the mug. She poured another cup for herself. The two sat down at Elisabetta's 1950s dinette set and helped themselves to cookies. Mia filled her in on Michael's "accident." Then her grandmother brought up Posi's unexpected appearance at the *Dons of Ditmars Boulevard* manufactured prom, which she'd heard about from Ravello. "They'll probably tack more jail time onto his sentence because of it," Mia said. "Even if they let it slide, which I doubt, he won't be released early for good behavior anytime soon."

Elisabetta grumbled a few choice Italian swear words. "I don't get the world today. Everybody, they want the attention. Why?"

"Money. Power. That's the end game. Producers, writers, performers, even average people. With social media, you can become a star by belching the national anthem or something. The more people get, the more they want. They become addicted to it. Look at everyone involved with this stupid show *The Dons of Ditmars Boulevard.* It's hard for the police to pin down a suspect when every single person involved is grabbing at the same gold ring. I swear, I never met so many manipulative backstabbers. They make the Family look like nonprofit volunteers."

"*Concordo,*" Elisabetta said, nodding agreement. She picked up a tricolor cookie. "I gotta ask you something. I ain't seen Shane sneaking out of your apartment in a while. *Che successe?* You two got problems?"

"No, not at all," Mia hastened to reassure her grandmother. "We're both so busy. We don't have time to pretend we're not in a relationship these days. That's all."

The doubtful look Elisabetta threw her way told Mia her grandmother didn't buy the excuse, which she had to admit was lame. Still, it was a better option than revealing to the octogenarian Italian that Mia's boyfriend was married, even if it was the equivalent of a technicality. She faked a yawn and stood up. "Boy, everything just hit me in a big way. I'm gonna take a nap." She planted a kiss on the top of Elisabetta's head. "Love you, Nonna."

"*Anch'io ti amo.*"

Elisabetta blew her a kiss and pulled out her crocheting. As Mia traipsed upstairs to her apartment, she felt a cloud of depression descend on her. The conversation with her grandmother made the next step in her relationship with Shane clear. There would be *no* relationship until his marital status was resolved.

In the morning, Mia broke the news to Shane when she reached Belle View. She swore there were tears in his peridot-green eyes, which she had to admit felt satisfying. "I hate that this is happening, but I get it and I respect your decision," he said. "Man, I regret all the dumb things I did in my youth."

"All? There are more?!"

"None this bad," he rushed to assure Mia. "I mean it as a general thing. It just sucks that I'm paying the price at thirty-two for things I did when I was twenty-two, or even younger. When I look at Donny Junior and Nicky, I see them following the same pattern. I wish I could use my own life experience to get the dons and donettes to think long and hard about the choices they're making."

"You do know Nicky's probably your age. And Donny is two years older than you."

"Seriously?" Shane, dumbfounded, took this in. "Wow. That's *bad.*"

"Uh huh."

"Well . . . both of them would do better if they took a look at the mistakes I've made and learned from them."

The sad expression on Shane's face made Mia ache to envelope him in her arms. Knowing there was no way this wouldn't morph into more romantic contact, she restrained herself. "Alrighty, enough about our *farkakteh* personal lives. We have work to do."

"*Farkakteh?*" Shane said, puzzled.

"At the bris a couple of weeks ago, I picked up a few Yiddish words. I love them. *So* expressive."

They took off in opposite directions, Shane to give tours, Mia to charm one of the facility's party-rental suppliers into cutting them a break on linens for a wedding with five hundred guests. At the end of the day, they met up with Guadalupe and Evans in Belle View's spacious first-floor main kitchen. The chefs had put together groceries needed at Casa Giovanni for the next *Dons* filming. Guadalupe went over her checklist. "Ten boxes fettucine, a crate of tomatoes, four jars of sliced olives . . ." She continued down the list. "Everything's there."

"These are the ingredients for pasta puttanesca," Evans said. "We're back there again?"

"Yup." Mia and the chefs chuckled.

"What do you mean 'again'?" Shane asked.

"I hosted a baby shower for my friend Nicole, and even though it was an afternoon tea, her nonna insisted we serve pasta puttanesca, aka streetwalker pasta, to let Nicole's stepmother know exactly what she thought of her."

"Ouch."

"Way more than ouch," Guadalupe said. "The stepmother's the one they found floating in the bay, strangled with her own gift ribbon. You can hear more about it on the podcast episode Cammie interviewed me for. If she ever gets the dang thing to air."

Evans began packing the ingredients into boxes. "And they're making pasta puttanesca on the show why?"

"Ariadne had the brilliant idea to shoot a scene where the dons make dinner for the donettes. I'm not being sarcastic. Considering all the dons still live at home when they're not living at Casa Giovanni, and their mamas cook for them, it's a disaster waiting to happen. Which is perfect for the pilot. And you know one of the donettes will call another one a *puttana* at some point, which should add to the fun. That last part *was* sarcastic."

They added ingredients for dessert, which would be tiramisu, then the four carted the supplies out of the kitchen to Mia's waiting car. "Let us know how it goes," Evans said.

"So you can share any good dirt with Teri?" Mia winked at him. "Sure."

They finished packing the car. "I'll go with you," Shane said.

He put his hand on the passenger-side door handle. "I got this," Mia said. She put her hand on his to prevent him from opening the door. The simple action sent a jolt of longing through her, and she pulled her hand away.

Shane got the message. "Okay." He backed off. "But if you need help, call."

Mia gave a brusque nod, avoiding eye contact with him. She got in the car and drove off.

When she arrived at Casa Giovanni, the dons helped her unload the car, transporting the ingredients into the kitchen, where Ariadne was issuing instructions to the production crew. She saw Mia and stepped away to peer into the boxes. "I see the pasta ingredients. What about the tiramisu?"

"It's all here." Mia opened the refrigerator door. "I'm putting away the perishable ingredients."

"It will make for a lovely food fight," Ariadne said with what Mia considered way too much pleasure. "You don't see too many pie-in-face sort of moments these days."

"Of course, since this is a 'reality show,' there's also the chance those moments won't happen, right?" Mia tried and failed to sound like she was making an innocent rather than a judgmental comment. "Sounds like you're taking over Michael's story brainstorming. How is he, by the way?"

"Fine." The vague response indicated Ariadne took an "out of sight, out of mind" approach to her employees. Mia wondered if anyone from the show would even claim the body if Michael passed away at the hospital.

"Yo." Little Donny clapped his hands to draw attention to himself from the dons, who were checking out the dinner ingredients like they'd fallen from outer space, confirming Mia's assumption the cooking in their lives was left to their mamas. Donny held up a sheet of paper. "We're gonna be making my mother's recipe for pasta puttanesca. I made paper copies for whoever wants, but I also sent the recipe to your phones."

The dons ignored the paper and opened their phones to access the recipe. Lysette's assistant-turned-cameraperson Cindy focused her video camera on the dons. "Alright, gang," Lysette called out, "let's get cooking."

Curious to see how the scene played out, Mia found a spot in an alcove to watch the filming. She had to admit watching the clueless guys take on the simple task of boiling linguini was amusing.

"Can I join you?"

The whispered request came from Violet. Mia nodded and moved over to make room for the co-producer. Nicky emptied a huge pot of pasta into a colander to drain. A cloud of steam enveloped him. "Mutha-effah, I'm getting boiled alive here."

"It's good for your pores," Donny Junior joked. "Makes your skin all soft, like a baby's butt." The other dons chuckled.

"I'm not the butt around here," Nicky retorted, unamused. He took the colander and returned the pasta to the pot, adding a heavy dose of olive oil. "Keeps it from sticking. I know my way around a kitchen, unlike you goombahs."

He held up the bottle with a flourish. Slippery with oil, it dropped from his hand to the floor, shattering and spraying olive oil. He cursed, while the dons roared, Donny laughing the loudest. "Ha! And that's it for kitchen tips from chef and head goombah Nicky Vestri."

Donny's phone pinged an update. The ping echoed from all the phones in the room. Donny took a look at his phone and instantly stopped laughing. Disbelief replaced amusement. "What the f—?"

Mia checked her own phone, which had alerted her to the notification. It came from a reality show gossip blog. A headline blared REALITY ROMANCE! in large black letters. It was the picture below the headline currently turning Little Donny's disbelief into all-out rage.

A picture showing Ariadne St. James and Nicky Vestri locked in a passionate embrace.

Chapter 25

Donny Junior bellowed with the rage of a bull who realized the guy in the ring with the red cape was out to get him. He went to punch Nicky but slipped on the olive oil. Nicky, who jumped back, also slipped, and the two dons landed on the floor. Donny went after Nicky, who fought back. The other dons yelled like they were watching a prize fight.

The commotion attracted the donettes, who'd been giving each other facials in another part of the house. They ran into the room sporting clay masks and joined the action as equally loud spectators. Torn between wanting to help Donny and not wanting to find herself on camera in any way, Mia elbowed Violet. "Someone's gonna get seriously hurt. Make them stop!"

"Why?" Violet watched in awe. "This is what you Yanks would call good stuff. I must say, Ariadne's simply brilliant."

Donny, coated with olive oil, managed to get hold of the kitchen island's edge. He hoisted himself up to standing. He grabbed the pot of pasta and dumped it on Nicky's head. "I swear, I'll kill you for messing with my girlfriend." He reached down to grab his cousin but slipped and wound up on his backside once again.

"Stop!" Ariadne finally called out. Lysette motioned to the camerawoman to stop filming.

"Mental note to always end on a big moment," Violet murmured. "I'm learning so much on this shoot."

Ariadne went to the two prone dons, making sure to avoid errant puddles of olive oil. "That's enough, both of you. Donny, love, it's not what it looks like. Nicky pushed himself on me. The next photo would have been me pushing him off."

"She's lying," Nicky said, "because she doesn't want to hurt your feelings. She finally figured out what we all know. You're a loser. We all pretend you're not, to be nice, but everyone knows where the power is around here." He thumped his chest. "With *me*. Nicky Boldano Vestri."

Donny let out another roar. Fury gave him the strength to propel himself at Nicky and wrap his hands around his throat. Motivated by terrified screams from the donettes, the dons finally sprang into action and pulled the cousins apart. Donny, oil-coated and breathing heavily, rose to his feet and faced Ariadne. "Tell me the truth."

She responded with a defiant glare. "Get out of this kitchen. You're done for the day. And possibly the entire shoot. Your anger is out of control. I didn't want to believe you might have killed Giles. But after what we all just witnessed . . ." She trailed off. When she spoke, her voice was thick with emotion. "Go. *Now.*"

Donny deflated. Head bowed, shoulders hunched, he dragged himself from the room. Mia, feeling for her lifelong friend, started to follow. She stopped when she saw Violet surreptitiously snapping pictures. "What are you doing?"

"Nothing," she said, with a guilty expression. She hurried to put her phone in her tote bag, but Princess stuck her head out, knocking the phone from Violet's hand. Mia grabbed it. "Give me that back."

Mia used one hand to hold off the ersatz producer. She used the other to scroll through the photos, finally landing on what she was looking for. She held the phone up to Violet, displaying the sexy photo of Ariadne and Nicky. "You took this. And sent it to the gossip site. The whole thing was a setup."

Violet grabbed the phone. "All I'll say is this *is* a reality show and there *is* reality in that photo."

She scurried out of the alcove, leaving Mia to try and make sense of her cryptic declaration.

On the ride home from Casa Giovanni, Mia was so distracted by the circus of thoughts whirling through her mind that she had to pull over to the side of the road to settle down. Parsing Violet's odd sentence about the incriminating photo of Ariadne in a lip-lock with Nicky led Mia to believe there was something at play besides the reality show. She wondered if Nicky might be right about his status supplanting Little Donny's with both the Boldano organization and in Ariadne's heart. The producer seemed to possess a gravitational pull toward power. More than one sign pointed to her interest in Little Donny cooling off. Was she now setting him up to take the fall for Giles's murder?

Mia tapped the car video screen connecting to her cell phone. Big Donny's voice soon came through the auto's speakers. "*Mia bambina.* Sorry I been out of touch. Aurora's losing her mind over the rehearsal dinner we're hosting tomorrow. Since it's gonna be in Connecticut, she wants to make sure it's what those people'd expect and not one of our *cafone* parties. Translation: no Jordan almonds in little gauze bags with the party date attached."

"That's disappointing. Going by the lack of food at the last Connecticut party, those almonds would've come in handy."

"How are you, *cara mia*? You get my son off the hook yet?"

"Working on it," she said, hoping she'd dodged a more specific answer, which would show she was coming up short on the assignment. "I'm calling because I was wondering . . ." Mia chose her words carefully. "What's the feeling in the family about Nicky Vestri?"

"Is that family with a big or little eff?"

"Both."

"Got it. Regarding the little eff, the general feeling is he's a bragging bigshot in his own mind who could use a swift kick in the a— . . . in the tush. If we're talking about the big eff"—Donny Senior also chose his words carefully—"as in Family, all I'll say is there are those who believe he has a glimmer of future potential."

"More than Little Donny?"

His father gave a sardonic snort. "No comparison. The only time my son's name comes up is when people suddenly remember I'm there and feel obligated to throw it into the conversation."

The answers on both counts came as no surprise to Mia. "Thanks, Mr. B."

"Why the questions about Nicky? Is he in trouble?" Donny Senior sounded hopeful.

"No. I'm only asking because I'm trying to figure out dynamics between the *Dons of Ditmars Boulevard* cast and crew, and how they might figure into Giles's murder."

"And the guy who got pushed into the Hudson. I heard about that. Seems like the stuff happening off camera is more interesting than whatever's happening on."

"It's sure a lot scarier." A car wanting to claim the place where Mia sat parked with her headlights on honked for her to move. "I gotta go."

"See you tomorrow night. I may need your help keeping Aurora from tossing herself onto the Connecticut rocks if the rehearsal dinner's a dud."

"I'm sure it will be wonderful. But if you need me, I'll be there for you."

Mia pulled out of the parking space and drove toward home, where she lucked out and found an open spot on the street directly in front of the house. She was getting out of the car when the vibration of an incoming text tickled her stomach. Mia took out her phone and read the disheartening text from Little Donny: **Dianopolis wants 2 talk 2 me at the station AGAIN!!!**

Fearing her worst fears about Donny being set up were coming to fruition, Mia's heart sank.

* * *

Pilgrim's Perch, the old-money colonial estate belonging to Madison's uncle, Garrison Campbell, sat on a promontory above the rocky Worthington coast. A full moon helped garlands of fairy lights illuminate the grounds, which were occupied by rehearsal dinner attendees milling about the manicured backyard grounds during the evening's cocktail hour.

Mia, a glass of pinot grigio in hand, made casual conversation with Madison, off to the side from her coworkers. Big Donny and wife Aurora had generously paid the cost of closing Belle View for the weekend to make sure the facility's employees could attend the wedding festivities. They'd also provided limo service to transport everyone, although Ravello chose to drive his family, along with girlfriend Lin Yeung, in his own Cadillac Escalade. Shane also drove separately. Originally, Mia had planned to ride with him, but the current circumstances involving his marital status negated that plan.

"I love your dress," Madison said to Mia.

"You should. I got it at one of the sample sales you hosted." Having learned her lesson from the fashion debacle of the Wythe barbecue, Mia had eschewed naval-themed attire for the simplest of little black dresses paired with sensible pumps. She took a sip of wine and drank in the lovely, old-fashioned setting. "Your uncle's home is wonderful. Very tasteful. It must have been cool growing up with a gay relative."

"He's not gay," Madison said. "He's what we call Connecticut straight. That's a man who never bothered to marry and is perfectly happy living as a confirmed bachelor."

"Is that so?" Mia responded, contemplating the concept, which was alien to her people.

Donny Boldano Senior approached the two women. Elegantly attired in a bespoke gray suit, he would have blended in perfectly with the Connecticut gentry but for the tie clip and cufflinks sparkling with diamonds. He took turns giving each woman a kiss on both cheeks. "So, whaddya think? We do this party up right for you, Madison?"

"It's lovely, sir." Madison gave her soon-to-be-father-in-law a warm smile.

"Aurora was so nervous about this whole shindig, I can't even tell you." Donny Senior gestured to the party in progress behind him. "She tried to hire Martha Stewart to run things but never heard back from her. Luckily, she found a book online that helped a lot."

"What book?" Mia asked. "Maybe we can use it at Belle View if a crowd like this ever books a party with us."

"*Entertain Like Your People Landed at Plymouth Rock: A Prepster's Guide.* Very helpful." Donny Senior took a silk handkerchief from his suit pocket and used it to mop his brow. "Phew, it's a hot night. Here's hoping the giant fans we rented to cool the dinner tent will take the edge off." He glanced past the women. "There's Ravello and Elisabetta. I need to welcome them. *Ciao,* ladies."

Mia bid him goodbye. Madison stayed silent. Mia noticed she'd gone pale. "You don't look so good. What's wrong?"

Madison gulped. "That book Mr. Boldano mentioned? It's a *parody.* It's not meant to be taken seriously."

Mia's eyes widened. "It's not? Really? *Marone.* This is gonna be one interesting party." Unable to restrain herself, she burst into a fit of giggles.

The color returned to Madison's face. "That explains the Cheese Whiz and Ritz crackers appetizers," she said, generating peals of laughter from the two.

Mia gasped for air. "We have to stop. My makeup's gonna smear." She wiped her eyes, then noticed *Dons of Ditmars Boulevard* director Lysette and her assistant step out of the mansion's French doors onto the flagstone patio. Cindy carried the ever-present video camera. "You're letting the show film this weekend?" she asked Madison, surprised.

"Only events involving cast members who are invited guests. I convinced Jamie we should do it to support Donny Junior. I want to kick off my marriage on the good side of my brother-in-law."

"Smart move. Here's Little D now, with his date . . ." Mia registered surprise. "Who is not Ariadne."

Donny Junior, clad like his father in well-cut, traditional men's garb, appeared on the patio clasping fellow cast member Chiara by the hand. A moment later, Ariadne appeared—hand in hand with Boldano cousin Nicky. Madison followed Mia's gaze and paled again. "Maybe letting them film wasn't such a great idea."

"It's bad enough these show bizzers hijacked your bachelorette party. No way it's happening to your wedding events. Go mingle. I have work to do."

Mia marched over to the appetizer buffet table, where Guadalupe, Evans, and Teri had relocated. "You want a deviled egg?" Teri asked. "There are, like, five versions of them."

"And whole bowls of potato chips and bowls of pimento olives," Evans said. "And chipped beef on toast. I thought they only served that to sailors at sea."

"A lot of this crowd does sail," Mia said. "Maybe Aurora thought they'd appreciate eating it on land for a change."

Guadalupe held up her full plate. "I don't care what they're serving as long as I don't have to cook it for a change. You know, a deviled egg bar isn't a bad idea for a cocktail hour."

"Noted," Mia said. "But I need to draft you all into a nonculinary task. Madison's trying to make nice with her future brother-in-law, so she and Jamie gave the *Dons* crew permission for discreet filming focused only of the cast members. Little Donny's here with Chiara as his date and Nicky's with Ariadne. Everybody's using somebody to make a point, and I refuse to let things get ugly and spoil the weekend festivities. Can you keep your eyes on all of them and intervene if you have to?"

The others voiced agreement to help. "Do you want me to bring Shane in on this?" Teri asked, sensitive to the distance Mia was trying to put between herself and her inamorata.

"Yes, thank you," Mia said, grateful for Teri's sympathetic take on the situation. "If you need me, I'll be with my dad and nonna."

She maneuvered her way through the guests. Seeing Cammie and Pete arrive, she stopped to exchange greetings and air kisses. "We're late because we did a little real estate shopping," Cammie informed Mia.

"You're not going to quit the job you barely

show up to, are you?" Mia asked, worried nonetheless."

"Never," Cammie said. "You'll have to carry me out of Belle View in a body bag. If I bothered to show up that day, of course. No, I thought we'd look at condos for weekend getaways. If we get back together, right, Pete?"

"Right." Pete grabbed a glass of wine from a passing waiter and chugged it.

"There are the others. I'm gonna say hi."

Cammie traipsed off. "You know what else is a never?" Pete said to Mia, speaking sotto voce. "Us buying some overpriced condo probably made with Chinese drywall. But don't tell Cammie I said that." He guzzled the wine, grabbed a second glass, and followed after Cammie.

The rest of the cocktail hour proved uneventful. Mia caught Shane casting wistful glances her way a few times. She hardened herself to them, turning away quickly each time their eyes met. She saw Little Donny shoot Nicky an ugly look, which his cousin responded to with a smirk. They stepped toward each other, but Evans got between them and directed each back to his corner. A cowbell announced dinner, and the guests made their way into a party tent to take their places at long tables set up for family-style dining. The meal was being served buffet-style, with stations set up on each side of the tent. Mia noticed a preponderance of casseroles lining the serving table she strolled by. "Is that—?"

"Tuna fish casserole with a crust of crushed potato chips?" Her father's girlfriend, Lin, elegant in a forest-green wrap dress, carefully examined the dish. "It appears to be."

"I've never seen one before except in pictures."

Elisabetta made a dismissive sound. "I may skip dinner and go back to playing with those golden retriever puppies. *Cosi carina.* So cute."

"Puppies?"

"I guess you missed them," Lin said. "Golden retrievers and Irish setters. Aurora explained it was from the chapter on entertainment in the book she used to plan the party."

Mia and Lin shared an amused expression. Lin addressed Ravello, who'd already taken a seat. "Ravello, should I make you a plate?"

Mia's father shook his head. Despite the fans, the air in the tent was tepid and humid. Ravello's red, perspiring face indicated it didn't agree with him.

Mia and Lin exchanged another glance, this time one of concern. "Dad, it's warm in here. Take off your jacket."

"You won't be offending anyone, dearest," Lin said. "A lot of the men have already taken off theirs."

"I'm fine," Ravello insisted. "You know what, I will have some of that white stuff." He pointed to the tuna casserole.

"*Testardo,*" Elisabetta said, shaking her head.

"As a mule," Mia agreed, earning a chuckle from Lin.

They filled plates and joined Ravello at the table. Lin placed his plate in front of him. As the others ate, he pushed the casserole around with his fork but didn't ingest a bite of it.

Whether it was the heat, the unusual menu, or the tension emanating from Little Donny and Nicky, Mia couldn't shake a sense of foreboding.

Overcome with anxiety, she stopped eating after a few forkfuls of casserole, which proved unexpectedly delicious.

She heard a rumbling of anger coming from a nearby table. Her frayed nerves frayed further when she saw Little Donny and Nicky standing face-to-face, making threatening gestures. She started to rise, but Shane beat her to it, thrusting himself between the cousins. The ambient noise of party chatter made it impossible to hear what he said, but Little Donny and Nicky reluctantly returned to their tables. Shane caught Mia's eyes. Instead of breaking contact this time, she mouthed "Thank you." He smiled and gave her a thumbs-up.

Madison's brother, Scooter, easy to spot in his kelly-green slacks and bright plaid sport coat, made his way to the front of the tent. He tapped a full highball glass with a knife to get everyone's attention. "When my sister's almost mother-in-law asked my advice for a special way to entertain you all tonight and honor the bride and groom-to-be," he said into a microphone, "it took me all of a split second to come up with the answer. Ladies and gentlemen, help me welcome Yale University's oldest a cappella group, the Spizzwinks!"

The applause broke neatly down the middle: thunderous from the New England crowd, polite from the Queens brigade. "What's a Spizz . . .whatever he said?" Elisabetta asked, confused. "It sounds like a bug."

"They sing," Mia said, "I guess."

A group of college students smartly attired in tuxedo tails assembled at the tent's front. "Congratulations, Jamie and Madison," their leader intoned into a mic. "We wish you all the best. And in the spirit of tonight's events, we'd like to invite any former Spizzwinks to come up and join us."

More than half a dozen men, including Scooter and Madison's father, Topher, leapt up from their seats and joined the group. The leader blew into a pitch pipe. The men responding by harmonizing a note. Then the singers launched into a rousing rendition of "Alexander's Ragtime Band." *Come on and hear, come on and hear, Alexander's Ragtime Band . . .*

Mia politely joined in clapping along to the song. The sound of a chair being knocked over distracted her.

Come on and hear, come on and hear, it's the best band in the land . . .

"What the hell's going on?" Ravello asked, unreasonably aggravated.

Mia craned her neck. To her alarm, she saw Little Donny raise a fist to Nicky. Shane rushed to pull him away from Nicky, who Evans fought to restrain.

They can play a bugle call like you never heard before,
So natural that you want to go to war . . .

Ravello slammed a fist on the table. "I've had it with those two mooks. If Big Donny ain't gonna do anything about it, I will."

He rose to his feet and staggered. Then he turned whiter than the creamy sauce covering the tuna casserole. Mia jumped up and reached out to him. "Dad—"

"I don't feel so—"

Ravello fell to the ground as the Spizzwinks continued to extoll the talents of Alexander's Ragtime Band.

CHAPTER 26

For the third time in less than two weeks, someone had passed out at Mia's feet. And now, for the second time in less than a week, Mia found herself spending several hours in an ER waiting room—albeit one slightly more upscale and much less frenetic than the one in lower Manhattan where she'd waited for news about Michael Planko. And this time, instead of being alone, she was with loved ones, including Shane.

"Dad was conscious when they put him in the ambulance." Mia repeated the detail she'd already shared more than once, desperately trying to mine good news from the awful event. She shivered, more from shock than the room's chilly air. Shane put a comforting arm around her shoulder, and she let it rest there.

Pete and a doctor emerged through swinging double doors. "Who is the family of Mr. Carina?" the doctor asked.

"We all are," Mia said. "Even the ones who aren't."

"I already explained what's going on to Detective Dianopolis—"

"I only wanted to make sure what happened to Ravello wasn't related to recent criminal activity," Pete explained.

"Very smart of you, honey," Cammie said. Her ex drank in the compliment.

"I was able to assure the detective Mr. Ravello's situation is purely a health issue. X-rays showed possible blockages in Mr. Carina's arteries. He gave us permission to perform an angioplasty. We found eighty percent blockage in his left main artery—"

"The one they call the widow maker," Pete added, causing Elisabetta and Lin to burst into tears.

"Not helpful," Mia said with a glare, trying to hold back her own tears.

"Sorry," Pete said sheepishly.

"We inserted a stent into the artery," the doctor continued. "There's evidence of plaque in other arteries, but we can take a wait-and-see approach to those. We're going to hold him overnight for observation, but we should be able to release him in the morning."

Mia thanked the doctor. They exchanged contact information, and he left to continue his rounds. Lin collapsed onto a chair. "This is my fault. I should have known Ravello's system couldn't take a sudden switch to a healthy lifestyle."

Mia and Elisabetta sat down on either side of her. "Lin, the switch probably slowed down the deterioration of his arteries and saved his life."

Elisabetta gave a vigorous nod. "What Mia said."

She handed Lin a large, crocheted square in bilious colors. "*Ecco.* To wipe your eyes. You can keep it."

Lin looked askance at Elisabetta's hideous handiwork but responded with polite appreciation. She dried her eyes and stood up. "I'm going to spend the night here with Ravello."

"I'll stay too," Shane said. "As a precaution."

Overwhelmed with gratitude, it took every ounce of self-restraint on Mia's part not to throw herself into his arms and sob all over his suit jacket. "You all go back to the rehearsal dinner," she told the others. "I know everyone there is worried. Let them know what happened and that Dad will be fine."

"You sure?" Teri asked.

Mia nodded.

"Won't the party be over by now?" Evans asked.

"I texted Cammie, and she said the Spizzwinks old and new are still singing. They were founded over a hundred years ago, so I guess they know a lotta songs."

Cammie replaced Lin in the seat next to Mia. "I'll stick around with you and Elisabetta. Pete, you help the others get back. I'll meet up with you back at the B&B. And shoot a text to the real estate agent about the last condo we saw to find out if that's the owner's best price. That view . . ."

Cammie mimed a chef's kiss. The expression on Pete's face made Mia fear he'd be joining Ravello in a hospital room. "Okay, hon," he croaked.

Lin and Shane left to find Ravello. Pete led the rehearsal dinner contingent back to the party, leaving Cammie with Mia and Elisabetta. Mia noticed her grandmother looked drawn and worn out. "We should get you back to the B&B, Nonna."

"I don't need sleep, I need food." Elisabetta patted her stomach and whined, "*Sono fame.*"

"Me too," Cammie said. "I'm starving."

"I could eat," Mia agreed. "Let's find a place. It's the 'burbs, though, so it may be tough at this hour."

They exited the ER to the street. Elisabetta grabbed Mia's arm. "*Guarda, guarda*! Look!"

Mia looked to where her grandmother was pointing to see a neon sign reading LA FAMILIA ITALIAN CUISINE, along with a neon Italian flag. A smaller neon sign announced it was open. "We're in luck," Mia said. "They must stay open for the hospital employees and visitors. Let's go."

"Real food." Elisabetta crossed herself and gazed upward. "*Grazie Dio.*"

"You gotta try this eggplant parm," Cammie said. "It's delish."

Within twenty minutes of entering the restaurant, the three women were gorging on traditional Italian dishes, along with a bottle of Montepulciano wine. The setting was equally traditional, befitting a restaurant whose menu proudly announced it had been in business for fifty years. The décor of paneled walls, red vinyl banquet seating, and faded posters of Italian hot spots circa 1970 confirmed this.

Elisabetta, whose health and energy were restored by the meal, scraped the last bite from her plate. "I never been so glad to see lasagna *in vita mia.*" She helped herself to a taste of Cammie's eggplant parmigiana, then gestured to Mia's barely eaten plate of spaghetti and meatballs with her fork. "You gonna finish that?"

Mia pushed the plate toward her grandmother. "It's all yours. I don't have much of an appetite. I can't stop thinking about what happened to Dad." She took a shaky sip of wine to quell her emotions. "It's embarrassing to admit, but I kind of thought he'd live forever. This is a real wake-up call."

"Hella *si.*" Elisabetta took a bite of meatball. "You never want your children to go before you. If anyone's gonna croak around here, it should be me."

"Nonna, no!" Mia cried out. "Don't even think that. You need to live forever, too."

"No, it's true. Look at me. I don't eat good." She referenced the meatball, then took another bite of it. "I don't get much exercise. I'm an old lady. Cammie, I'm saying this here so Mia can't say she didn't know. My will is in a Polly-O ricotta container under my bed. Not the whole-milk container. That one's got my wedding ring and a couple of other pieces of jewelry in it. The will's in the part-skim container."

"Elisabetta, I'm honored you gifted me with this knowledge," Cammie said, choking up. "Should we talk about any other details? Funeral arrangements? You know, music, the luncheon, favorite flowers—"

"Stop!" Mia waved her hands in the air. "Let's talk about something more pleasant, like murder." A waiter picking the cash tip from the table next to them paused and shot Mia a nervous look. He pocketed the tip and quickly moved on. Mia faced Cammie. "Has Pete shared anything new with you about Giles's murder, or the poisoned water bottle, or what happened to Michael? Even the smallest, tiniest clue would help."

"Believe me, I've tried to pull something out of

him. I spent a hundred bucks—his money, of course—on new lingerie and modeled it for him. Nothing. I don't get why he's holding back. I think that, aside from Little Donny, no one else has a hard target on them. At least that NYPD has been able to zero in on. It's nuts when you think about it. There's tons of video to sift through. That's all these people do. Film stuff. But so far, Pete hasn't found anything incriminating anyone."

"I wonder if that's intentional." Mia put an elbow on the table and rested her chin on her fist. "It's like what magicians call misdirection. I've met enough of them through children's parties at Belle View to get how they work. They steer your focus one way so you don't notice what they're doing the other way."

"How does this apply here?" Cammie asked.

"If a crew member knows where the camera's going to focus, they also know where it's *not* going to focus, and that's the sweet spot for where they can commit a crime. You know, like they make sure they're safely off camera when it comes time to get rid of Giles or poison Ariadne's water bottle. Which makes it much more likely this is an inside job on the part of someone with Giles St. James Productions rather than Little Donny."

"What about Michael's head injury? It was you and him. No cameras."

"I know. With all the puzzle pieces here, that's the piece that feels like it's from a different puzzle. Then again, someone could have followed us and, knowing how popular Little Island is, blended in with the crowd to give him a shove, then disappeared." Something niggled at Mia. She rubbed her eyes. "I'm missing something. It flashed through my brain and disappeared. Argh." Her phone pinged a text. She read it, and her mood lightened. "It's from Shane. He's with Dad. He said Dad's awake and feeling good. The doctor says they can release him in the morning."

Elisabetta closed her eyes and muttered a prayer. She crossed herself and opened her eyes. Mia saw tears in them. She took her grandmother's hands in her own and squeezed them. Tears dripped down Mia's own cheeks. "Thank God. I was so worried." She took a hand off her grandmother's and placed it on her heart. "I swear, I feel like I may faint. Considering how many people have done that around me lately, I feel like I'm owed a turn."

Cammie placed a hand on her shoulder. "You're tired. Let's get you back to the B&B." She waved a credit card at the waiter. "I'm adding three cannolis to go. Don't worry, it's all on Pete."

"You mind putting in another order for lasagna?" Elisabetta asked. "I can have it for breakfast."

Haunted by the evening's events, Mia slept fitfully. But the morning brought good news. Not only was Ravello officially released from the hospital, Delany, Madison's official maid of honor, was out of rehab and ready to resume her duties. This allowed Mia to return to the less-demanding position of bridesmaid.

Since she wasn't required to show up at Pilgrim's Perch until late afternoon, to prepare for the evening wedding, Mia spent the morning helping Lin relocate Ravello from the hospital to a suite at their hotel. The couple planned to rest for a few days and pay a follow-up visit to the cardiologist who'd inserted the stent to make sure Ravello was in the best shape possible before they traveled back to Queens. They sent their regrets to Jamie and Madison, sad to miss the wedding. "But," Ravello told his daughter when they had a moment alone, "there may be another wedding in our future. Mine."

"Oh, Dad . . ." Mia teared up.

Ravello put a finger to his lips. "Shhh. It's not gonna happen for a while. I gotta be at a hundred percent when I pop the question. I don't want poor Lin to think she's signing on as a nursemaid."

"I won't say a word. But I'm excited to have a stepparent I actually like." Her mother Gia's second husband having been an odious and dangerous thug, Mia couldn't have been more sincere.

After a quick brunch with Ravello and Lin, Mia returned to the capacious Victorian bed and breakfast where she and Elisabetta were staying, along with the Belle View crew. Unfortunately, several of the *Dons of Ditmars Boulevard* crew and wedding guests were also being housed at the B&B. Mia committed herself to ignoring them. She needed a break from the drama they constantly manufactured. This day was about Jamie and Madison finally tying the knot. Everything else, including proving Little Donny's innocence, could go on hold, at least through the weekend.

Mia entered the B&B's lobby, a confection of antiques set against a backdrop of white wainscotting and chandeliers dangling from ornately carved plaster medallions. She poked her head into the front parlor to see if Elisabetta might be there. She wasn't, but the production company's middle-aged accounting intern, Jason, was. He sat at the room's antique secretary's desk, vigorously typing on a laptop. A file folder sat next to the computer. "Hi, Jason," Mia said.

Jason started, letting out a cry, startling her in return. He quickly closed his computer. "Sorry. I didn't hear you come in."

"No reason you should. I was just looking for my grandmother."

"Haven't seen her."

He rose from his chair, tucked his laptop under his arm, and hurried from the room. *Okay, that was weird*, Mia thought. She glanced back to make sure he was gone, then went to the desk. In his haste, he'd forgotten to take the file folder. Mia saw it was marked "Private and Confidential." She debated for all of a second, then opened it. The top sheet titled "ASJ" listed items like cars, apartments, and travel. She peeked under it at what appeared to be a daily log of Ariadne's activities

Mia heard heavy footsteps and quickly closed the file. Jason appeared in the archway. "I was going to come look for you," she said with the sunniest smile she could muster. "You forgot this."

She picked up the file and handed it to him. He responded with a look that spooked her, then muttered a thank-you, and slunk away.

Mia was pondering Jason's strange behavior when her grandmother appeared in the archway. She held a large gift bag. "Good, you're back," Elisabetta said.

"Is that for Dad?" Mia had already brought her

grandmother up to speed via a phone call on the car ride back from her father's hotel. There'd been no mention of a gift.

"No, it's for you. I woke up early and finished it."

She handed over the bag. Mia reached in and brought out a beautifully crocheted black slip dress. "Nonna . . . this is gorgeous. Is it a swimsuit cover?"

"Swimsuit? Meh, what are you talking about? It's a dress. It goes over the slip in the bag. You can change into it after the ceremony for the reception." She started up the staircase, motioning for Mia to follow. "*Andiamo.* I want to see it on you."

Once inside her B&B bedroom, Mia retrieved a black slip from the bottom of the gift bag. She removed her jeans and T-shirt, replacing them with the slip and crocheted sheath, which she guessed weighed a good five pounds, probably more. Still, she couldn't deny her grandmother had finally created something classy and flattering, even if it was the heaviest piece of apparel she'd ever worn. "I love it," she told her grandmother, happy not to be lying about one of her grandmother's crocheted creations for a change. "It's perfect for the reception. *Mille grazie, Nonna.*" She showered a beaming Elisabetta with kisses.

"I'm glad. I know it's not so colorful, but I ran out of the other yarns. Don't worry. I'm gonna get a big bag when I get home and make you something that'll be like wearing a rainbow."

"Yay." Mia tried her best to sound enthusiastic. To her relief, her grandmother bought it.

Once Elisabetta left, Mia focused her energy on preparing for the wedding. She napped for an hour, after which she showered and used hot rollers to turn her long, dark brown hair into a mass of luxurious waves. She applied makeup, outlining her eyes with a navy that accentuated their bright blue and opting for lipstick in a subtle, natural tone. Makeup and hair completed, she slipped on her bridesmaid's dress. As usual, Madison's terrific taste made for a fabulous choice of a tea-length gown in a pale steel blue chiffon cut on the bias with a deep V-neckline. As a veteran of hideous bridesmaid's gowns that friends and relatives insisted "you can wear out for parties after the wedding," Mia was thrilled to finally own one that lived up to the promise.

She slid on silver Jimmy Choo sandals, then picked up the on-trend silver mesh clutch purse Madison had gifted to her bridesmaids, in addition to a simple silver bracelet from which a small heart dangled. Mia checked out her reflection in the bedroom's full-length mirror. Satisfied with the image reflected back to her, she went to the room's large bay window to see if the limo that was to transport her to Pilgrim's Perch had arrived yet. Instead, a far more interesting sight met her eyes.

Nicky Vestri pulled into the B&B's circular driveway in his ostentatious black Cadillac Escalade with tinted windows. He hopped out of the car, glancing around nervously. He lit a cigarette and affected a casual pose. Violet, dressed in a snug satin suit whose color matched her name, came out of the B&B and went to him. They exchanged a few words, and he extended a hand to her as if to shake. But instead, he pulled her toward him for an extremely unbusinesslike kiss. They separated reluctantly. He helped her into the passenger seat, hopped into the driver's seat, and tore out of the driveway.

Considering Nicky's date to the wedding was Ariadne and that Violet hadn't been invited to the wedding, Mia was unable to resist marking this odd development. She broke her vow to ignore all things related to *The Dons of Ditmars Boulevard* and texted what she'd witnessed to Teri Fuoco. The reporter instantly responded with an exclamation mark. Mia put away her phone and once again checked the driveway for the limo. She raised both eyebrows at an even more surprising sight. A familiar face crept out of the woods. But someone lingered behind. Mia leaned in closer to the window to get a better look. She saw a flash of white and suddenly recalled the missing image she'd blanked on at during dinner the night before. She sucked in a breath and grabbed her phone to text Teri about yet another development. Teri shot back a row of exclamation marks.

Mia sat on the bed. She contemplated a theory, running through events dating back to the day of Giles's murder to see if they lined up to verify it. Elisabetta yelling from outside her bedroom door snapped her out of it. "Messina Carina, the limo is here. Didn't you hear the honking? It's driving us *pazzo*!"

"Oops. Sorry."

Mia stuffed her phone into her evening bag and ran from her room to the limo waiting outside. Sleuthing would have to wait. She had a wedding to attend.

Chapter 27

The rose garden at Pilgrim's Perch, where the wedding ceremony would take place, basked in the golden glow of twilight. The scent from the garden's wide variety of roses perfumed the air. Mia huddled with her fellow attendants in a patch of wooded glen next to the garden, staying out of sight from the guests. Not wanting to reveal her dress to her groom until she walked down the aisle, Madison chose to have photos taken of the entire bridal party after she and Jamie were officially man and wife. But she'd given the go-ahead for the photographer to take pictures of the bridal party without them prior to the ceremony, so at least that task was done.

Mia peeked through the trees to study the arriving guests. Chiara came on Little Donny's arm. She threw him annoyed glances he didn't see because his eyes were on Ariadne, arriving on the arm of Nicky. Any hope Donny had of making her jealous seemed ill-fated. She seemed the definition of a woman who'd moved on.

Aside from donette Francesca, whose parents were long-time friends of the Boldano family, there were no other guests from *The Dons of Ditmars Boulevard.* Forbidden to film the ceremony, crew members from the show hovered discreetly on the sidelines.

"Mia," a woman's voice hissed. "*Mia.*"

Mia turned to see Teri beckoning to her. They rendezvoused under a large sugar maple tree. "Update. I saw—"

"No names," Mia cautioned. "The trees have ears. Okay, that sounded nuts, but you know what I mean."

"I do. I saw suspect number one making what looked like a very sneaky phone call. So I 'accidentally' "—Teri mimed air quotes—"bumped into them and knocked the phone to the ground. When I apologized and picked it up to return, guess who was on the other end of the call?"

"Suspect number two."

"Exactly."

"Did you tell Pete?"

"Instantly. He's got an eye out. On a couple of people."

Noise from the garden caught the women's attention. They turned to see Nicky suddenly leap up from his white folding chair. He reached into his inside jacket pocket. Mia gripped Teri's arm.

"Don't anybody move!" the don yelled. The guests froze. He removed his hand from his jacket . . . and tossed a handful of flower petals into the air. "Since Jamie and Madison don't have a flower girl or boy, I'm the flower dude."

He removed a plastic bag stuffed with petals from under his chair and sashayed down the aisle, scattering petals on the white carpet leading to the arbor where Jamie and Madison would exchange vows. The guests laughed and applauded. Nicky did a victory dance a la Rocky Balboa in the movie *Rocky* and sauntered back to his seat next to Ariadne. Mia and Teri were close enough to hear their exchange. "Got it," Ariadne said, holding up her cell phone.

"Awesome. They can cut it into the other footage, right?" The producer responded with a yes. Nicky put his arm around her shoulders and leaned back in his chair with a self-satisfied smirk.

"If I murdered him," Mia whispered to Teri, "there's not a jury in the world that would convict me."

"It would be like the Agatha Christie book where the killers lined up for their turn to take a knife to a horrible guy," Teri agreed.

A bagpipe's screech startled them. Madison's uncle Garrison, clad in full Scottish attire down to the kilt of his Campbell clan, assumed position at the head of the bridal party, who lined up behind him. "The ceremony's starting," Mia said to Teri. "Go sit. I'll touch base with you after."

Teri left to join the Belle View crew. Garrison, blowing a bagpipe tune that sounded a tad mournful to Mia's ears, led the bridal party down the aisle. When they reached the arbor, the men and women split off, with ushers going right to the groom's side and bridesmaids forming a row on the left in front of the bride's friends and relatives. A string quartet took over musical duties, playing soothing classical music as Aurora and Big Donny slow-walked Jamie down the aisle. He looked supremely elegant in his peak-lapel traditional tuxedo.

His parents kissed him, wiped tears from their eyes, and took their seats next to their family priest, who would not be performing the ceremony. That honor fell to Uncle Garrison, who turned out to be a retired minister. Mia wasn't sure which Christian denomination he represented. They tended to blend together in her mind.

Uncle Garrison put down his bagpipes. The quartet paused. The guests rose to their feet. Madison appeared at the top of the aisle, a parent on each arm. She looked stunning in a wedding gown handed down through generations of brides on her mother's side. It was a simple 1930s ivory satin gown cut on the bias, embellished with delicate crystal flowers around the V-neckline. A satin cap trailing a lace veil topped her beautifully coiffed blond hair. Her beauty earned a well-deserved gasp from the guests.

The quartet played Madison down the aisle to Jamie's side, where her parents bid her goodbye. As the sun setting in the west cast a glow over Long Island Sound in the east and Jamie and Madison exchanged heartfelt personal vows, Mia recalled her own impulsive, slapdash wedding to the hopefully deceased philanderer Adam Grosso. *I want this someday,* she thought, filled with emotion. *A real wedding with a man I know I'll spend the rest of my life with, in front of all the people I love more than anything in the world except for him.*

Mia removed a tissue hidden in her bouquet and dabbed her eyes. She felt the sudden sensation of someone watching her. She looked to the guests, and her eyes met Shane's. His eyes also glistened with tears. The expression on his face, a combination of longing and sadness, made her heart clutch. She tore her eyes off him to ward off bursting into tears.

"I now pronounce you husband and wife," uncle and officiant Garrison Campbell declared. Jamie and Madison kissed to whoops and cheers. Garrison picked up his bagpipes and blew a loud note to punctuate the moment. The newlyweds marched triumphantly up the aisle, followed by their bridal party.

After posing for the requisite photos, Mia was relieved from bridesmaid duty. She found a powder room on the main floor where she changed into Nonna's crocheted creation and black ballet flats before joining her friends and Elisabetta in the party tent, where the reception was in full swing. "Awesome dress," Teri said. "One of yours, Elisabetta?"

"*Si*," the elder Carina answered with pride. "I'll make you one. My connection says she got a ton of orange and lime green yarn waiting for me."

"Orange and lime green, huh? Wow." Mia enjoyed seeing the reporter become slightly green herself.

Cammie and Pete appeared, each carrying a plate of appetizers. "Big improvement on the rehearsal dinner," Pete said, munching on a giant shrimp. "Can't say I'm a fan of aerosol cheese."

Mia pulled him aside. "Any developments regarding the suspects I mentioned?"

Pete shook his head. "I've had my eyes on them all night. I guess crime's taking the night off to enjoy the wedding."

The loud braying of Uncle Garrison's bagpipe made everyone jump. He spoke into the DJ's microphone. "If you will all turn your attention to the

Sound, we're celebrating the marriage of Jamie and Madison with fireworks."

Guests crowded to the side of the tent featuring a vista of Long Island Sound. All the lights in the tent went off, plunging the party into darkness. There was a rumble, then a massive multicolored display erupted in the sky. The guests reacted with delight, oohing and ahhing at each explosion. The show finished with a truly impressive display of one heart exploding into another and another until the sky filled with hearts. The guests roared their appreciation.

The hearts disintegrated, replaced by the pitch black of night. The lights suddenly popped on, along with the song "Celebrate!" by Kool and the Gang. Mia's friends took to the dance floor, leaving her alone, blinking to adjust her eyes to the brighter environment. She saw Donny Junior searching the crowd, a perturbed expression on his face. In another corner of the tent, Nicky was doing the same thing. They each noticed Mia and made their way to her.

"Whoa," Mia said. She spread her arms out wide. "Safe distance, please. I don't trust the two of you getting near each other."

"I don't care about him," Little Donny said with disdain. "I'm looking for Chiara. I haven't seen her since the fireworks started."

"Same deal here," Nicky said. "I can't find Ariadne."

Alarm bells louder than Uncle Garrison's bagpipe sounded in Mia's head. "They're both missing, huh? Excuse me."

She ran onto the dance floor, elbowing her way past party revelers until she located Cammie and

Pete, who were doing the bump to KC and the Sunshine Band's hit song "Get Down Tonight." Mia yelled over the music to get Pete's attention. "Ariadne and Chiara are missing."

"This is Cammie's favorite song." Pete tapped hips with his ex-wife. "They're probably in the little girls' room."

"You know that's doubtful, and never call it the 'little girls' room' again. It sounds sexist and a little pedophiliac." She grabbed his arm. "We have to find them before something terrible happens."

"It's okay, hon," Cammie said to Pete. "I can dance with someone else."

She reached out to a handsome twenty-something groomsman and yanked him onto the dance floor. Pete glared at Mia but followed her off the dance floor.

The two rounded up Evans, Teri, and Guadalupe to join Little Donny and Nicky in the hunt for the missing women. Shane ran up to the group as it was leaving the tent. "What's going on? Something is, I can tell." Mia explained the situation. "I want to help," he declared. "I've been wandering around the grounds doing a lot of thinking, and I know the layout of this place pretty well by now."

Much as Mia wanted to press Shane on what he was thinking about during his wanders, she restrained herself. "Fine. Let's go."

The group scored flashlights from Uncle Garrison's housekeeper. After scouring the woods to no avail, they moved on to the coastline. "There!" Evans shouted. "I see someone!"

Mia shone her flashlight on an outcropping of rocks along the edge of the water. The bright light exposed a gagged-and-bound Ariadne being hustled over the rocks by Chiara and a cohort. Mia moved her flashlight, revealing the donette's partner in crime to be none other than segment producer Michael Planko. The large white bandage on the back of his head confirmed he was the person Mia had spotted rendezvousing with Chiara in the woods outside the B&B.

"Are they filming this?" Guadalupe asked, perplexed. "Is it for the show?"

Mia's flashlight illuminated Ariadne's expression of sheer terror. "No," she said tersely. "For a change, this is very, very real."

Chapter 28

"Stop in the name of the law!" Pete yelled down to the three on the rocks.

Whether they didn't hear him due to the crashing waves or chose to ignore him, Chiara and Michael moved toward the sea with their captive. They stumbled on the rocks but managed to regain their footing.

The others ran toward them. Nicky hesitated. "Is it safe? It looks like high tide, and I'm wearing my best shoes."

Little Donny shoved him out of the way. Nicky gave an angry cry and grabbed Little Donny's ankle, taking his cousin down with him. Mia leaped over them. Unencumbered by heels or slippery Italian leather soles, she reached the miscreants and their prisoner first.

Chiara flashed a switchblade at her. "Don't even think of trying anything," she said with a snarl. "I'll cut her."

"Switchblade? 'Cut her?' What, did you fall into

a time tunnel to the nineteen-fifties?" Mia deftly negotiated the rocks.

"Honey, don't go rogue," Michael cautioned Chiara. "Remember our original plan."

"There is no plan anymore, you moron!" the donette screamed at him. "We can't kill Ariadne now. We can only use her as a hostage to trade so we can get away."

"Oh. Right." Sweat streamed down Michael's nervous face. "This is way more complicated than in the movies."

He and Chiara scrambled up a rocky outcropping that formed a low cliff above the water. Angry waves crashed too close for comfort as Mia scrambled after them, followed by the others.

"I'm warning you, Mia."

Chiara delivered this with a snarl. She swung her switchblade around, finishing with a poke in Ariadne's side. The producer let out a cry muffled by the gaffer's tape over her mouth.

Michael let go of Ariadne's arm. "I don't like this plan. It's got a stink on it."

He began scrambling over rocks to reach flat land and get away. Apparently still feeling the after-effects of his injury, Michael staggered. But he regained control and took off running. Pete and Evans gave chase. "Loser!" Chiara yelled after him.

With Chiara distracted by Michael's defection, Mia saw an opportunity and went for it. She whipped off her crocheted dress and flung it over the ruthless donette. The dress acted as a net, trapping Chiara. She struggled to free herself, letting go of Ariadne in the process. Still bound by tape, Ariadne fought not to lose her balance. As Mia reached out to grab the producer, the heart on her silver bracelet snagged on a crochet stitch, attaching her to Chiara. The donette tumbled backward, dragging Mia and Ariadne with her, and the three women fell off the cliff into the water below, narrowly missing the jagged rocks.

Mia let go of Ariadne, who rolled herself toward shore. The water wasn't deep, about four feet or so, but unable to detach herself from Chiara, Mia was in danger of drowning with her. She realized too late that, once drenched with water, Nonna's crocheted creation had turned into an anchor. Mia swallowed seawater as Chiara thrashed and alternated choking on the water with screaming a stream of panicked profanity the likes of which probably hadn't been heard on the Connecticut coast since a whaling ship sank in the nineteenth century.

Exhausted by the effort to save herself, Mia was a step away from giving up and bidding a silent goodbye to her loved ones when strong hands reached under her arms and pulled her up. She found herself face-to-face with Shane. Meanwhile, Evans did the same with Chiara. He grabbed the switchblade she'd managed to hold on to and brought it down on the tangled stitch attached to Mia's bracelet, finally separating the two women. Evans dragged Chiara through the water to the shore. But Shane lifted Mia into his arms. "You can put me down now," she told him when they got to dry land.

"I don't want to."

"Please."

He reluctantly released her to standing. But he

kept his arms around her. Sopping wet and freezing despite the warm evening air, Mia didn't object.

Pete hurried toward them, huffing from overly exerting himself. He took off his jacket and handed it to Mia. "You look cold. Here."

"Th-th-thank you."

"Hold on."

He pulled a pair of handcuffs from one of the pockets. "You carry those with you to parties?" Mia asked, slipping on the coat.

"To be honest," Pete said, moonlight exposing his blush, "they were for later if I got lucky with Cammie."

"Of course they were." Mia pulled the jacket close around her. "What happened to Michael? Did he get away?"

Pete grinned. "He wishes."

He gestured over his shoulder. The others looked in the direction he indicated. Guadalupe loped toward them. She had the segment producer in a chokehold and dragged him along with her. "We done here? I don't wanna miss the wedding cake."

"Almost," Pete said. "Worthington PD is on the way."

"The injury made me do it," Michael said with a whimper. "It affected my brain."

"Nice try," Mia snapped. Cold and still recovering emotionally from her near-death experience, she had no patience for his bull. "You were in perfectly good health when you killed Giles."

The segment producer began protesting, but Pete cut him off. "Save it for whatever squirrely defense you try pulling on a jury." The detective motioned to Guadalupe, who dragged her captive closer to the detective. Pete slapped one cuff on Michael and the other on Chiara. "Michael Planko and Chiara . . . what's your last name?"

"I never use it," the donette said, trying to hold on to one last shred of dignity. "I wanna be one-name famous."

"Fine," Pete said. "Michael Planko and Chiara One Name Famous, you're under arrest for murder, attempted murder, and ruining my flippin' evening."

Chapter 29

Mia sat at a table under the party tent, surrounded by her friends. She wrapped herself tightly with the Campbell plaid shawl Uncle Garrison graciously lent her. Elisabetta had already left the party, taking Mia's bridesmaids dress with her, so the kind host also donated a kilt and accompanying garments for Mia to change into after she showered off the seawater from her ocean tumble.

"You look like you should come with a side of haggis," Teri commented about her outfit.

"Unfortunately, Nonna's dress didn't survive Chiara."

"I'm happy to donate whatever creation she's crocheting for me. Orange and lime green are definitely your colors."

Mia gave Teri the side-eye. "They are so not. Besides, I wouldn't want to miss the sight of you in that creation."

Teri held up a beer bottle to Mia. "Touché."

Jamie and Madison approached the table hand

in hand. "Are you alright?" Madison asked Mia, concern etched on her face.

"Fine. I'm so sorry those criminals hijacked your wedding celebration."

"Are you kidding? Worthington hasn't seen this much drama since the Women's League changed the date of their annual bake sale from spring to fall."

The bride and groom pulled chairs between Evans and Guadalupe "It sounded like everybody had it out for that Giles guy, including Donny," Jamie said.

"You're right about that," Mia said.

"So what made you suspect Chiara and the producer?"

Mia finished the last drop of wine from a glass Shane had thoughtfully fetched for her. "When it came to motive, it was pretty much a case of take a number. And we were all at Casa Giovanni when Giles was killed, so we all had access to the barbells. But something didn't sit right. With all the filming they were doing, it seemed pretty convenient everything around the pool house, the murder site, was off-limits. That reduced the suspect list to whoever had the power to make that decision, which was basically the producers, which included Michael, and Brian, the director, a guy who had one foot out the door the entire time he worked on the show."

Shane appeared at Mia's side holding another glass of white wine. Like Mia, he'd traded his wet clothes for one of Garrison's donated kilts, as had Evans. Shane handed her the wine. "I thought you could use another one."

"Good call. Thank you."

Their fingers touched as he transferred the glass to her. They exchanged a heated look, then broke eye contact. "No problem," Shane mumbled.

He took a seat across the table, putting distance between him and Mia. She inhaled a breath to steady herself, then exhaled and continued. "There was something else that made me think they might be in on it together. It happened at the airport in New Orleans. Chiara was still weak from drinking the poisoned water. Michael was helping her sit down in the lounge, and there was an interaction between them that seemed . . . intimate. I thought he winked at her but wasn't sure, so I forgot about it. But it came back to me when I looked out my B&B window this morning and saw her sneaking out of the woods, and then a flash of white that I could see was a bandage on a man's head. I'm guessing they were going over their plot to get rid of Ariadne by making it look like she went for a walk during the wedding and slipped and fell to her death in the ocean."

Madison scrunched her face. "It's all so confusing. Why did they do it? In New Orleans, was the water in the bottle really poisoned? I don't get it."

Cammie briefly took the conversational reins. "We'll know more once Pete gets one of them to rat on the other. He and Worthington PD are escorting Chiara and Michael back to Queens to face charges. My money's on that Michael guy breaking first. He was crying when Pete put him in the patrol car." She gave a shudder of delight. "Pete's so hot when he's in tough-cop mode." She pointed a finger at the group. "Do *not* tell him I said that. It'll tip the balance of our relationship toward him, and I will *not* be happy."

"I can answer the water question," Mia said. "Yes, it was poisoned. My guess is by Michael and Chiara, and she grabbed it by accident. Something else just came back to me. When Chiara was sick on the street in New Orleans and Michael and Ariadne tried to help, he asked me where the water bottle was. But Kelvin told me Ariadne was being stingy with the bottles. He was trying to get people to drink from cups to make the water go farther. So, how did Michael know Chiara got sick from a water *bottle*?"

"He'd know if he and/or she were the ones who poisoned it and marked it for Ariadne," Teri said. "You can bet the executive producer wasn't drinking from some Dixie cup. And I'll take a crack at the why, Madison. A murderer's motivational trifecta: fame, power, and money." She mimed climbing a ladder. "One leads to the next, then the next, then the next."

Jamie stood up. "You'll have to text us updates. But now my *wife* and I have to get ready for our flight in the morning."

"Where you headed on your honeymoon?" Evans asked.

"Where else? Italia!"

Jamie took Madison's hand and led her in a brief tarantella. The others laughed and applauded. Madison grew teary. "I love you all. You're my new family."

"Awww." Everyone laughed at how they said this in unison.

After a long round of hugs and best wishes,

Jamie managed to coax Madison away. They left to make the rounds of other guests, finally reaching Little Donny, who was sitting by himself at a distant, empty table. Donny gave the happy couple emotional hugs goodbye. Once Jamie and Madison departed, Donny sat down again. He fiddled with a full tumbler, his expression alternating between wistful and glum.

Mia felt for the Boldano's eldest offspring. "Little Donny's by himself."

"That happens when your date's arrested for murder," Teri said.

"We invited him to join us, but he passed." Guadalupe held up a cake plate. "I got his piece of cake. A little heavy on the buttercream, but not bad."

"I'll go talk to him," Shane said.

He started to rise, but Mia held up her hand. "No, I will. I promised Mr. B I'd keep an eye on him."

She left the group's table for Little Donny's, where she pulled up a chair next to him. "Hey," she said, sitting down.

"Hey." He didn't look up from his tumbler.

"I'm sorry about Chiara."

He shrugged. "No big surprise there. I only brought her as my date because I was ticked off at Ariadne for hooking up with Nicky. I get what Ariadne's about now. She's what my dad calls an operator."

"Yes, she is. I'm glad you finally see that."

He gave a mirthless snort. "Took me long enough." He nursed his drink. "Nicky was right about one thing. I *am* a loser. And everyone knows it."

An emotional Mia placed a hand on her friend's arm. "You are not, Donny. Are you perfect? No. You can be a pain and arrogant and kind of a—"

"Could you move on to the part where this is supposed to make me feel better?"

"Yes, right. You're a truly good person. You're smart and funny and passionate. I know when you find someone truly worth giving your heart to, you will make an amazing boyfriend and husband someday, and a great dad. You *will* find your purpose in life. But to be honest, I don't think it's as a reality star. I'm sorry. I don't mean to hurt your feelings."

"You're not. Being on one of these shows is way less fun than I thought it would be. Especially with people getting murdered and stuff." He pushed his drink away. "Thanks for not writing me off like everyone else. It means a lot to me."

"I think more people have faith in you than you know."

He glanced at Mia, and she saw something in his eyes she hadn't seen in a long time—hope.

The Belle View crew walked over to their table. "We're going to an after-party on someone's big sailboat," Evans said to Mia. "Apparently that's a thing in these parts. Y'all wanna come with?"

"Why not?" Little Donny said. "Might as well finish off the night with some fun. Or seasickness. Or both. Mia?"

Mia rubbed an abrasion on her leg. She winced. The injuries from her fall into the water and struggle with Chiara were minor but still painful. "I think I'll pass. I'm pretty wiped out by everything."

"Understood," Evans said with a sympathetic nod.

"I'll pass too," Shane said. He made a tentative offer to Mia. "I can give you a lift to the B&B."

Too tired to debate whether close proximity to Shane in a car was a good idea, she accepted the ride. "But first we need to make plans with Uncle Garrison to return these." She gestured to her kilt and Shane's.

Teri snapped her fingers like she was having a "Eureka!" moment. "I finally figured out what your outfit's missing." She flashed an impish grin. "Bagpipes."

Chapter 30

A couple of empty days on Belle View's event calendar allowed Mia to take a day off from work and get a late start the day after. She used the time to pay her brother Posi a visit.

She was happy to see regular guard and family friend Henry Marcus on duty in the Triborough Correctional Facility's visitor's room. "Henry, so glad you're back. How was Disney World?"

"Lotta walking in the heat and humidity for a man my age," said the guard, who Mia pegged as being in his early sixties. "I got what they call Disney Rash. My legs were red all over. I'll show you a picture."

Henry called up a photo on his phone and showed it to Mia, who did a double take at the image of his two dark-brown calves covered with a flat, mottled red rash. "Henry, that looks awful. Was it painful?"

"Nah. Red and itchy is all."

"*Hellloooo.*" An annoyed Posi waved from where he sat behind the visiting room's shiny new table.

He waved to Mia. "Remember me? The person you're supposed to be visiting?

Mia wagged a finger at him. "Stop with the self-involvement. We owe Henry here a lot. If it wasn't for him, you'd be in solitary for that stunt you pulled at Belle View."

"Getting him off with a slap on the wrist didn't take much doing," Henry said with much modesty. "I explained to my superiors that Belle View was the family's business and Posi wanted to see his beloved sister. The temp guards owned up to not knowing the area and being distracted, which helped his case."

"Well, we can't thank you enough. And we'll remember what you did come Christmas and your birthday." Mia took a seat opposite her brother. "So they didn't slap any more time on your sentence?"

"They did not," Posi said with a cocky grin. "I'm good to go in nine months. Although I'll miss Henry."

"I'd say same goes here," Henry responded, "but you'll be back."

"You know me so well, my friend." Posi winked at the guard. Then an expression of concern replaced the grin. "Nonna came by yesterday. She told me about Dad."

"He's gonna be okay."

"Thank God." Posi crossed himself. The cocky grin reasserted itself. "Someone else stopped by. A guy by the name of Shane Gambrazzo."

Mia tensed. "What? Why?"

"To assure me his intentions to you were honorable—"

Mia bristled. "Why is that any of your business?

I'm the only one who should care about that. I make my own love-life choices."

"Says the woman who married professional lowlife Adam Grosso."

"Point taken," Mia said, abashed.

"He also asked my advice on how to handle the Petra Vilsni sitch."

"Why you? What kind of advice?" Mia asked this with alarm as she ran through a dozen possibilities, none legal and a couple lethal.

"Relax, sis. He came to me not as a mobster offspring but as one extremely handsome man to another."

"What did you tell him?"

"To flip the script. He made the mistake of telling Petra the truth. He needed a divorce because he wanted to be with someone else. Who wants to hear that?"

Mia pursed her lips. "I wouldn't have minded hearing it from my ex instead of him cheating on me behind my back."

"Stay on topic, please. I told Shane, go to Petra and sell that you're not good enough for her. Not by a mile. You've accepted that and have chosen to settle—"

"*Ouch.*"

Posi crossed his arms in front of his chest and gave her a baleful look. "You want him to get this divorce or not?"

"Yes," Mia said, still pouting.

"I told him to totally give her the upper hand. Let her announce to the world that she's the one divorcing him, shedding someone who isn't worthy of her and moving on with her life."

"That's really good advice."

"You're welcome."

"You're the best brother ever." Mia impulsively reached toward Posi to hug him, eliciting a warning from Henry. She sat back. "Sorry. I need to get to Belle View. Cammie texted Pete is there with updates on the Giles St. James murder."

Posi looked glum. "It sucks I'm not in that *Dons* pilot."

"No, it doesn't. If you don't believe me, I'll send Little Donny over for a talk."

On the drive away from the correctional facility, Mia allowed herself cautious optimism about the future of her relationship with Shane. She said a prayer that Petra responded positively to his new tack at securing a divorce.

When she reached Belle View, she found Pete in Cammie's office dismantling her podcast set up. "Moving on to the next hobby?" she asked her friend, amused.

"Yup. I've learned podcasting is not for me. I'm more of a visual than an aural person." Cammie pointed to her ears, from which dangled gaudy 1980s earrings.

Pete wound Bubble Wrap around a microphone the size of a forearm. "I wonder if I can make my money back selling this stuff online or if it's like a car, where you lose value the minute you drive it off the lot." He gave a glum sigh. "I'm guessing it's the second."

Mia dropped onto a folding chair. "So, you have updates on the Michael-Chiara sitch?"

"Yup. Whoever had money on Planko folding first can collect." Pete picked up an unopened box. "Cam Cam, please tell me you have a receipt for this so I can return it."

"I don't do paper receipts anymore. I'm trying to save the planet. But I hate all those e-mail receipts clogging up my inbox."

"So that's a no."

"You were saying Michael folded?" Mia prompted.

"The man's desperate to cut a deal. He's also desperate to have a successful show business career, which is what led to murder. Remember that day at Casa Giovanni when you overheard him and St. James going at it?"

"Since it's the day the guy was murdered, it's kind of hard to forget."

"The argument didn't end there. Planko followed him into the pool house to plead his case for a promotion. Giles finally made good on his threat to fire him, and Planko snapped. His words, because he won't come out and admit he bonked him on the head with barbell. But the dots are there to be connected."

"Saved his job and removed an obstacle," Mia commented.

"That was just the beginning. He found a partner in Chiara One Name Famous, who apparently never heard the old Hollywood joke about not sleeping with the writer to get ahead. He ratted on her as the brains of their lame operation."

"Brains being used loosely here."

"Oh yeah. They teamed up on a plot to get more screen time for Chiara and the promotion to executive producer for Planko. Ariadne was the next human bump in the road they had to remove. He insists poisoning the water bottle was Chiara's idea. But they got their wires crossed, and she didn't know Planko already planted and marked the bottle for Ariadne."

"I thought maybe Chiara drank it on purpose. It sure got her more screen time."

"The upside to an attempted murder gone wrong. But it wasn't enough for Ms. One Name."

"What about the attack on Michael when we were at Little Island? Or should I put quotes around the word attack?"

"Yes to that. Again, he says meeting with you and planting the fake story about the camera-woman and production assistant plotting to take over the company was all the donette's idea. She figured that would make Lysette and Kelvin suspects in St. James's murder and the attempt on Ariadne's life. On his partner's instructions, Planko faked the push that landed him in the river. He jumped in himself. Unfortunately, he hit his head on an old piling in the fall."

Dumbfounded, Mia took this in. "So basically, in trying to kill—or frame—other people, those two almost killed themselves."

"You have no idea how many dumb criminals I meet up with," Pete said. "I see TV shows and I wanna scream, How do you guys get these great cases when I'm across the table from a guy who committed a robbery barefoot so the shoeprint wouldn't give him away and then got his feet stuck to wet rock salt when he ran outside in winter?"

Cammie patted his cheek. "Poor baby, you have such a tough job."

He eyed her with a worried look. "You landed on a new expensive hobby, didn't you?"

"Maybe." She winked and blew him a frosted-pink lipstick kiss.

"Moving on," Mia said, to get Pete back on track.

"How did Violet figure into their plans? With her as co-owner of the company, she had to."

"The goal was to get rid of Ariadne and replace her with Violet. Being new to the business, Violet needed them more, and they assumed they could manipulate her better. But if Violet wasn't willing to promote Planko or make Chiara a reality star, you can bet her fluffy little kitty would've ended up orphaned."

"We're done, hon." Cammie clapped her hands together to rid her original white-lace fingerless gloves of dust they'd attracted.

"Your desk is clear now," Mia said. "Lots of room for the files from our bookings."

Cammie chortled. "I love how you think that's gonna happen."

Mia rose from her chair. "Thanks for the intel, Pete. I guess that's that."

"Not exactly." Pete assumed a crafty expression. "Before *The Dons of Ditmars Boulevard* even started casting, NYPD received an anonymous tip about some sketchy doings at Giles St James Productions. How would you like to take part in a sting operation?"

Chapter 31

Mia was a bundle of nerves waiting for the sting to commence the next day. Pete refused to give her any details about what he was planning. On his orders, she sent the cast and crew invitations to an impromptu screening of the *Dons of Ditmars Boulevard* pilot, which would take place in the second-floor Bay Ballroom. The first floor's Marina Ballroom was playing host to the goldfish memorial Shane had booked.

Mia peeked into the Marina Ballroom, where a slide show commemorating the lives of Bubbles, Buddy, and Goldie played on a large screen for the Woods family of four: father Tom, mother Kelly, ten-year-old Brianna, and grieving goldfish dad, six-year-old Justin.

"This is the sweetest thing," Mia whispered to Shane, who stood watching from the back of the room.

Shane, holding back his emotions, gave a brusque nod. "Just so you know, I'm not charging them for the room or the luncheon. Which will be fish-free.

I didn't bother to run this by you because if you didn't approve, I'd pay for it myself."

"Of course I approve." She noticed something orange sticking out from under Shane's arm. "What is that?"

"A goldfish." He showed her the large, adorable goldfish plushie under his arm. "I bought it for Justin. I thought it might make his loss a little less painful."

"Ooooh . . ." Mia swallowed back tears. "I'm sure he'll love it."

Hearing muted conversation coming from the lobby, Mia left to see Nicky Vestri enter, with Ariadne on his arm once again. She welcomed them with a polite greeting. "I need to freshen up," Ariadne told her date. "I'll meet you upstairs."

"You got it, babe."

He sent Ariadne off with a pat on the backside, much to Mia's disgust. She decided to confront him. "I saw you with Violet. Outside the B&B in Connecticut. I know you're up to something."

Nicky held up his hands. "Just keeping my options open. Like I do with all the super-hot ladies. Feel free to count yourself among them."

"Hard pass on that."

Nicky responded with a casual shrug. "By the way, Violet sends her regrets. She can't make it today. She had to take that furball of hers to get groomed. So I'm here with her co-boss. While she's in the john, I'm gonna give you one last chance. Say the word and I'll fit you into my sex schedule." He wiggled his eyebrows suggestively.

"You make me physically ill," Mia said, grossed out. "Go upstairs. *Now.*"

She dodged her own backside pat from the don, who scampered up to the Bay Ballroom.

Belle View's lobby double doors flew open, and the *Dons of Ditmars Boulevard* cast and crew poured in. The space rang with excited chatter about the pilot screening. Francesca gave Mia a hug. "How are you?" Mia asked. "I know you were kinda-sorta close to Chiara."

"I'm . . ." Francesca mimed her head exploding. "It's so crazy. I blame this stupid show. I'm never doing another one." She blushed and added shyly, "I registered for classes at Queens College."

"Francesca! That's so great."

The donette gave an embarrassed shrug. "Yeah, well, I decided instead of playing a feminist on TV, I should become one in real life. I'm gonna be a women's studies major. Who knows? Maybe I'll become a lawyer someday."

"If you become a defense attorney, you already have a client list." Mia gestured to the dons milling close together. The women chuckled without any idea how prophetic Mia's joke would prove to be.

Director Lysette stood in front of a large screen Belle View kept on hand for when organizations renting out the banquet facilities needed to display visuals at their events. "Welcome, everyone, to our surprise screening."

"It's a surprise to me, and I'm the producer," Ariadne said with a flip of her dark mane, to scattered laughter from the attendees.

"Just to warn you, this is a rough cut," Lysette said. "Some of the footage is grainy. Especially where it was shot by a hidden cell phone camera."

A murmur of confusion and fear rippled through the viewers. Mia, standing in the back, found herself joined by Pete, his partner Ryan, and several uniformed officers.

Lysette gave the high sign to Kelvin, who was operating an electronic projector. A logo for *The Dons of Ditmars Boulevard* flashed on the screen, earning applause and whoops from the cast. However, the scene appearing onscreen was new to everyone. As Lysette warned, it was shaky and grainy. Nicky sat on the bed in his New Orleans hotel room, talking to a couple of his fellow dons. "I'm telling you, the crew on this thing is a bunch of idiots. They got no protection on what they're shooting. My hacker's got copies of every scene. I got a guy in China I already sold a few days of stuff to. You gotta come in on it with me."

"Wha-wha-wha . . ." Nicky followed the stutter with a choking sound.

"How exactly does it work?" said the unseen person he was talking to. Mia recognized don Vincent Moltisani's voice.

"NO!" Nicky yelled this as he jumped out of his chair. He went for the projector, but two of the uniformed officers grabbed him. Vincent strode in from the outer hallway. Gone were the don duds, replaced by a sport coat and jeans. He flashed a badge at Nicky. "Nicholas Cariolo Vestri, you're under arrest for video piracy and sale of stolen goods."

"That's where the water flats went," Kelvin exclaimed.

"Among many other set items." Ariadne glared at Nicky, who Vincent was in the process of cuffing. "And our footage. You're despicable. What's that American expression? I hope they throw the book at you."

Vincent led a very unhappy Nicky up the aisle. Francesca reached out to stop him. "You're an undercover cop? That is *so* hot."

Vincent responded with a sexy grin. "We'll talk."

Ariadne placed a manicured hand on her heart. "This has certainly been illuminating. I don't know about anyone else, but I could use a drink."

Pete stepped forward. "Sorry, but that'll have to wait." He sauntered to the front of the room. "Detective Moltisani's undercover operation was separate from ours. He got clued into Mr. Vestri's illegal actions by a fellow don. But prior to that, we received an anonymous tip regarding the financials of St. James Productions."

Intern accountant Jason Stern stood up. He waved. "Not anonymous anymore." He held up a flash drive. "Here's a copy of all the documentation I turned over to NYPD showing a pattern of off-the-books compensation on the part of Giles and Ariadne St. James in the form of apartment rent, vehicle rent, entertainment expenses . . . I could go on and on, but I don't want to bore you with dull felony financial details." He fixed a speechless Ariadne with a dark stare. "You better think twice before you ever hire a professional accountant to do an intern's job. Not that you'll be doing any hiring from jail."

"He's going to make a wonderful chief financial officer for the newly formed St. James, Stern, and Princess Productions, don't you think, love?"

Violet St. James, clad in her requisite tiny skirt and sky-high heels, made a grand entrance into the room. She delivered this statement to Ariadne with a sneer. Mia could swear kitty Princess Kate also sneered at the producer being handcuffed and led out of the room by Pete and Ryan.

The room erupted into a cacophony of chatter prompted by the dramatic events that had unfolded before everyone's eyes. Mia made her way to Lysette. "How'd you like being part of a sting?"

"A little scary, but I like the results," the director said with a satisfied smile.

"I bet you wish you could've filmed it."

"We wouldn't have a place to use it. The pilot's not moving forward."

"Really?" Mia said, surprised to hear this.

"Yeah. Someone put out the word to potential outlets it would be in their best interests not to buy it. But that's okay. Violet okayed putting Kelvin's documentary project into production. With me as both the director and executive producer on it."

Lysette went to join up with her crewmates, leaving Mia to assume the person who just texted her was also responsible for scaring off the pilot's potential buyers.

EPILOGUE

Mia re-read the document on her computer screen one last time. Violet St. James had requested a proposal for an event celebrating the launch of her reorganization of the company founded by her late husband, Giles, and his potential felon of an ex-wife, Ariadne. The proposal was pro forma. Violet's gratitude for Mia's help in nabbing her husband's killer guaranteed Belle View would get the job.

Mia hit Send. She heard someone at her door and looked up from the keyboard.

"Hey, boss."

Mia glanced around her computer screen. The person standing in her doorway wasn't who she was expecting to see. "Little D, hi."

"Forgot I worked here, didn't ya?"

Little Donny flashed a grin. Once annoyed by his arrogance, Mia now welcomed it as a sign he was back to his old self. He'd shaved, too, getting rid of the stubble that made him look like a parolee on the lam rather than a hipster, and had trimmed his thick black hair, which was held in place by product.

"To be honest, I did. You worked here, what? All of a day or two? But we're happy to have you back."

"Actually, I just came by to give notice. That's how they say it in business, right? As a nicer way of saying you're quitting?"

"You could put it that way. I appreciate the sensitivity." She motioned for him to sit down. He parked himself in one of the office guest chairs and put his feet on her desk. Happy for another sign he was on the mend after the *Dons* debacle, Mia didn't swat them off. "You have any plans for the future?"

"Big ones." Little Donny helped himself to a handful of the Jordan almonds Mia kept in a bowl for visitors. Their candy coating crunched as he spoke. "Working here taught me something."

"Really? I thought you hated it. You sure seemed miserable the whole short time."

"I know. I think because I was miserable about my life in general. But I liked the event-planning stuff. You know, shaking down suppliers for the best prices. Coming up with party ideas." He paused. "I wanna say shaking down suppliers for the best prices again. That really felt like it was in my wheelhouse."

"It was. It is."

"I know, right?" He beamed. "Anyway, I was at Singles the other night, drinking away my sorrows, and I got to talking about all this to the owner. He offered me a job drumming up events and running them."

"So now you're my competitor." Before he could protest, Mia held up a hand. "I'm kidding.

Plenty of room in Astoria for all of us. Besides, we'll have very different clienteles. I've been in the Singles event room. My first piece of advice is to fumigate it."

She made a face and pinched her nose. Little Donny laughed. "Yeah, twenty years of booze, BO, and barf." He leaned back in the chair. "I finally got what you said about how good it feels to help people make memories through events about the most important moments of their lives. I even turned down a chance to be in Violet's new show to take this job."

"She's doing another reality show?"

"Not just doing, starring in it."

"I'm almost afraid to ask what it's about."

Little Donny let out a guffaw. "You should be. It's called *Hot Young Widow.* Thirty guys compete to hook up with her. No pilot this time. Got what they call a straight-to-series order."

"Speaking of pilots . . ."

Mia stood up. She walked to the office door and closed it, then returned to her office chair, pulling it closer to Little Donny. "It was you, wasn't it? You're the one who killed the *Dons of Ditmars Boulevard* pilot."

"I can neither confirm nor deny this," Little D said, cagily. "I'll just say I'm happy certain TV people saw how important it was to step up and do the right thing."

"So, it's a yes." She mimed clapping. "Nicely done. Can I assume you're the one who narc'ed on Nicky about the piracy and stolen goods?"

"Any one of us could've done that, he was such a loudmouth about it. But . . . maybe." Little Donny stood up. "I gotta go."

"You sure? Why don't you stay for lunch?"

"Can't. I ran into this model in the lobby out there. She took a ride share here. I offered to drive her back to Manhattan."

Mia's heart hammered. "It's not Petra Vilsni, is it?"

"Sure is. She told me she's here to see Shane. The way she said *Shane*"—Little Donny delivered the name with a lot of disdain and a slight Eastern European accent—"told me I got a shot with her."

He flicked up his shirt collar and left the office with a swagger to his step.

Mia placed a hand on her heart, willing it to ratchet down its heavy beating. She picked up her cell phone to text Shane, then put it down. After the fourth time of repeating the gesture, a knock on the office door distracted her. "Come in." *And please be Shane with good news.*

The visitor was Shane. He waved a sheath of papers in the air. "You're looking at the ex-Mister Petra Vilsni. Woot woot!"

Mia's usually reserved boyfriend hopped around the office in a happy dance while he continued his joyous shouting. Mia jumped up from behind her desk. He grabbed her hands, and they jumped up and down together. Mia suddenly stopped. "I feel bad for Petra that we're celebrating like this."

"Don't worry. Posi was right. The minute I flipped the script and said the divorce was about me not being good enough for her, she was on board. Like, instantly." He sounded a little insulted. "I saw her in the lobby flirting with Little Donny, and then they left together, so I think we're good on the divorce." He took Mia in his arms. "I'm really, really sorry I put you through this."

"All is forgiven." She lifted her lips to his. After a

steamy interlude, Mia pushed him away. "Stop. We still have an issue we need to resolve."

"We do?" Shane appeared confused as well as worried.

Mia, hating to ruin the moment, wrinkled her brow. But she persisted. "When you sent me to see Petra at her apartment to try to talk me into the divorce, she said you'd replaced your drug and drinking addictions with another one. I know this happens with people fighting addictions, and I understand and sympathize. But I need to know what it is before we can move forward." *Please don't say it's sex, please don't say it's sex, I will* never *be able to trust you.*

Shane grimaced. "Ugh. I've been working through it. I was hoping you'd never find out."

It's sex. He's another Adam Grosso. Whaaaaa!!

Shane took Mia's hand. "Come with me. I need to show you something."

He led a wary Mia to his office, shutting the door behind her. He leaned over his computer keyboard and typed. "Come see this."

Mia reluctantly made her way to the computer. She scrunched up her eyes, fearful of what might be on the screen. Then her eyes popped open. Before her was an image of bobblehead dolls—hundreds of them filling one shelf after another in what looked like a storage facility. "What is this? I don't get it."

"Petra was right. I did develop an addiction. To collecting bobblehead dolls. I moved them out of the house to help me break the habit. I've been selling them off."

Mia peered at the screen. "Is that a Mets player?"

"I've got the whole 1969 World Series Mets

bobblehead lineup." Shane shared this with pride, then added hastily, "But I've put it up for sale on the Internet. I think it's gonna generate a bidding war."

"Nice."

"I know it's weird." Shane's brow creased with worry. "Are you gonna break up with me?"

"No. But if we move in together, we're not decorating with bobbleheads." She glanced at the screen. "Except for Dolly Parton. *Love* her."

"And I love you."

The two stared at each other, their lives forever changed by Shane's blurt. "I do, Mia. I love you," he repeated.

Mia drew in a deep breath. "I love you, too."

She responded quietly in an effort to control her emotions. Shane enveloped her in his arms. She rested her head on his shoulder. "The day we met," he said, "I knew you were the one. Don't ask me how I knew, I just did. It really hit me at the memorial for Buddy, Bubbles, and Goldie."

"Such perfect names for goldfish."

"I know. Watching how much respect the Woods showed Justin . . . how the family came together to help him through a tough time . . . I had this moment where I saw you being a mother and me being a dad, walking our little boy through the first loss of his life and teaching him to be stronger for it. And it hit me how much I want that. With you. For the rest of my life."

He placed his hands around Mia's waist. He bent down and was about to kiss her when Cammie appeared in the doorway. "Sorry to interrupt you non-dating lovebirds. I was heading out to meet Peter. I've traded doing podcasts for making videos, and we're going shopping for high-end equipment like ring lights and, of course, a professional makeup artist and fashion stylist. There's a couple in the lobby waiting for you, Shane."

Shane dropped his hands. "The Aguilars, right. I'm giving them a tour. They're thinking about booking the Bay Ballroom for their daughter's quinceañera." He gave Mia a smoldering look. "We'll pick up where we left off later."

He hurried out of the office. The women walked down the hall in silence. They reached Mia's office. Cammie studied her. "Everything good between you two? You seem, I don't know . . . not all here."

Mia cast a glazed glance toward the lobby. "That's because"—feeling slightly faint, she paused—"I think Shane just proposed."

RECIPES

Pasta Puttanesca

If you read *Long Island Iced Tina,* you'll know that pasta puttanesca figures prominently in that storyline. You'd think I would have included this recipe in *that* book—and you'd be right! What happened? Simple. I forgot. But I'm making up for it here, lol. I hope you enjoy the recipe.

Ingredients

1 lb. pasta of your choice
3 Tbsp. virgin olive oil
1 tsp. dried oregano
2 tsp. minced garlic
2 tsp. anchovy paste
½ tsp. red pepper flakes
1 28-oz. can diced tomatoes in juice
2 Tbsp. drained capers
½ cup chopped, pitted Kalamata olives
Pinch of salt (optional)
¾ cup chopped fresh basil
Grated parmesan cheese, to taste

Directions

Prepare the pasta according to the instructions on the box. Drain, toss with one tablespoon of the olive oil, and set aside.

In a medium to heavy 12" skillet, cook the garlic, anchovy paste, and red pepper flakes in the remaining 2 tablespoons of oil, stirring occasionally until fragrant—about two minutes.

Add diced tomatoes and juice, the capers, and the chopped olives to the mixture in the skillet. Lower the heat and simmer for around 5 minutes, stirring occasionally. Taste and add a pinch of salt, if necessary.

You can go one of two ways from here. You can add the pasta to the sauce and stir to combine, then divide into 4 bowls and serve. Or you can divide the plain pasta into 4 pasta bowls and spoon the sauce evenly on each bowl of pasta.

Top with evenly divided fresh basil and grated cheese to taste.

Serves 4.

Italian Wedding Cookies

You don't have to wait for a wedding to make these delicious, crumbly cookies.

Ingredients

1½ stick unsalted butter
¾ to 1 cup powdered sugar*
¾ tsp. salt
1½ cup finely ground nuts (I use slivered unsalted almonds and grind them with a Magic Bullet. But you can use a food processor or blender.)
1½ tsp. vanilla extract**
3 tsp. almond extract***
3 cups all-purpose flour
⅓ cup powdered sugar for rolling the cookies

Directions

Preheat oven to 325 degrees.

Cream the butter in a large bowl. Slowly cream in the powdered sugar and salt until well combined. Cream in the ground almonds (or your choice of nuts), then the vanilla and almond extracts. Add the flour slowly—½ cup at a time. The dough will be extremely crumbly. I sometimes use my hands—very clean hands!—to combine it.

Using your hands, take about a tablespoon of dough and form it into a ball or crescent. Place on an ungreased cookie sheet and bake for 15–20 minutes. You don't want the cookies to get too brown.

Place the ⅓ cup of powdered sugar in a small bowl. Let the cookies cool a little—you want them to harden so they don't fall apart, but to retain a little heat so the sugar will stick to them—and roll them in the sugar.

Servings: about 30 cookies. For more cookies, you can make the balls or crescents smaller. But adjust the cooking time so you don't burn them.

*I use 1 cup of powdered sugar because I like the cookies a little sweeter. But ¾ cup is fine to use and may make the dough a little bit less dry.

**If you're like me and can't get enough almond flavor, substitute additional almond extract for the vanilla, so you're adding 4½ teaspoons of almond extract to the dough. If you don't want almond flavor, use 4½ teaspoons of vanilla.

***You can also substitute anise or do a mix of anise and vanilla for another traditional Italian flavor.

Coconut Amaretto Bread Pudding

Ingredients

4–5 cups torn croissant pieces
½ cup sliced almonds
3 large eggs
¾ cups sugar
1 cup milk
⅓ cup Amaretto liqueur, plus 1 tsp.
½ cup heavy or whipping cream
1 tsp. vanilla extract
1 tsp. almond extract
¼ tsp. salt
6 macaroons, crumbled
2 Tbsp. unsalted butter
1 Tbsp. dark brown sugar

Directions

Dry bread uncovered at room temperature for 12 hours. (You can also dry the bread in a 250-degree oven for one hour.)

Preheat oven to 350 degrees.

Butter a 13" x 9" (or larger) baking dish.

Arrange the croissant pieces in the baking dish. Sprinkle the almonds over the bread, making sure they're evenly dispersed.

In a bowl, whisk together the eggs, sugar, milk, ⅓ cup of Amaretto, heavy cream, vanilla and almond extracts, and salt. Stir in the crumbled macaroons. Pour the mix slowly and evenly over the bread.

Cream the butter with the brown sugar and teaspoon of Amaretto, then dot the pudding with the mixture.

(Note: You can chill the pudding, covered, for anywhere from an hour to a day before baking, but this is optional.)

Bake the pudding in the middle of the oven until it's slightly puffed and golden and the middle has set—about 40 minutes.

OPTIONAL SAUCE: In a double boiler, whisk together ⅓ cup of Amaretto, ¼ cup of heavy cream, and a pinch of salt until combined well. Serve warm. Notice that there's no sugar in this sauce recipe. That's because I find the bread pudding to be sweet enough. But it's a pretty hard sauce without it, so feel free to add sugar according to your taste.

Serves 6.

Tricolor (Tre Colore) Cookies, aka Rainbow Cookies

Ingredients

4 large eggs
1 cup sugar
3½ oz. almond paste, softened for 30 seconds in microwave and cooled slightly
1 cup flour
1 cup butter, melted and cooled
½ salt
1 tsp. almond extract
6–8 drops red food coloring
6–8 drops green food coloring
¼ cup seedless raspberry jam or apricot jam

Chocolate glaze

1 cup semisweet chocolate chips
1 tsp. vegetable shortening (more if needed)

Directions

Preheat oven to 375 degrees.

In a stand mixer, preferably, beat the eggs and sugar together in a large bowl until the mix is thick and a pale yellow. Gradually add the almond paste. It's important it be softened; this will make it easier to mix. But it shouldn't be too warm because that will affect the eggs.

Gradually add the flour, butter, salt, and extract. Make sure to space out the flour and butter, adding by ⅓- or ½-cup portions; otherwise, the batter will splatter.

Divide the batter into thirds. Tint one batch red and one green. Leave the third portion un-tinted. (These are the colors of the Italian flag!) Spread each portion in a separate, well-greased 11" x 7" baking pan. (If you don't have pans this size, you can use 8" x 8" or 9" x 9" pans. The batter may not spread all the way to the edge, but you only need a square, thin layer, so try to spread the batter in the shape of a square.)

Bake each layer between 7 and 10 minutes. Check at 7 minutes because, being thin layers, they tend to cook fast. The center should be springy and the edges lightly browned. An inserted toothpick should come out clean.

Cool the layers completely.

Gently remove the red layer and place on waxed paper. Spread with half the jam. Place the plain layer on top of the red layer, and press down gently. Add the remaining jam, then the green layer, and press gently.

To make the glaze, melt the chocolate chips with the shortening in the microwave, checking every 30 seconds. You don't want to nuke the chocolate too long because it will be clumpy instead of melty. If that happens, add more melted shortening to create a glazed consistency.

Spread the glaze over the top layer, and refrigerate the whole assemblage until it hardens.

Once the pastry has hardened, cut into thin, rectangular cookies about ½" by 2" long. A pizza cutter is a great way to cut through the hardened chocolate. A sharp knife will also work.

Servings: about 30–40 cookies.

Tuna Casserole

I know this isn't an Italian recipe, but I had to include it. It does include pasta, so . . . Italian-adjacent? This recipe makes enough for a party—16 servings! To make a smaller batch, halve all the ingredients.

Ingredients

2 cans (10¾ oz.) cream of mushroom soup (I go for reduced fat whenever possible)
2 cans all-white tuna fish, drained
2 cups milk (chef's choice; I use skim)
1 cup finely diced onions or shallots
2 cups shredded cheddar cheese
1 cup cooked peas
1 cup cooked chopped mushrooms (I like to roast mine for extra flavor)
2 cups cooked farfalle pasta
2–3 cups crushed potato chips

Directions

Preheat oven to 425 degrees.

Mix the soup, tuna, and milk in a large bowl. Add the onions, peas, and mushrooms. Stir in the cheese, and mix well to incorporate all the ingredients. Add the pasta, and gently stir to combine.

Pour into a 12" x 17" baking dish. Sprinkle all over with the crushed potato chips and bake for 20 minutes. Check the center to make sure the casserole is thoroughly cooked.*

Serves 16.

*If you've halved the ingredients, use a 9" x 12" baking dish, and bake for 15 minutes. Check the center to make sure the casserole is thoroughly cooked.

Event Tip

If you're hosting or helping to plan a destination event, here's a tip that will help you avoid the disaster that befell the bachelor and bachelorette party guests who forgot their passports. Gift attendees with a folder or portfolio to house the important documents they'll need to travel. You can find items like plastic accordion folders at dollar stores.

For a bachelorette party, add the name of the bride's and the event on the front with a permanent marker—for example, "Madison's Bachelorette Party." You can even throw a pre-party where guests decorate their folders or portfolios with stickers and markers.

If it's a larger event like a destination wedding, suggest the bride and groom give affordable personalized portfolios or travel wallets to attendees as a wedding favor. But in this case, make sure they distribute the favors to guests prior to departure.

Acknowledgments

I'm grateful to my terrific agent, Doug Grad, who found the perfect home for The Catering Hall Mysteries, as well as the perfect editor, John Scognamilio. *Mille grazie* to both of you, as well as Larissa Ackerman, Lou Malcangi, Lauren Jernigan, and everyone at Kensington. You are all absolutely wonderful to work with, offering energy and enthusiasm that inspire me.

A shout-out to my fabulous partners in crime (writing) at chicksonthecase.com. Chick Vickie Fee gets a special shout-out for fact-checking my Catholicism! Can't thank you enough, Vickie. More love to my fellow eleven members of Cozy Mystery Crew, especially fearless leader and fellow Kensington author Libby Klein. Fellow Fearless Foursomeers Gigi Pandian, Lisa Q. Mathews, and Diane Vallere—I heart you. And even more love to the bloggers and reviewers who toil away to support us, their only payment being our undying gratitude. I'm talking to you, Dru Ann Love, Mark Baker, Lesa Holstine, Lisa Kelly, Sandra Murphy, Lorie Hamm, Kristopher Zgorski, and Debra Jo Burnette—profuse apologies but much love to anyone I missed. Not only have you rewarded me with kind words, some of you have also rewarded me with treasured friendships. Extra thanks to the lovely Cindy Silberblatt for being, well, wonderful. And to Malice Domestic and Left Coast Crime for their incredible support and encouragement. I would not be here without them. Lysette House, thanks for your generous bid at Malice. Hope you enjoy being in the book!

As always, I have to thank husband Jer and daughter Eliza for their endless patience. And as always, profuse thanks to my Italian family, primarily mama Elisabetta DiVirgilio Seideman—and my brothers Tony and David, who gets extra thanks for taking such good care of Mom during multiple tough times. Love you ALL!